The McIntyre Saga: Quest for the Librarian

Prologue

2008

Global News Headquarters in New York

"I'm James Powell and this is the top of the news at the bottom of the hour." He hesitated a moment before staring directly at the camera. He didn't look well. *"I've been reporting the news for a long time and honestly, this feels strange standing here. I have contracted the Omega virus and I'm dying. Those of our team who are working with me today have the virus also. We are using what time we have left to make this broadcast because while we're not going to beat the disease, we can*

at least flail away at Omega doing what we do best…report what we know."

"It has been almost five years since Omega was introduced into the world's population. The threat of a "superbug" that could overpower our medical capabilities has been around for decades. But that "superbug" has been recklessly unleashed. A mutated smallpox virus is seemingly here to stay. The best research scientists in the world, including those who helped create the virus, have been stymied. The virus appears to be unstoppable and has invaded almost every corner of the globe. It was hoped, that given time, the virus would grow weaker, but it has not. The numbers of people who have died and who continue to die, is staggering. Sociologists are asking the question; is this end of the human race? If nothing changes, what will the world look like in ten years or in a 100 years?"

J.P. shifted his gaze to a map of the world, then back to the camera. "The upshot is this: Omega has won, at least for the time being. I am assuming that a remnant will survive and a weapon to fight Omega will be found. We, at Global News, are working with a skeleton crew and this will be our last broadcast. Industry and commerce have been shut down. The electricity for this broadcast is coming from a Vanderhooten

Electrical Power System which some of you would know is ironic."

Sweat was beginning to pour down J.P.'s thin face. "Schools are closed. Not much of a social structure remains, but a few churches still hold services. Gangs of thugs seemingly rule the streets."

"Every industrialized country in the world is collapsing into chaos. Not enough people have survived to build, run or maintain the complex machinery of a complex civilization. Government sponsored crematoriums have cremated tens of millions of people, but it is not enough. Many of the dead are simply stacked like so much firewood in empty buildings or fields. Anarchy has become the rule rather than the exception in many parts of the world."

"Large cities have been transformed into ghost towns. Smaller populations of people in more remote areas, like Hawaii and other island archipelagos, are reportedly doing pretty well considering how many infected people came to the islands before air flights in and out came to a halt. Those who live in small isolated villages in Africa and the jungles of South America seem to be fine. The people with little or no contact with the modern world seem to have the best chance

of survival. It may well be that the meek will indeed inherit the earth."

"Some of you have heard about what has occurred on the west coast. The destruction caused by the massive earthquake is staggering, but because of Omega there is no one left to fight the fires, to look for survivors or rebuild what was destroyed. Seeing photographs of the Golden Gate Bridge collapsed into San Francisco Bay is heartbreaking."

"But Omega is really all that matters right now and it has brought this country and most of the world to its knees. Since this is my last report, I'll end my time with you with a personal observation."

He coughed. "Ultimately the Omega virus was a human invention. The hubris of the scientists who created this monstrosity is stunning. What were they thinking? That it was the perfect weapon? That it could not escape its watery grave? If their idea was to kill off the opposition; it has worked all too well. For the few of you who are watching, I'm James Powell. May God have mercy on us all. This is Global News. Goodnight and goodbye."

The Aftermath of Omega

"Man has lost the capacity to foresee and to forestall. He will end up destroying the earth." *Albert Schweitzer*

Almost two centuries have come and gone since Omega struck and the world is a much different place, especially on the west coast of North America. Fifty-one years after the virus was unleashed, the San Andreas Fault moved almost 100 feet. It generated a 9.0 earthquake ripping apart large metropolitan areas like Los Angeles, San Francisco and Sacramento. The California earthquake triggered other massive earthquakes as far south as Chile and north into the Seattle area of Washington State. Tsunamis pounded some areas taking much of the rubble of earthquake damaged buildings and massive numbers of the dead out to sea. The devastation was horrific.

Those same earthquakes triggered undersea avalanches of incredible magnitude. Whole ranges of undersea mountains disappeared while new ones were created. The landscape at the bottom of
the Pacific Ocean changed dramatically, upsetting the food chain and redirecting massive ocean currents that flowed along the bottom. The unparalleled changes in ocean currents has caused a shift in weather patterns for the coastal regions of North America and other parts of the world.

Average temperatures have risen, while rainfall totals in areas west of the Sierra Nevada Mountains have decreased. Storms now drop a lot of their moisture between the Sierra Nevada range and the Rocky Mountains.

Not much is left of a technologically advanced society. The World Wide Web of communication has collapsed, as have radio and television services. Power companies are failing to produce electricity. Even the mighty Hoover Dam no longer generates power. Without workers to maintain the system, the intake valves of the dam receiving water from Lake Mead have clogged up causing the massive generators to shut down. With very little water coming through the dam, the once mighty Colorado River below the dam had shrunk to a small creek. Lake Mead, itself, began to fill to capacity. Almost five years later, water began to pour over the emergency spillways and the Colorado flowed once again, but at a reduced rate.

Industry of every kind has collapsed. Without people to maintain buildings, structures and equipment, rust, rot and corrosion have attacked everything man-made. Airplanes no longer fly, cars and trucks are no longer seen on the road except as burned-out, rusted hulks. Mechanical transportation has long ago ground to a halt. Decaying trains sit idly on the tracks. Not much is left of them, either. Old cars that have survived in dry areas in garages, basements or car showroom floors have become decorations for the rich and powerful, where wealth is measured not by gold, but by the size of your army, the productivity of your land and the number of cattle, goats or sheep owned. As a result, America has become almost medieval in nature. Towns have become ghost towns. Those who have survived and are strong enough in a military and economic sense have become the feudal lords of the day.

The people who have not succumbed to Omega, live with great difficulty. It has become a case of the survival of the fittest. With only 5-10% of the population surviving Omega and the earthquake, some will do anything to live and the result has been utter chaos. The basic needs of each day for the survivors has come down to three things: avoiding contact with anyone who is ill, finding enough food to eat and a safe place to sleep.

The good news is that the pandemic called Omega has slowed down. With so few people left to infect, the virus has all but disappeared in many places. But what has not left is the concern it could return. So people choose to live in small isolated groups. The fear of strangers is huge. Every village or community has an isolation station where newcomers, or those who develop Omega-like symptoms, are sequestered for a week. The security around the stations is intense.

With the collapse of federal, state and local governments, the artificial boundaries between the states, counties and cities have dissolved. General regions or territories have replaced them.

Mountain ranges, rivers, deserts and major highways are now seen as boundaries. In these areas, anyone with authority over a dozen men can, and have, transformed communities into military style posts. Ammunition and weapons stored by the ancients in weatherproof boxes and found in archeological digs, are highly prized and even fought over.

The rugged Rocky Mountains and the Sierra Nevada mountain range have kept the western territories pretty much isolated from the rest of the former United States of America. Contact between the west and the rest of the country has faded. A loose system of communal government has emerged; much like it did in the Dark Ages of distant centuries past. Memories of a technologically advanced society have become part of fanciful tales parents tell their children at bedtime, about a people who are now called the Ancients.

After the earthquake and the fires, schools, colleges and prisons still standing have become the places where many of those who have survived, live in poverty and subjugation to those who have power and weapons. Those who are able to work doing something to support the community, live; those who do not...don't. The elderly are rarely seen anymore. They are not useful in a society where your value is dependent on what you produce, what you do in the fields or in digging up what the Ancients left behind.

The exceptions are those people who live in smaller, more remote communities in the mountains or desert. They live a quiet existence where the church, family and hard work are still a valued commodity. The elderly are seen as a source of wisdom, as well as being great babysitters allowing both parents to work on the difficult task of survival.

The marvels of modern society have fallen into ruin, but some of them, buried and hidden under the rubble for hundreds of years, are being uncovered and even restored.

A class of people have emerged who make a living out of discovering and restoring that which was lost. They are called diggers. The Ancients may have called them a type of archeologist. Often well-educated and mechanically inclined, these diggers have given people new hope for the future, as the past is brought into the light of day. But as they work, life is hard, except for a privileged few.

Then there are stories about the Librarian, someone who has the knowledge of the Ancients and may know a cure for Omega. The rumor is the Librarian is a woman, locked up in a glass cage by those who want to keep any cure for themselves. They want to rule what is left of the world. True or not, the result is that people have hope and many are convinced God will provide someone who will lead them into a new golden age. Amidst the desolation, the light of hope is burning.

"We should now give some real thought to the possibility of reforming our technology in the direction of smallness, simplicity, and nonviolence." *E.F. Schumacher*

Chapter 1

Sometime around the beginning of the 23rd Century....

Camilla McIntyre stood on the remains of one of three massive piers protruding into the mouth of the Columbia River, as it emptied a half million gallons of water a minute into the Pacific Ocean. That was just an estimate, of course. Her husband had read that at one time the river poured twice as much into the ocean. Later measurements would prove Henry's calculations weren't too far off.

Directly ahead of her in the water sat the badly rusting remains of a large cruise ship that had been scuttled offshore, long before she was born. A powerful storm had unceremoniously tossed the cruiseship onto its starboard side. Not much was left above water. A portion of the port side was exposed a few feet above the water. The faded name of the ship was just barely visible; Pacific Voyager. Camilla had witnessed its slow disintegration for most of her life. Fortunately for what was left of Astoria, the tsunamis caused by the Pacific Northwest earthquake did not travel far up the Columbia River. A few buildings had withstood the ravages of the earthquake, time and natural decomposition, but not much was keeping them in a vertical position.

Camilla was tall and somewhat thin. She had a pleasant face with high cheek bones, a firm jaw line and full, pouty lips. A striking feature was her long ebony-colored hair, usually pulled back tight against her head into a pony-tail. But what caught most people's attention was her wide, toothy smile and easy laugh. Her husband had fallen in love with her, not when he first saw her, but when he heard her laugh.

Shifting her gaze to the right, she looked up Industry Street. The sign identifying it as such, hung precariously from a tall pole. All of the unreinforced brick and stone structures had collapsed during the big earthquake. Most of what was left consisted of piles of broken brick, stone and rubble which were partially obscured by vegetation. For the past two hundred or so years, diggers had been combing through the debris of the past hoping to find something useful for the present. Because of the devastating impact of the Omega virus, finding the bones of those who died over the last couple of centuries, was still a relatively common occurrence for the diggers.

Anything useful that was easily found had been scavenged long ago. Old cars, trucks and the buildings still standing were covered with various varieties of climbing plants thanks, in part, to a warmer but somewhat drier climate. For diggers, it was a matter of cutting through the vegetation and rubble to reach the decaying remnants of places and things abandoned and buried long ago. Sometimes it was just the vines that kept a wall from collapsing. The work was dangerous, but rewarding. The Ancients had left a treasure of useful tools, household items, clothes and machinery buried in basements and collapsed warehouses. Often as not, many diggers like those in her family, had the know-how enabling them to unlock the secrets of useful mechanical marvels, large and small, found under the surface. Rust and rot had claimed a lot, but not everything. Some items had been wrapped in a thin, clear covering resembling a piece of transparent cloth, and they survived. Diggers frequently found cardboard boxes in dry digs which were used to store things the Ancients had made. Sometimes inside the box was a white but very lightweight material that surrounded an item. It obviously was used as protection from potential damage. Once the white stuff was removed the item itself could be seen. Those items appeared to be in perfect condition and in good working order, especially if they were mechanical in nature. Diggers found everything from kitchen dishes to wearable clothes, especially if they were made of synthetic materials that didn't rot. Two classes of working people became highly prized; those who could sew and those who could

find, repair or restore that which the Ancients produced long ago.

Camilla turned her gaze to a boat anchored out about a hundred feet from Pier 2. It was a 70 foot long sail boat, without the rigging or sails. It had been stripped long ago. But the hull, the mainmast and main cabin were intact. Interestingly enough, the *Adelene Marie* was constructed of cement. She thought to herself. "How on earth does one build a cement boat?"

Seeing something shiny in the sand regularly deposited by storms, she leaned over and picked up a partially flattened aluminum can. Five letters and a logo could be still seen on the side. Pepsi. She recognized it as a popular drink for the Ancients. She shook her head. Like the Coke can she found the other day, the beverage probably didn't taste very good.

She smiled as she looked back at the *Adelene Marie*. Little did she know that the sturdy cement sailboat was centuries old. The commandant had found the boat several years previous. It was partially buried on the riverbank. The deck and woodwork had long since rotted away, but the cement hull was intact. Dozens of men spent almost two years rebuilding the deck and woodwork, including the mainmast. Now it floated gracefully a few hundred feet from shore. Her son, Cooper, said one day he would sail on the boat. She had no doubt he would. Her son was a determined young man. She heard a series of howls and looked in that direction. Packs of vicious dogs still roamed the streets and were dangerous to anyone caught out in the open. Many cities did not have to worry about cremating all those who had died. Wild dogs ate the flesh of the dead while being impervious to the virus.

Human bones were piled up wherever the dogs had feasted.

Astoria was once a robust community of about 25,000 people before Omega struck. Now, about 500 people called Astoria their home. Aided by the warmer climate, the Oregon wilderness was reclaiming most of Astoria. The people who remained, eked out an existence, living in a half dozen communes that had taken up residence in various buildings, schools and office buildings which managed to survive the devastation. Because of chain-link fences surrounding schools and some businesses, the people who lived inside were more easily defended against wandering tribes of marauders by hired mercenaries who were just a little more civilized.

The marauders were an interesting cultural phenomenon. Rather than work for their food and a place to live, they simply stole. And if anyone got
in their way, they were summarily killed without hesitation or thought. It was their right to take what they needed to survive, or so they thought. The marauder camps moved from place to place following searchers whose job it was to find basic supplies and whatever they deemed to be the necessities of life. Whole families lived in the camps and generations of children were raised up

to become marauders, and they were a fanatical bunch.

Camilla reached down to pick up the six foot long rusted iron bar Henry had seen earlier. It was heavy, but she could drag it with relative ease. She had no idea why the bar was needed, but was certain he had a plan to reach an as of yet undiscovered cache of what the Ancients left behind. She smiled at the thought of her husband, a usually gentle and thoughtful soul. A well-educated and hard-working man, he was the kind of guy you wanted to be around when trouble arose. He was fond of saying, "Don't argue or complain; work the problem!"

The McIntyre family had reached almost legendary status for their ability to discover, recover and repair usable items. She smiled slightly. The McIntyres had been part of the Northwest Territory for a long time. Stories had been passed down from generation to generation. Her husband was only too glad to tell them to anyone who would listen. She shook her head slightly. The tales were almost too good to be true. One fantastical story told of how some McIntyres ended up on a Hawaiian island in the Pacific Ocean, days after the Omega virus was first exposed to the population. True or not, they were entertaining stories, to say the least.

She looked up river. The once mighty Columbia River was no longer the dangerous waterway the Ancients navigated. As the Northwest climate warmed, the accumulation of snow in the mountains had decreased, as did some of the runoff. The warmer climate provided rain, but not in the torrents that described the storms of centuries past. The river was no longer as difficult to navigate as it once was, and had become a major supplier of fish for the community. In the distance one could see what was left of the once beautiful Astoria Bridge. Henry had shown her photographs of the bridge in its original state.

His collection of books was growing extensively. One volume was almost entirely made up of photographs of the Northwest. Only the Commandant had a library with more volumes than Henry's. It was too bad the Commandant was illiterate. Very few people had any education beyond what was necessary to survive. When Astoria's library collapsed during the earthquake that occurred long before she was born, very few books survived the ravages of time and weather. But Henry had uncovered part of the basement which was still reasonably intact and dry. He found hundreds of books and magazines. Since the Commandant often rewarded Henry with some of what he found and had no idea as to the content of the books, Henry kept the most valuable volumes. Camilla smiled to herself. She and Henry, her two children and only a handful of other people knew how to read. It was a tremendous gift of God to be able to read what the Ancients wrote, and to see photographs of what once was.

As Camilla walked back toward the dig she looked again at the ravaged bridge. Most of it had fallen into the river, but miraculously, one section still hung delicately over the water, as it clung to one of the massive pillars that had managed to survive. A single car could be seen still caught in the debris.

The date under the old photograph of the bridge before the earthquake that Henry had shown her was July 1966, long before Omega. But, since no one knew the current day, month or year, it really didn't have much significance other than knowing that it was a long time ago. Henry had guessed maybe 210 years had come and gone since the Omega virus struck, but even he didn't really know for sure. Henry was working on developing a calendar based on the movement of the earth around the sun, the phases of the moon and the summer and winter equinox.

For most people, the passage of time was marked by changes in the seasons. Her son,

Cooper, was born on a hot day in the middle of summer and was recorded as such in their family Bible. Maggie was born just as the leaves began to change color with the onset of fall. Henry put a check by their names in the Bible each year that came and went. By that reckoning, Cooper was a little over seventeen years old and Maggie had just turned sixteen. The two were working closely with their father a short distance away. As Camilla threaded her way through the rubble, Henry looked up at his wife. "Thanks, honey. This is exactly what I need."

As she handed him the iron bar she said, "A pack of dogs are nearby."

"I heard'em. Don't worry, they usually don't come down this far anymore."

Cooper pointed. "Uhh...Dad, that one did."

Henry looked up to see a big black Rottweiler about 40 feet away, who was literally foaming at the mouth. As the dog charged toward them, Maggie took three quick steps, stooped down, picked up her modified crossbow and aimed carefully. She pulled the trigger. The ten inch arrow-shaped bolt struck the vicious animal, burying itself into the dog's massive chest. The iron bolt slowed the dog down, but he kept coming. Cooper, who was already big and strong, grabbed the iron bar from his father and ran toward the furious animal, now bleeding from the mouth. As the two closed in on each other, Coop swung the bar like a baseball bat and hit the Rottweiler squarely in the head knocking the dog backward. Blood, bone and brains sprayed everywhere. Camilla's face turned ashen as she looked up the street. Henry saw the oncoming pack of dark colored wild dogs and yelled, "Run for the pier!"

Like black ghosts in the night, without making hardly a sound, the dogs chased after them. Henry and his family made it to the end of the pier, with the maniacal dogs close on their heels. At Henry's bidding they jumped into the water and began swimming toward the *Adelene Marie*. When the McIntyres reached the anchor chain, Maggie easily pulled herself up hand-over-hand toward the boat deck, followed by Camilla, then Cooper. It was then the dogs began to bark and howl as they danced on the end of the pier, frustrated a meal was so close, yet so far. As Henry began to climb up the chain, his son pulled out a powerful sling shot and several handmade lead balls. His aim was deadly at anything under 40 feet; this was about 100. He picked out a half inch sized ball and tucked it into the leather pocket. Pulling the leather pouch back with his thumb and forefinger, he aimed high toward the center of the pack knowing, he would at least hit something. He released the pouch and almost immediately a dog yelped. As his dad climbed onto the deck, he sent another and had a similar result. After being pelted a dozen times, the wild dogs finally lost interest and trotted off back up the street. When they reached their fallen comrade, they ripped him apart.

The four McIntyres lay almost spread-eagled on the wide open deck in front of the main cabin that was locked shut. The warm summer sun felt good. Camilla sighed, "Let's not do that again." She sat up. "Okay, everyone strip down and lay your clothes on top of the cabin. It won't take long for

them to dry." Most families lived in relatively close quarters. Modesty was a luxury few could afford.

Cooper smiled. "Mom, what's the point? We have to swim back to the pier."

His dad shook his head. "No, son. You have to swim back." He pointed to a portion of a small dock that still remained afloat after the ravages of time and wild weather. It was several hundred yards away. Tied to it was a fairly large rowboat. You are, by far, the best swimmer among us. So you get the honor."

Coop stared toward the dock. "Why didn't we just run for the rowboat?"

"I decided the water off the pier was a lot closer and wasn't sure how fast those dogs could run. I think I chose wisely."

Cooper muttered to himself as he stripped off his clothes. "Yeah sure, that's because you don't have to swim all that way."

"What did you say, son?"

"I said, it's not too far to swim all that way."

"That's what I thought you said."

Unsure of the water's depth, Coop jumped in and began swimming toward the dock. His lean but well-muscled arms and legs enabled him to almost churn through the water. He resembled his mom in the face, but looked like his dad from the neck down. Camilla laid her son's clothes on the cabin roof and watched as he swam. She looked at her husband. "He is becoming a big man, isn't he?"

Henry nodded. "In another couple of years as he gets a little taller and his body fills out, he will have the size of some of the legendary football players of the Ancients. It also doesn't hurt he has inherited his mother's brains."

Camilla grinned. "But he must have gotten the unforgettable memory part from your side of the family. None of us Andersons have his kind of ability."

Their daughter stretched her long and lithe body on the deck, warming herself in the sun. "What did I get from you, Mom?"

Without hesitation her Dad answered, "You've inherited her personality, her gorgeous hair, that fantastic smile and her intellect." He thought for a second and then added, "You are also totally fearless like your mom. It's not that she is never afraid, but rather she will stand face to face with evil and not flinch. You have that quality, as does your brother. I was proud of the way you stood up to that Rottweiler."

Maggie closed her eyes, turned over onto her stomach and wondered quietly to herself, "Do any McIntyre women have unforgettable memories like Cooper?"

Her dad did not mention she was by far one of the prettiest women around. She was tall like her mom, but had a face and figure that turned the head of many men. She snoozed a little, but then sat up to check on her older brother who had just reached the dock. He pulled himself up and into the boat. Coop carefully searched for the oars and couldn't find them. He extended his arms in frustration.

"Uhh, Dad? The oars are missing."

Henry sat up. "Now that I think about it, why would the Commandant keep the oars out in plain sight? He must have hidden them."

"Not to worry, Dad, Coop will find something."

Coop stepped out onto the dock and walked up onto the shoreline. He disappeared from view for about ten minutes but returned carrying two oars he had confiscated from a sunken boat. Stepping back into the rowboat, he slipped each oar into its davit and began a lot drier trip back to the *Adelene Marie.*

Maggie gave her dad a smug smile, but didn't say anything. However Camilla did. She looked forward and then toward the stern. "If this boat had sails and rigging, what would keep us from sailing away from here?"

Henry stared at his wife. "Once we learned the basics of sailing....nothing. Are you thinking we should change our plans?"

"Not all. But it's always nice to have a back-up plan. We should probably keep the *Adelene Marie* in mind, down life's road."

Maggie grumbled loudly. "Where's that brother of mine, I'm getting hungry."

Coop had covered the distance in less than half the time it took him to swim. As he approached the *Adelene Marie* he yelled, "I heard that Sis. You're always hungry."

Fifteen minutes later they were all walking up the pier back to their dig. With the wild dogs around, Henry thought about abandoning their work, but decided to keep at it. He had a feeling something useful was buried there.

Maggie was thinking about her mom's question, so she asked, "How did the Ancients build boats out of cement?"

Coop politely waited for one of his parents to answer. His dad finally answered. "I haven't a clue, but I suspect Cooper might."

His son nodded. "I remember reading some stuff on boat construction. The Ancients built boats mostly out of wood and a material called fiberglass. But cement was also used. It was a specialized cement mixture that was pushed into layers of chicken wire and steel reinforcing rod laid over a boat-shaped mold. The exterior was smoothed out with trowels. After curing, the mold was ripped out
leaving just the hull. You know the swimming pool in back of the commandant's apartment?" Maggie nodded as he continued. "The construction technique resembled building a swimming pool inside out. Most conventional boats made of wood or fiberglass fell victim to some of the tsunamis that followed the great Pacific Rim earthquake and being relatively fragile, were sunk or destroyed. But because of its hull strength and presumably being anchored well, the *Adelene*

Marie somehow survived. I understand she was in pretty sad shape when the commandant found her. But he has done a nice job of restoring her, and uses the boat as a place to relax with his choice of entertainment for the evening."

Maggie grimaced slightly. "He's a dirty old man. His lieutenant asked me on the commandant's behalf, to join him on the *Adelene Marie.*"

Everyone looked at her. It was Henry who responded. "Why didn't you say something? If I would've known, he and I would have had words."

Maggie shook her head, "And you would've ended up in the cooler. I just ignored the request and nothing else happened."

Cooper was fuming and Maggie knew it. "Look big brother, getting into it with the commandant, when we are so close to leaving this dump, wouldn't be a good thing. Right?"

Coop was definitely the kind of guy you wanted around in a fight. Not only was he big, he was smart and fast. He didn't respond as they passed the bloody patch of ground where the dead dog had laid. Absolutely nothing was left. When they reached the dig, Henry picked up the iron bar and motioned to Coop and Maggie. "We are going to use this bar to lift the end of that beam."

Cooper and Maggie wrestled with a large chunk of concrete and placed it about two feet in front of one end of a thick beam that held up a pile of debris. Henry jammed one end of the two inch thick iron bar under the edge of the beam and set the rod against the piece of concrete to act as a fulcrum. He and Cooper began to pull down on the opposite end of the rod. Nothing happened. Camilla joined them and the beam suddenly moved up about six inches. Maggie stuffed pieces of wood and rock under the beam as her dad adjusted the lever. Working slowly and methodically they were able to raise one end of the beam about two feet. Once the beam was secured, Cooper crawled under the beam and into a partially collapsed room untouched by diggers since the earthquake. He lit a candle and covered it with a glass chimney. Henry yelled, "What did you find, son?!"

Even the usually taciturn commandant was stunned by what the McIntyres brought back to the commune.

"The secret of happiness is freedom, and the secret of freedom....courage." *Thucydides*

Chapter 2

Commandant Clark Cable stroked the smooth surface of the wood as he examined the exquisitely constructed coffin. "So, where did you find this?"

Henry smiled, "Under the rubble of a building down by the old shipping pier. It appears we uncovered a workshop of some sort."

"I suppose you made sure the coffin was empty."

"Of course, sir."

"Very good. What else did you find?"

"Some unusable electrical equipment and a few serviceable woodworking tools. I brought back a few for your collection."

"Did you keep some for yourself?"

Henry did not hesitate, knowing the commandant had an uncanny knack of figuring out when someone was lying. "Yes sir. They will come

in handy when we are repairing or rebuilding things useful to you."

He spoke the truth as far as the question was concerned. He did not say anything about the other treasures found in the shop, things with no value to the commandant, but were invaluable to the McIntyres. They had discovered general construction plans for everything from buildings to boats and more. From his perspective, Henry believed they had found the equivalent of a cache of gold. He was sure the plans would come in handy someday.

"Okay, Henry, keep up the good work. Have my stewards put it in the main warehouse."

"Very good, sir."

Henry and Cooper walked out the door. Coop had not said a word, knowing he was not permitted to speak unless the commandant invited him to do so. Life in the commune was becoming intolerable.

The next morning Cooper and Maggie walked back down to the dock. Earlier, he had noticed a sunken canoe on the opposite side of the Commandant's rowboat. It looked to be made of a material his dad had called fiberglass.

When they reached the dock, Coop emptied his pockets and placed the contents on the top of a short post which the dock was secured to. Maggie wrapped the worms in a damp piece of cloth and sat it next to her brother's stash. They both jumped into the clear, slightly cool water and swam down about ten feet to the sunken canoe. The salt water stung their eyes and blurred their vision, but it seemed like the craft was not damaged. Inside one end lay a mooring rope. He pointed it out and Maggie grabbed the end. When they reached the surface, Cooper let out a war-hoop. "Waahoo!! We have transportation!"

They both pulled on the rope, but the canoe didn't budge. Fortunately, the rope was long enough for them to reach the dock. With more solid footing they pulled once again. This time the canoe moved. Eventually, and with considerable effort, the two siblings managed to pull the canoe onto the shoreline and turned it over to empty it of water. Much lighter now, they sat the canoe back onto the water and it floated nicely. Ten minutes later, using an oar from the rowboat, Coop and Maggie moved steadily out into deeper water. Pulling the oar out of the water for a moment he turned and offered the oar to Maggie.

She paddled the canoe out where more fish were likely to be found. In his pocket Cooper had a wooden dowel with about 30 feet of fishing line wrapped around it. He had found fishing line and some hooks in another dig a few days back. In another pocket he had a few rusty nails and bolts to use as weights. His sister had the bait…a pocketful of large, juicy earthworms. "Okay, sis, I'll keep the canoe going in a sensible direction. You get to fish."

Without hesitation, she handed the oar to her brother and skewered one of the earthworms on and around a hook. Then she attached a couple of bolts to the line a few feet above the hook. Maggie smiled at her big brother as she dropped it into the water.

"Didn't think I could do it, did ya?"

"Just the opposite Mags; I knew you could."

Three hours later Coop and Maggie arrived home with their catch of fish, all cleaned and ready to cook. They had sunk the canoe again but tied it to a portion of the dock under the waterline making it easier to find and use again.

Coop took the prerequisite fish tax to the commandant's office as his mother prepared dinner. He dropped the fish off without saying a word and returned home.

As soon as he walked in the door, he could smell his mother doing her magic. Fish and poultry were the main sources of protein for almost everyone. It was the eggs of the hens that were consumed, not the chickens themselves. They were too few and too valuable to eat. The wild dogs made sure of that. The same was true of cows. Their milk was far more valuable than the meat they could provide in the short term.

During the time Coop was gone, his mom had made a simple crust using hand-ground flour, a couple of eggs, some lard and milk. Rolling it out onto a lard greased piece of polished metal, she placed the fish onto the crust. After stuffing it with herbs and spices, she placed another rolled out crust on top of the fish and pinched the edges together, lathering the top with more lard. To the side of their home sat a small brick oven Henry and Cooper had built. She slipped the fish into the oven and closed the metal door. An hour later, it was time to eat.

The McIntyre family sat around an old card table Henry McIntyre had found in an earlier archeological dig in downtown Astoria. During the last couple of years he found an abundance of useable or repairable items in the ruins of the town. He was a good digger and the commandant let him keep the card table as an expression of appreciation. The only reason why the table had survived through the centuries was it was found in a dry dig, a dig that had not seen much moisture at all, which was rare in a rainy and more tropical climate. A dry dig usually provided the best of what the Ancients had. In this case, a collapsed roof had kept it so.

They all sat and stared at what sat at the center of the table. It was a 2 liter bottle of fresh water. What was truly unusual about the bottle was that it was glass. Virtually all liquids found to date were in plastic bottles. It was labeled Spearhead Springs. Coop asked softly, "Did this water actually come from a freshwater spring? I've heard of them, but never seen one."

"Apparently," said his dad with a smile. "The commandant gave up on the dry dig a week ago, but yesterday I found the bottle. I was alone at the time, so I just stuffed it in with some of the junk we'd dug up at another dig, and brought it home."

Maggie reached over and touched the bottle. "Are more bottles like this one around?"

Her dad nodded. "I'm certain of it. More will be uncovered as time goes on."

Camilla McIntyre placed on the table a bowl of freshly boiled potatoes and carrots, both of which had come out of their garden. Next, came the fish Maggie had caught. After offering a prayer of thanks, the family dug in.

Every family in the commune was expected to keep a vegetable garden and to give half of the produce to the commandant. Camilla pulled a small shaker of salt from the pocket of her well-used apron. She sprinkled some on the vegetables. Salt was difficult to find but her husband made sure they and their friends had a supply.

Henry opened the cap on the bottle of water and poured a half-cup into everyone's glass. Coop sampled his. "Wow, this isn't bad....no yucky after- taste."

The water they and everyone else at the commune usually drank came from a well in the middle of the compound. It was often dirty and had an odd taste. Henry had built a filter system that cleared up the water a great deal, but it still wasn't great. There was a lot about living in the commune that was less than desirable.

While they had all benefited somewhat from being part of the commune, life was progressively becoming intolerable as the commandant became more and more demanding. He wanted more production and less complaining. Some of those who did, were beaten, but not to the point where they couldn't work. No one was permitted to leave the compound, unless escorted by a guard. The

McIntyres and two other families soon planned to ignore the rule.

Two months earlier, Henry had proposed a plan to escape the compound and to venture south. But now the plan was becoming a reality and in a few days they would leave the homes they had lived in for more than two summers. It was either face the marauders who wandered the countryside, or live in relative safety inside the compound and work as servants. The McIntyres had been hiding most of what they had personally collected from various digs over the last two years, and did so in plain sight. The commandant's warehouse was a perfect place. It was wildly disorganized and Clark Cable had long forgotten what was stored in the building, which was formerly a gymnasium. The only person who knew exactly where everything was located, would soon leave.

The grounds were surrounded by a ten foot tall chain link fence topped with barbed wire. But that wasn't a problem for the McIntyres and their friends
on the night of their departure. A noisy and violent storm had struck the area and the three families simply walked past a guard post that had been abandoned because of the fear of lightning. It had struck the post several times during a

previous storm. A copper covered figure on a nearby flag pole was proved to be an excellent lightening rod.

Walking on long and crumbling roads, which had been abandoned, they hid in an underground shelter Henry and Coop had found while scavenging outside of town. The Commandant often sent Henry out to rummage through old buildings and stores in old Astoria looking for anything that was still usable or valuable. People who dug through the trash of previous generations were derisively called "garbage diggers." Henry preferred to be called an archeological digger. It referred to those who saw themselves as archeologists who dug up the past. Most people didn't even know what an archeologist was. Coop thought the name digger was just fine.

The initial plans for the journey south were fueled by a story his dad, William McIntyre, told saying

they had family who had traveled to and were living in Yosemite Valley, a place with almost mystical qualities. The trip would not be easy, especially in the California territory where it was said thousands of marauders ruled the landscape. Some of those marauders had moved up into the

Oregon territory and had killed Henry's parents when he was a young boy.

Finding an intact basement beneath a home that had collapsed was ideal. Sharing what little food and water they had, they planned to stay out of sight until the soldiers gave up searching.

By candlelight, Coop lay on his bed mat and wrote in one the most precious things he had, a journal. Actually he had several. He chewed on the end of his pencil, then finally asked, "Dad, I'm one of the McIntyres who has an unforgettable memory. Why am I writing all of this down?"

"It's for those who do not have a memory like yours, like me for instance. If I want to know what happened seven days ago and you aren't around, all I have to do is look it up in your diary."

Cooper nodded. "Do you know other people who have an unforgettable memory?"

"No, but I've heard they exist. Your grandfather believed every other generation of McIntyres had at least one person with a memory like yours. The Ancients called such a memory, photographic. But I prefer to use the term unforgettable, since you literally cannot forget anything. With so much of the population gone, I'm glad we have a few people like you, to help us keep things straight. We've lost so much, but people with memories like yours or even close, can help us rebuild and restore what was lost."

Henry shifted his weight in the broken down old chair. "I've read that more than 250 million people lived in America before Omega came. I've come across centuries old newspapers wrapped in plastic bags that have said millions died just on the West Coast alone. We have no idea how many people are left or what parts of the world are still populated."

"Unfortunately, all of the books we have uncovered so far were written before the Omega virus struck. So we know a lot about what life was like before Omega, but not after. Oral history is all we have now." Looking at Coop he smiled, "You have a big part to play in keeping history alive, at least until we can, once again, make paper and print books."

Henry looked around at their cramped quarters. "The last 200 years have led us into a period of cultural darkness. I am hoping you and your sister can help change that, along with our friends. The world emerged from a period called the Dark Ages a long time ago. I am confident that it is happening again and we are part of it."

Henry stopped to finish his meal, then continued. "Part of our family oral history says the McIntyres have roots right here in this area. When Omega struck, some members of our family and their friends ended up on some islands way out in the Pacific Ocean. Several generations later, it is believed a few of them returned to the West Coast."

From the other side of the underground shelter, Davy Jones asked, "Is that why we're going to this Yosemite place…to re-invent ourselves?"

Henry smiled. "Yes it is. I believe some of our McIntyre ancestors are living there, or at least have lived there and have established a place of learning and culture. Our goal is to help build on whatever we find. The isolation of Yosemite Valley can be the perfect place to rebuild our society without interference from those who don't give a damn."

Camilla spoke firmly, "Henry, watch your language"!

A few days later, leaving their hideaway, the three families hiked in a southerly direction walking on a long abandoned freeway. A barely legible sign identified it as highway 101. Henry had decided to make their journey to the south as near to the coast as possible. It would give them access to various kinds of ocean fish and maybe a few crabs. In addition, they were bound to come across deer, rabbits and other animals that would provide fresh meat.

Very little was left of abandoned cars and trucks. Sometimes, all that remained was the frame and part of an engine block or transmission. On occasion the travelers would see old rusted signs identifying towns and roads. The towns themselves, reminded Cooper of pictures that he had seen in books of cities that had been bombed during various wars. Much of the land was being reclaimed by nature. In a few places where water was plentiful and the rains fell more abundantly, green vegetation grew but for the most part, the land through which they walked was much drier than it once was. Coop looked skyward. The dark night sky held an explosion of stars and the moon appeared to be almost close enough to touch.

For almost six months, the families eked out an existence, fishing where they could, picking fruit and berries in some areas, but continuing on their quest to find sanctuary in the Yosemite Valley. Often hiking at night through and around towns by rivers and lakes where marauders often camped, they turned to the East and eventually came across another freeway that took them further south. They came across the Merced River and the remains of the city. Because of the abundance of rain in the mountains, the river was full, but not much was left of the town. Turning east toward the mountains, they followed the river up into the mountains. The McIntyre entourage stopped at a small village. An old barely readable sign identified it as El Portal. Only two brick buildings stood. All the others were piles of rotting wood and fallen debris. Everyone was amazed that the area seemed to be a virgin site. Diggers had not yet discovered the town. The McIntyres decided to stay for a few days to see what could be found, while the others were eager to press on. During the next few days they found a treasure trove of useable tools, odd looking clothing, a few readable books and other gear, much of it wrapped in clear fabric. A most amazing find was fishing tackle and a hunter's bow and arrow set, including both practice and razor sharp hunting arrows.

One job the McIntyres had at the compound, in addition to being diggers, was fishing. Henry used a pole and crude tackle that belonged to the Commandant. When they left Astoria, all they had was Cooper's rudimentary fishing gear. Now they had their own fishing tackle and it was good stuff. The trout were plentiful, so before they left, the family ate well.

Maggie expertly turned some fish cooking in a cast iron skillet. She had used the last of their cooking lard. As the fish popped and sizzled,

Camilla was cooking up some fresh vegetables in another skillet. Amazingly, weeds had not yet chocked out the vegetables of a long abandoned garden. It was still producing.

Ten minutes later, the family sat cross-legged around the fire, each with a plate full of deliciously smelling food.

Henry prayed. "O Lord, once again we are enjoying the bounty you have so graciously provided, and we thank you. We pray for our friends, who are ahead of us, and ask for your protection and blessing on them. Grant us a good night of rest, as we prepare for the adventure of tomorrow. Amen"

The next morning using two partly rusted, but usable wheel barrows they had dug out of the debris, the McIntyres carried away as much as they could and continued their trek up the river. In a few days, they hiked up and around a natural dam that had been formed on the river by an avalanche. They caught up with their friends who had stopped to rest for a few days when one of their party badly twisted an ankle.

But now all three families walked down into an open area. They discovered the beautiful and amazing Yosemite Valley, through which the river ran. On their left, they all stared in awe at a massive rock face soaring thousands of feet toward the sky. A fallen sign by the road identified it as El Capitan.

Birds and squirrels filled the trees and deer were seen by the hundreds, feeding in the tall grass on either side of the river. Walking further into the valley, they found dozens of collapsed and decaying buildings, and a few signs made of faded plastic identifying areas in different parts of the valley as Yosemite Village, Curry Village and Ahwahnee. The metal and wooden signs had disappeared long ago. While exposed wood and metal had long ago succumbed to rust and decay, a few things remained standing. Off to the left of the road, Coop spotted the falls that tumbled gloriously over the side of the cliff. Another intact sign identified it as Yosemite Falls. They walked up a litter covered trail leading toward the cascading falls. Climbing a hill, they came upon a stone bridge straddling a sizable creek. Like the stone aqueducts built by the ancient Romans, the construction stones of the bridge had withstood the ravages of time and nature. The three families all stared, almost transfixed as the mist from the falls blew over them.

Returning to the main road, the families decided to split up; one would go toward Yosemite Village, another to Curry Village, and the last to Ahwahnee. The McIntyres headed toward

Ahwahnee. An hour later they walked past a small stone gatehouse and followed the road, as it curved to the right. They were stunned by what they saw. It wasn't a town...it was a huge castle-like building and was five or six stories tall. Situated in a heavily forested valley between towering granite cliffs on one side and a massive granite dome of rock on the other, the Ahwahnee took one's breath away. Tall stone columns five or six feet wide supported the structure. Between the columns were massive paned windows and doorways. Many of the windows were of beautiful stained glass and were still intact. It was apparent that someone had been maintaining the structure, at least for a while.

The road was littered with branches, fallen trees and debris, but it led them to a large covered portico where an old car sat rusting. Henry imagined this was a drop off place for those who lived or visited. They followed a wooden walkway about a hundred feet long. It was in amazingly good repair. Only a few boards had rotted away. It led them to the main doors that were slightly ajar. Pulling with difficulty, the large doors opened revealing a lobby, complete with a fireplace and a tall desk. Keeping to their right, they walked into another lobby with another massive fireplace. Walking further, they came upon a cavernous room filled with broken tables, chairs and overturned furniture. From the amount of litter on the floor, it was obvious the room had not been used in a while. Dust and dirt was everywhere. Several of the massive windows were broken and signs of animals and birds littered the floor.

They found themselves staring up at the ceiling and beams of an expansive room. At one time, it must have been quite elegant. On either end were large open fireplaces and large stacks of firewood to burn in each. But it was clear, fires had not burned in either for quite some time.

The four McIntyres immediately went to work picking out the usable furniture so they would have someplace to sit in front of one of the fireplaces. Beautiful glass chandeliers hung from a ceiling. They had to be thirty feet high. Well-worn tapestries and artwork adorned the walls. With a little help, it could be, once again, an extraordinarily beautiful place.

Within an hour, a fire was burning. Cooper and his sister plopped down on a sofa. Coop smiled, "This is pretty comfortable. I'll sleep here tonight." Henry looked around. "This is what the ancients called an Inn or a Lodge. I'll bet hundreds of people stayed here on a regular basis."

Above the impressive stone fireplace was a large painting. It appeared to be a painted glass image of the Ahwahnee. Off to the right imbedded in the stone at eye level was a piece of polished metal. It looked like brass. Most of the letters on the metal were worn off. Coop walked over and placed his hand on it. It was warm to the touch and he heard a slight hum. Suddenly, an image that moved and spoke replaced the motionless scene on the glass.

"I never think of the future. It comes soon enough." *Albert Einstein*

Chapter 3

Henry and his family stood with their mouths agape at the apparition of an old man on the glass continued.

"Welcome to the Ahwahnee Lodge. My name is Ezra John Wayne, the 5th or is it the 6th? I don't remember now. No matter, it is Friday, June 21st in the year 2161 A.D. In case your education is incomplete the letters A.D. are an abbreviation for the Latin phrase Anno Domini...in the year of our Lord. Our traditional calendar is based on the years before the birth of Jesus Christ, B.C. or after, A.D. representing the reality that Jesus rose

from the dead and is yet alive sitting at the right hand of God the Father Almighty."

"Some yahoos have tried to change the designations from B.C to BCE (before the Common Era) and from A.D. to A.C.E. (after the Common Era), therefore eliminating the need to refer to Jesus Christ as the center point of history. The whole thing is ridiculous since, in either case, we are still talking about the dates of history before or after the birth of Christ."

"Oh my stars, there I go again. I must apologize. It's just that we don't get many visitors up here anymore, hardly ever unless it's the marauders, and they are mindless thugs. Watch out for them, they would just as soon kill you as spit."

"Anyway, since you are watching this video, I'm either out walking in the woods or in the latrine that's out back. I'm 85 years old, you know. That's pretty old in this day and age. It may be that I have died. In that case, you are likely to find my emaciated and decaying body lying around somewhere….unless some animals drug me off. It's possible the marauders came up from the valley and finished me, but I doubt it. But of the entire family of forty, I'm the only one left. I've outlived them all, except for my son Ezra who left the valley thirty years ago. I haven't heard from him since. One of the McIntyres from Yosemite

50

Village left about a 100 years or more ago. Nobody heard from him either."

"Just so you know, to my knowledge the Omega virus doesn't exist in the valley. But since I'm left handed, it wouldn't affect me anyway. As you may or may not know, left-handed people seem to be immune to Omega."

"In this part of the country, the Ahwahnee Lodge is probably the finest building left in existence, especially with all that is going on these days. We have worked hard for over 150 years to keep this place a testimony to the beauty of God's creation, and to establish an outpost of learning for future generations, should they exist and find their way here. Obviously you have, so I hope you enjoy your stay. Pick any room you like. They're all available. Just sweep out the spiders and such."

"Every floor of the hotel has part of an extensive library we have collected over the years during our travels. Please note that there is much MORE to our library than meets the eye."

"As you have noticed we do have electricity which is a rare thing in many parts of the world today. It is provided by a very old VEPS unit that has been rebuilt dozens of times; a couple of times by its inventor, so I'm told. If it gives you any trouble, you may have to jiggle a few wires. Other than that, read the instructions."

"There are hiking trails all over Yosemite and plenty of game and fish. Be careful of the rock falls that occur from time to time near the cliffs. If you do find my body, please bury me in the cemetery out back. The grave is already dug. Just plop me in there, throw in some dirt and say a few words. But hopefully I'll be walking in to greet you sometime soon. If not...much obliged."

Cooper's dad exclaimed, "Son, what did you do?"

He shrugged his shoulders and pointed, "I merely touched that metal plate. Maybe we have just seen some of our past come back to life."

"The simplest and most complex examples of life and the universe itself, are in themselves so awe inspiring as to be a sufficient proof for the existence of God." (The Author)

Chapter 4

The McIntyres stood there staring at the screen that had returned to what it looked like originally. Finally Coop spoke, "Who was that guy?"

His dad smiled, "In all likelihood, he was a distant relative of ours. The name Ezra goes way back in our family history along with other names like Cooper, Kate, Maggie and Camilla. The McIntyre that left from Yosemite Village may have been my grandfather or great grandfather, but my dad rarely talked about family. He was too busy trying to feed us and put a roof over our heads. I don't ever remember him taking a day off. We actually saw very little of your grandfather, and he died too early for any of you to remember him."

Henry looked around at the mess that still surrounded them. "Let's get to work."

Over the next several months, they reclaimed the Ahwahnee. Coop numbered the days in his diary, figuring them to be sixty-three since they had arrived. He put a line through the days on the handmade calendar his dad designed and hand-drawn for the families in Yosemite.

In their digging, they had come across old calendars the ancients used. But society had long ago lost track of the days, months and even the current year. While the McIntyres kept the same names for the 12 months of a year and the number of days in each year and month, the days of the week was a different story. The very ancient Roman designations for the days of the week (Monday, Tuesday and etc.) were not helpful in planning the central activities of a week. So Cooper and his dad came up with a five day week. Part of the activities of every day included a special focus. The first day was Worshipday, which was a day of honoring God and of rest. Then came Schoolday. Including Cooper and Maggie, there were seven who attended school. On Washday the morning was set aside to do laundry. On Bakeday, women gathered to bake bread and pastry for the week. Then came Marketday, which was a day set aside to barter goods and services. Each month, then, had six weeks in it. The five day week worked well and had become an accepted part of life in Yosemite.

While in Astoria, his dad had used an old wind-up clock Coop had repaired, to discover the longest night of the year. He decided the next day was Worshipday, January first in the year 2216. He, of course, had no idea if it was accurate, but wanted to start somewhere. Coop looked at his calendar. It was a good beginning. He smiled. Tomorrow was Bakeday, his favorite day of the week.

A large workshop was behind the Lodge, along with a small blacksmith shop containing tools and supplies. Those tools enabled them to repair much of what was damaged and to reconstruct the greenhouse that had partially collapsed.

Coop found the remains of old Ezra on a small bed in the basement near a smaller workshop, along with an assortment of items on which he had been tinkering. The skeletal remains suggested he had been dead for a long time. On his workbench they discovered a manual for the Vanderhooten Electrical Power System. They buried Ezra John Wayne in the grave he, himself, had likely dug. All of the other graves had numbers on them. A journal found in the solarium, told of the identity of each person and had a synopsis of their lives. Maggie wrote what she could about the old man.

Maggie and Coop cleaned up the solar power unit, replaced a few wires and, as long as the sun was out, it produced electricity. The batteries no longer held a charge, and Henry had not yet discovered how to repair them. Using the few power tools still working, the tools revealed a whole new world of wood-working possibilities for father and son. But each evening, when the sun went down and darkness enveloped the Ahwahnee, Coop could be found sitting next to the fire, reading. The bookshelves contained thousands of books. Since he had inherited from somewhere along the family genetic pool a memory that forgot nothing, he spent most of his free time reading. All he had to do was look at a page and all the material was indelibly imprinted in his brain. He would almost rather read than eat...but not quite.

Several weeks later, Coop's mom handed him a plastic bag filled with leftover food from the previous day. He and Mary Kate, who had introduced him to the some of the pleasures of a boy/girl relationship, were headed out for a picnic. She met him at the head of the trail leading them down river to one of their favorite spots. Mary Kate was the oldest daughter of the Wilsons, who were staying at Yosemite Village. She spread out a blanket on a sandy part of the riverbank. After an hour of intense relationship building, they had not yet touched their lunch. The two young lovers were thankful this part of the river was partially shaded. Laying on their backs for a moment, Mary Kate offered, "Maybe we should take a break and go for a swim to cool off."

Cooper smiled at his first real girlfriend. "Sounds good to me. But the water might be a little chilly though. You go first."

She sat up on one elbow and looked at him almost solemnly. "Are you the one?"

He answered a little perplexed, "One what?"

"You know, the one who'll lead us out of the Dark Ages, as your dad describes it."

Cooper laughed, "What on earth makes you think that?"

She continued, "My mom thinks you are. She says you're far and away the smartest person she has ever met and, like your dad, you're a good leader. From my perspective, you're not afraid of anything, in fact your self-confidence is almost irritating."

Cooper shook his head. "Even if all those things were true, none of them qualifies me as the one you're talking about. As far as I'm concerned, while I may know more than my Dad, he is far smarter than I am. There's a huge difference between knowing something and knowing how or when to use that knowledge."

She wouldn't be dissuaded. "Maybe you're our next Moses or Daniel, leading us out of the lion's den that we live in, because of Omega."

He scowled, "What do you know of Moses or Daniel?"

She replied indignantly, "You're not the only one who reads, Mr. Smarty pants." She pouted slightly. "It's just that my mom is a pretty good judge of people and is the reason why we came with your family in the first place. She's rarely wrong about stuff like this."

Cooper reached out and touched her cheek. "Don't you think God would kinda let me know if I was the one?"

She grinned, "Maybe you haven't been listening. Are you hungry yet?"

He rolled over on top of her. She said softly, "Guess not."

Coop pulled her close kissing her mouth and then the side of her neck, taking her by surprise. He pulled back, passion still smoldering in his eyes. She looked up at him touching her mouth where his kiss still lingered. She murmured, "You're a fast learner, McIntyre."

After a few minutes, they laid back on the blanket and stared at the beauty of Yosemite Valley. She asked, "Are we always going to live in Yosemite?"

"Not sure. More than likely, some will stay, but others will eventually leave. I suspect I'll be one of the latter."

She added with a concerned voice. "I hope you don't. I like it here. I hope we stay forever."

Mary Kate continued in a soft tone, "Do you think God had a specific purpose in creating places like this? I never tire of just looking at the trees, the river, the mountains and animal life. And don't get me started about what the sky is like at night.
The explosion of stars is incredible."

Coop replied as he sat up, "I think God created areas like this all over the world, to remind us of His power, His loving-kindness and the value he places on having a relationship with us. How can we not think of God when we see nature in all its glory? How can people not believe in God?"

Mary Kate commented, "Sometimes, I think God talks to me, when I'm all alone, and staring at the stars. Do you hear God sometimes?"

He responded quickly, "I think I've heard God in a lot of different situations, whispering things in my head. Does that sound crazy?"

She leaned over and nuzzled her boyfriend's ear. "Not at all."

It was late in the afternoon when they strolled back into the kitchen of the Ahwahnee. Cooper had brought along his fishing gear and handed his mother the catch of the day. They could hear his dad speaking in the room next door. Camilla smiled, "Your dad has been talking for some time with Mary Kate's parents about God's plan and purpose for us. Cooper and Mary Kate slipped in trying to be as unobtrusive as possible.

Henry continued, "As difficult as all this has been for the last two centuries, I'm convinced God preserved a remnant he would use for His purposes, in rebuilding and restoring His creation." He looked at his left hand. "We are it. The only remaining question is, are we willing to be a part of God's plan, whatever it is." Henry looked at Mary Kate as she and Cooper walked in. "How was lunch?"

"Great!"

He smiled, "Do you even remember what it was?"

Mary Kate blushed deeply. "Mostly fruit and vegetables, I think." She looked at Cooper for help who just grinned, but finally said, "We were preoccupied, Dad. We had a conversation about Daniel and the lion's den."

Henry laughed and looked at Mary Kate's parents. "So, is that what they call it now?" We thought you were "making out."

Mary Kate stared at Cooper and mouthed silently, "What's making out?" He shrugged his shoulders.

"Some books are meant to be tasted, others to be swallowed, and some few to be chewed and digested." *Francis Bacon*

Chapter 5

It was after dinner on the next day that the McIntyre family sat around the fireplace in the Library Suite's parlor room, enjoying a warm fire and talking about their day. Coop threw a piece of wood on the fire.

"Dad, when we got here Ezra told us about the extensive library of the Ahwahnee."

"And you son, have made fine use of it. So why do you mention it?"

"It is not nearly as extensive as I thought it would be. We had a bigger library back in Astoria. Ezra's choice of words has got me thinking. Do you remember when he encouraged us to 'please note that there is much MORE to our library than meets the eye?' Why did he emphasize the word *more*?"

Henry smiled. "I was wondering when you would ask about that. Your mom and I have wrestled with that odd emphasis for a while. The only thing that we have come up with is that the library may have more significant value than we can see at the moment."

Cooper nodded. "Yeah, I have been thinking along those lines myself. But what if the word *more* is a hint at something else?"

"Like what?"

"I'm not sure. But you yourself have said there are some inconsistencies around the Ahwahnee; like the fact the third floor library room is slightly warmer than any other room in the place. It is so despite being located on the coolest side of the building."

His mom smiled and looked at her son. "What are you implying, Coop?"

"I'm not implying anything yet. It is a mystery much like Ezra's emphasis on the word *more*. No matter how bizarre it seems, is there a possibility that the two are somehow connected? Obviously there is something else Ezra wanted us to understand."

Henry shook his head. "Why then, didn't he just come right out and say it?"

Cooper smiled broadly. "Because it's a clue he gave for only certain people to figure out...people like us. We're smart, dad; you've said so yourself. The word *more* must mean something else."

Maggie, who was sitting on the sofa with her older brother, punched him in the shoulder. "You're crazier than I thought. What else can the word *more* mean than just *more*?"

Cooper stood and grinned at his family. "What if it were a proper noun with the name More?" He spelled it out.

"So what, son? Where does that get us? There are likely to be dozens of book titles with the name Moore or More on them."

"Actually there are thirty three. I've read six of them." He picked up one of the glass chimney candles and ran upstairs to the third floor library. His family was not far behind. When he reached the right section, he began pulling books off the shelf. All the volumes were on the floor as his parents and sister caught up to him.

Henry laughed. "Okay Coop, now what?"

He drew closer to the empty shelf and looked carefully. It was barely visible and was behind the next book on the shelf, a biography of Sir Thomas More.

He pushed the small button and the whole bookshelf began to move. A four-foot wide section of the bookcase slid straight back a foot then moved to the left, disappearing behind the wall. A soft blast of warm air filled the room.

"Careful son," warned his dad.

Candle in hand, Coop stepped forward. Before anyone else could move, the four-foot section quickly returned to its original position. He heard his parent's yelling. He hollered back. "I'm okay! Give me a few minutes to check this place out!"

In the flickering candlelight he could see the room was fairly large, about twenty by thirty feet with a ten-foot ceiling. Two walls were covered with bookcases and books. A comfortable-looking reading chair was stationed on the third wall, accompanied by a twin-sized bed. On the fourth wall was a desk, on which sat a smaller version of what they saw in the Great Room. Next to the screen sat a tall box. A small light was flashing on both the screen and the box. Immediately to the right of the desk was a door. He opened it to discover a small bathroom and sink. To the right of the door was a small kitchen. Coop saw a larger red button on the edge of the bookcase and pressed it. The section slid back open. His parents and sister looked anxiously at him. His mom was actually furious with him.

"What were you thinking about going in there by yourself?!"

Risking further chastisement, Cooper smiled thinly and offered, "Mom, I wasn't afraid and I didn't know the bookshelf section was going to close so rapidly. I'm sorry."

As they spoke, the doorway closed once again. Henry asked, "What did you see in there?"

"It appears to be a secret room of some sort, complete with a small kitchen, bathroom, bed and a chair and surprise, surprise...floor to ceiling books. The spines of some appear to be made of leather which could make them very old even by the Ancient's standards."

Henry nodded. "Okay, I think we have had enough excitement for one day. We'll take a closer look at Cooper's hideaway tomorrow."

Coop smiled. "I saved the best for last. Sitting on a desk is a smaller version of Ezra's moving picture device. I think the ancients called them computers."

His dad's eyes widened. "Really...a working computer. There's a manual for a computer called Apple in the downstairs library. This could get really interesting....tomorrow. Off to bed, all of you."

The next morning after breakfast, Maggie and Coop explored the hideaway. An overhead light came on as soon as they entered. It was assumed VEPS was now supplying power to the hideaway. The computer was not an Apple, but had the two initials, *HP,* inscribed on the tall metal case and on the side of the moving picture screen. Coop was quickly scanning the *HP* instruction manual his sister had found in a desk drawer.

Maggie had recently made the transition from being a youth to a woman and had already made two trips to the small bathroom, which was quite functional. She began to notice she could read almost as fast as Coop and remembered most of what she had read. Maggie decided that memory skills must have leaked into her gene pool as a result of body maturity which was, in the McIntyre family, a trigger for a memory that didn't forget anything.

The two began to spend all of Schoolday each week, and any other spare time they had, pouring through the books in Cooper's hideaway. Coop spent a lot of time becoming familiar with the HP computer. The Vanderhooten Electrical Power System was, evidently, providing power for the computer and other electrical needs in the room, including a quartz rod space heater. Now it was understood why the third floor room was a few degrees warmer than the rest of the Lodge. The other families at Curry Village and Yosemite Lodge were fascinated with Cooper's hideaway as well.

As the months passed into years, each week the three families got together to share a Worshipday meal and to talk about what they had found in various parts of Yosemite. Mary Kate's family discovered what remained of a museum and what was left of an Indian habitation. It was clear someone in Yosemite had been working on preserving what they could of the Indian's culture. But very little was left. Eventually both families moved over to the Ahwahnee and worked together to build a small community. There was even talk of going back down into the valley to see if anyone else was interested in making Yosemite their home.

One of the older men was a martial arts expert. During the months and years that followed, he would teach Cooper everything he knew. Coop was an apt pupil, not only studying Jujitsu and karate, but also learning everything there was to know about the material contained on hundreds of DVD's and CD's. Seeing the past come to life was a life-changing experience. Recovering what had been lost after Omega, was now an all-consuming passion for Cooper.

"That which doesn't kill us, makes us stronger." *Friedrich Nietzsche*

Chapter 6

About three summers later, according to the number of months he totaled in his journals and on his personal calendar, Cooper McIntyre rolled out of his bed. He began the exercise routine that would forever be a part of his life. Now considered an adult, he was twenty years of age and could no longer be described as tall and gangly. He had filled out considerably. Running for hours at a time on the trails of Yosemite Valley, and with his mom's fine cooking, it all kept him in good shape. Cooper had read that because of the changes in weather patterns to the North, the weather in Yosemite had also become much milder and the winter snows were not nearly as harsh. As he stretched, his eye caught the fresh bread, an orange and piece of fish that lay on the table in his room. The supply of oranges and string beans from the heated greenhouse, over the winter was steady, but getting a little monotonous. The orange tree was the only one to survive among six that had been planted, by an unknown gardener. Animals had strewn the dried remains of vegetables on the greenhouse floor. Seeds found on the ground, were all carefully planted and nurtured, but only the string beans had sprouted.

There was hope other seeds found in the greenhouse would eventually be coaxed back to life. It wouldn't be long before he and his dad would begin to plant more wheat in the field in front of what was, as photographs had shown, a once beautiful meadow. The spring and summer months were wonderfully pleasant, and gave the valley an enviable growing season, as it did for much of the Northwes Panting from his rigorous set of crunches and push-ups, Coop lay on the wooden floor of his room and looked toward the window at floor level. One of the boards adjacent to the wall was slightly higher than the others. He pulled out the pocket knife his dad had given him, and crawled over. Prying up the board, he discovered a canvas bag.

He carefully opened the bag, and pulled out an object wrapped loosely in oilcloth. As he removed the cloth, he found an old revolver. Coop recognized it immediately. He had seen it in one of the books he had read on firearms. It was a Colt .45 dated back into the late 1800's or early 1900's. It had an easily removable cylinder that shot six times in rapid succession. It then could be exchanged for a full cylinder. Coop eyed the gun. The cylinder was full. He spun it slowly and cocked the hammer. All the pieces moved easily. It had been well cared for before it was wrapped in oil cloth. On the worn inlaid wooden handle was inscribed very neatly, the name Kate. He smiled. "I bet there's a story behind this."

Coop reached back down into the hidden chamber and removed several boxes of ammunition and two other full cylinders. There was a note.

"In case you haven't noticed, there are very few places where one can buy ammunition for anything. So when I use the Colt, I save the brass and reload them myself. There is a re-loader in the basement, including a couple of bags of gun powder, some chunks of lead and a cast-iron mold. Instructions are under the re-loader. After a couple of tries you'll get the hang of it. As for the gun, just point and pull the trigger. The Colt will do the rest. Take care of her. She has saved my hide more than once."

Coop re-wrapped the Colt, placed it back in the canvas bag and returned it to its hiding place. He carefully fitted the wood plank on top and ran downstairs to talk to his dad. Maybe he no longer had to hunt just with the bow and arrow.

In the lobby, Henry was arguing with three unfamiliar men. They were dirty and rough looking. He saw his son approaching. "Coop, please take Oscar out for a walk." It was a code phrase to be used only in an extreme emergency. Coop walked slowly back toward the kitchen, where his mom was working. Camilla looked up at the worried face on her son. "What's the matter, Coop?"

"We have to get out of here right now. We have unwelcome visitors. Where's Maggie?" Before she could answer, three other men burst into the room. A monstrously big man grabbed Cooper and tossed him brutally against the wall and beat him severely.

As he fell to the floor the man walked by and stomped on Coop's lower leg, breaking it. "Oscar will have to wait."

The man turned toward Camilla. "You're a mighty handsome woman. What say you and I dance a little?" She backed up to a table.

"Resistance is futile. It will only make me mad. I'm going to get you one way or the other."

She ripped open her bodice exposing herself. "Come get them, big boy." He rushed forward and buried his head in her chest, groping viciously. Camilla held his head with her left hand, while reaching for a long paring knife behind her on the table. She quickly shoved the blade into his left eye while twisting it savagely. He stood up screaming in anguish as he pulled out the knife. With blood streaming out of his eye socket, he grabbed Camilla's head and snapped it sharply, breaking her neck not realizing he was within moments of death himself. She was the last person who would die at his hands. Camilla fell to the floor in a heap. He collapsed on top of her. Cooper helplessly watched his mother die. The two other men ran back into the lobby. He crawled painfully to his mom and pulled the dead thug off of her. He covered her up and cried uncontrollably.

Screams began to erupt from different places at the Ahwahnee. Using his strong upper torso and arms, he dragged himself into the now empty lobby. His dad lay on the floor, bleeding from several terrible knife wounds to his abdomen. His last words before he died were, "Save your sister and mom. Get out of here." He didn't seem to notice his son was unable to walk.

With difficulty, Coop pulled himself up the stairs to his room and retrieved the revolver and the two extra cylinders. He lifted himself up to the window and sat on his knees. At least thirty men were grabbing what they could, including Maggie, Mary Kate and the other women right below his window. Their husbands were being knifed or bludgeoned to death where they stood. Coop broke the window and pointed the gun at one of the marauders. He pulled the trigger and the shot missed. The next shot hit the man in the chest. The men all looked around. It was rare to hear a gunshot anymore. Coop used their confusion to his advantage. He aimed and shot three more men, as he emptied the revolver. A red-headed man pointed up at him and yelled, "There he is!! Go get him, and I want that gun."

Several ran back into the lodge. Coop drug himself out the door and into the hall at the top of the stairs. He quickly changed out the cylinder. When the men appeared on the stairwell, he waited until they were about ten feet away, then shot them in succession. Four more men followed and as they rushed up, Coop fired at almost point-blank range. He popped in the last cylinder as the only remaining unwounded man tripped over the others. As the marauder looked up, Coop aimed carefully. It was one of the men from the kitchen.

With a grim smile he pulled the trigger. The force of the bullet snapped the guy's head back. No one else tried climbing the stairs. The marauders left the Ahwahnee with their screaming captives.

Hearing his sister scream, "*Cooper!!!*", he drug himself back to the window and yelled as loudly as he could as the marauders left, "I will find you Sis!!!"

"Although the world is full of suffering, it is also full of the overcoming of it." *Helen Keller*

Chapter 7

Fortunately, it was Coop's shinbone that had been broken, not the larger tibia in his lower leg. And it was a simple fracture instead of the more difficult complex break when the skin was punctured by broken bone. It was painful and awkward, but he managed to set his own leg, probing and pushing until he was convinced the two broken edges were close together. He wrapped the leg with a clean towel, then tied a half dozen wooden splints around the area where the break was.

It took days, but on his knees he dragged his mom and dad and the bodies of the others back around to the cemetery. Earlier he had found a pair of kneepads tile setters had used working on the Ahwahnee. The pads made the job a little easier. Coop was also thankful that an eight foot high wrought-iron fence set in a concrete footing, surrounded the cemetery. It would keep the carnivores from digging up his family. Rather than try to crawl back upstairs, Coop decided to sleep in the basement as old Ezra obviously did.

Earlier, after they had discovered Ezra's remains, they had changed out the mattress and put on fresh linen and blankets. It suited Coop just fine. The work shop down there was well tooled and someone had installed a small sink and shower with hot and cold running water. Ezra had used a hot plate to cook simple meals, so would Coop. An old pot-belly stove sat several feet away from the bed. Wood was still stacked against a wall. In the opposite corner he found a large Galileo telescope that had been covered with a light weight tarp. He remembered that Galileo Galilei had studied the heavens more than 600 years earlier with a primitive handmade telescope. He dared to publish his conclusions suggesting that the earth was not the center of the universe. Leaders in the church were none too happy. When Coop's leg was better, he planned to check out the moon, stars and planets. He doubted he would have much trouble with a church that had a lot more on its mind than any discussion about the universe.

His agile mind turned to a book he had read about space exploration. It was difficult to believe that man had once walked on the moon and lived for months at a time in an elaborate space station orbiting the earth. He read in a an old newspaper that had survived the ravages of time about several men and one woman who were left stranded on the International Space Station.

Coop wondered, could humanity recover enough of its technology and manufacturing expertise, in his lifetime, to at least fly once again? He decided anything was possible.

The water tower the Ancients had built on the hill behind the lodge had long ago rusted out. It had been replaced by a large wooden tank. Water from a nearby creek kept it reasonably full and the tank was a lot easier to keep in good repair. It leaked a little, but the runoff was funneled down to the greenhouse. There was a difference in height between the water tank and the lodge of about 50 feet. The PVC pipe that the earlier occupants had installed, carried the water at substantial pressure to the Ahwahnee.

The VEPS supplied power to a small 15-gallon electric water heater and a few florescent lights he had liberated from rooms that were not in use and placed in rooms that were. With difficulty Coop brought over several of the smaller electric powered tools from the larger workshop to help him with his projects.

The first thing Coop made in the shop was a pair of crutches. They helped him get around more easily and with greater speed. For food, he ate freely from the greenhouse garden and worked hard to keep it producing. Every other day or so he would make his way down to the Merced River to catch some fish. His diet was plain, but it kept him healthy.

Ezra had brought down from the main building hundreds of books representing various disciplines of study...medicine, engineering, science, physics, archeology, horticulture and animal husbandry. He also had thrown in a couple of murder mysteries including one called Murder at the Ahwahnee Lodge. They all kept Coop's mind active and sharp. But now something was gnawing at the edges of his unforgettable memory.

Using his crutches, Coop returned to his bedroom and knelt once more at the floor niche where he found his revolver. Reaching inside he explored the bottom with his fingers and discovered the small hole he had seen when he pulled out the handgun and ammunition. He inserted a small stick and pulled upward. The false bottom easily lifted. Inside, he found a gold pocket watch wrapped in a piece of oil cloth. On the reverse side a name was inscribed: Cooper McIntyre 1940. The watch must have belonged to his great, great grandfather. Coop wondered if he looked anything like him. He pushed a button that opened the watch. As the cover popped open, a faded picture had been secured inside. His grandfather was thin, but nice looking. Coop bore little resemblance to him. He asked aloud, "I wonder if he had an unforgettable memory?"

In just four months he was ready to leave the valley. His agenda for the moment was simple; find the group of men who murdered his parents and kidnapped his sister. He knew the marauder leader had red hair, a raspy voice and a face he would never forget. Of course, he couldn't forget any of them. And he would do everything in his power to find Maggie and the others, should they still be alive. He thought about what his dad said about being part of God's remnant. Evidently the number of those in the remnant was getting smaller.

Coop knew it was an audacious thing to do, but he was beginning to wonder about the nature of God's plan. He would never disbelieve God's existence, but was unsure of God's role in all that was happening. As he thought about it, did God just create the universe, then step back to watch it all unfold? And if God was an actual presence in the lives of people, why hadn't he yet brought forth someone to give direction and hope? If those in the remnant were going to restore and rebuild society, who was going to lead them? Maybe it was the Librarian. All he knew for sure was that it wasn't him.

He slung an official Yosemite backpack over his shoulder. It was filled with some basic things that would help him survive what he was beginning to believe would be a long journey. He tied his unstrung bow and a sleeping blanket onto the backpack, along with a dozen or so hunting arrows. His loaded Colt .45 was secured to his hip in a leather holster he had fashioned. He was ready. As Coop walked down the road toward the main gate he looked back at the Ahwahnee. Would he ever return?

A couple of hours later he passed the massive cliff El Capitan as it extended skyward on his right. He had read that people actually climbed that 2,000 foot high rock just for fun. He shook his head. They must have been crazy back then.

Instead of following the road out of Yosemite down the Merced River into the valley below, Coop followed another road that turned in a northerly direction headed up into the mountains outside of Yosemite. Two days later he came across a bridge. It had, at one time, crossed a rather formidable river but was now laying in pieces. In the distance he could see spirals of smoke drifting into the air. Somebody lived up there and he was going to find out who they were. To say he was about to be surprised by what he found, would be a profound understatement.

"The world cares very little about what a man or woman knows; it is what the man or woman is able to do with what he or she knows that counts. *Booker T. Washington*

Chapter 8

Coop crossed a tree-lined ridge and stared at a narrow valley below him. He was given directions to the valley by some people in a small village a day's walk outside of Yosemite itself. It wasn't as big as most valleys were; maybe four or five miles wide and seven or eight miles long, but was apparently quite fertile. The valley floor was sub-divided into sections. He pulled out a pair of binoculars he had found in one of Ezra's storage boxes at the Ahwahnee. The fields were separated by split rail fences and narrow dirt roads. Several sections were devoted to grazing sheep, cattle and horses but most were planted with various crops. Water from irrigation ditches were keeping the fields green. What was interesting was that some of the fields were filled with black sheep and others with white.

He continued walking down the crumbling and cracked pavement of the road until he came to a concrete bridge that had at one time straddled the river. The center portions of the bridge had collapsed into water that was fairly deep and was at least a 50 yards wide. Cooper guessed that over the centuries, strong currents of water had eroded the foundation piers of the bridge causing them to give way. Water tumbled over and around broken sections of concrete and steel rebar.

In the distance he could see with his binoculars the spires of a couple of churches extending above and through the trees. Somehow he would figure out a way to get across the fast-moving water. But that would be tomorrow's business. Right now he was a little tired and hungry.

An hour later his camp was set up and a couple of trout were frying in the small cast iron skillet he used to prepare most of his meals. He even ate from the skillet minimizing the cleanup.

Along with the Colt revolver and fishing tackle, he had brought along a few kitchen utensils, some spices and cooking lard. Coop had sewn on some heavy loops and pockets on the outside of his backpack to carry a few essential tools, a small hatchet and some rope. He had reserved two large zippered pockets for several handfuls of various sized nuts and bolts he had found in Ezra's workshop.

Coop used a hot pad to lift the frying pan from the coals of the fire and set it on a flat rock to let it cool for just a few minutes. He looked toward the fields across the river hoping he could find some vegetables to add to his mostly protein diet.

A half mile away up on a rock ledge, a large cougar rested comfortably as he finished eating a small coyote he had killed 20 minutes earlier. At almost eight feet in length and two hundred pounds, he was far bigger than most and powerful. The tawny colored cat lifted his head to catch scents that were vaguely familiar; fish being cooked and that of a man. But, satisfied for the moment, he just growled and laid his head back down.

Cooper heard the growl and turned his head up stream. He would have a restless sleep tonight even with his Colt at hand. Using a fork, he dug into his meal thanking God as he did so and praying for the safety of his sister and Mary Kate.

The next morning the sun had risen slightly over the trees to the east but its rays had yet to touch

Coop's camp. He snuggled a little deeper into the warmth of his sleeping bag. Then he heard a soft snap. Before he went to bed he had thrown some dried twigs in about a 12 foot circle around his campsite. Without hesitation he rolled out of his sleeping bag with his gun in hand cocked and pointed in the direction of the sound.

The intruder lifted his hands and said, "Good morning. Didn't mean to startle ya."

Coop holstered his gun as he stood up. "You should be careful about walking into a camp without announcing your intentions." He extended his hand. "Good morning."

The man backed up slightly. "You're an outlander, aren't ya?"

Coop dropped his hand and smiled. 'If you mean that I am not from around here, you are right. I've come over from Yosemite Valley. My name's Cooper. What's yours?"

The man eyed Coop carefully. "I'm called Jeremiah. We've heard stories about folk living up in Yosemite. Had one visit us a long time ago. I've never seen an outlander up close and personal. You got the sickness?"

"Nope. I'm left handed."

"What's that got to do with it?"

Cooper toed the dirt a little. "For some reason, those who are left handed cannot catch the

Omega virus. How long ago did someone from Yosemite visit your town?"

Jeremiah thought for a moment. "Not exactly sure, but it was a long time ago. He didn't stay long....about 10 years or so."

Cooper held his breath a little as he asked, "Do you remember his name?"

"Shore. He helped make our little town what it is today. Everyone knows about William McIntyre."

Coop looked over toward the river and then back
at Jeremiah. "My full name is Cooper Wellsley McIntyre."

Jeremiah's mouth dropped open. "The hell you say. Gotta go tell the town council." He started to leave but turned around and reached over to shake Coop's hand. "Don't go anywhere. I'll be a'coming back."

He promptly turned and quickly walked up river. Coop just watched as the man disappeared around the bend. He was more than a little odd. The man was dressed in black from head to toe. Even his beard was black.

Looking down, he toed the remnants of his fire to see if there were any hot coals left. Seeing none, he bent over and placed some tinder on the fire bed, covered it with some small dry twigs followed by some larger ones. He flipped open his old Zippo lighter and lit the tinder. He had found it and a full can of lighter fluid, in an old basement workshop in Astoria. His dad had said he could keep it and after all these years he had only lit the lighter a dozen times. A flame erupted and he concentrated on making the most of it, adding bigger pieces of wood. The flame began to die down, so he leaned over and blew gently.

A quarter mile away a hungry cougar had left his morning lair and crept silently down to within 25 feet of his prey. He was eyeing the man carefully. He had eaten the flesh of a human once. A bear had been interrupted in his meal and he managed to sneak off with part of a leg. It was good eating, nice and tender. He sprang from his crouch and was on the man in seconds. The big cat heard a terrible scream as he sank his teeth into the neck of his victim.

Coop heard the scream and in moments was running upstream as fast as he could. He saw the cougar throwing Jeremiah around as if he were a toy. When he was about 20 feet away he knelt, aimed carefully and pulled the trigger three times in succession. Each shot echoed in the valley and hit the animal; once in the hip, once in the gut and the last managed to graze part of his heart. The cougar dropped his meal and began to run away only to collapse after about 30 feet. He growled at the second man who walked up and put a bullet in his brain.

Cooper stepped back to the man in black. From the huge chunk of flesh missing from his neck and the amount of blood on the ground, he knew the man had died almost instantly, thank God. He stripped Jeremiah of his coat and placed it over his head as he mused aloud, "And just exactly where were you headed?"

He walked along the river's edge for another five minutes and saw the miner's cart dangling from a cable stretched over the river. The ore cart was attached to a three wheeled trolley system sitting on the cable. Coop trotted back to his campsite and returned with his backpack to where Jeremiah lay. Fortunately, he was not a big man and Coop was able to carry him to the cart. After placing the body inside he examined the cable and cart system to see how it worked. The cable was set at an incline. The frame that held the cable and cart up on the other side was built higher than the frame on his side. Gravity brought it over. But going back up that incline was another matter.

He spotted a half inch thick polyester rope hanging off the front edge of the cart and extending all the way up to the frame on the other side of the river. A geared winch was attached to the front of the cart. He wrapped the rope a couple of times around the drum and began to turn it by hand. In a few minutes, the old ore cart was moving steadily toward the opposite side. Looking toward his goal he suddenly noticed about a dozen people quietly watching him. They didn't appear too friendly.

The men wore conservative black clothes and the few women with them were dressed all in white. Cooper simply said, "Hello. Sorry to meet you under such difficult circumstances." He glanced down at Jeremiah. From their position on the platform, they could see their dead friend. So far, no one had said a word or even changed their expression. Finally a woman spoke. She was dressed as the other women but wore a red sash around her waist.

"We've been watching you ever since your arrival." She pointed toward a 30-foot tall watchtower off to her right. "We saw what happened to Jeremiah and are grateful for your efforts to save him." She hesitated then said, "But as an Outlander, you're not welcome here."

"I came from Yosemite Valley so if that means I'm an Outlander...so be it."

She repeated, "Outlanders are not permitted on this side of the river. Jeremiah was not authorized to contact you and I apologize for his actions. Our men will remove his body and you will return to the other side of the river. It may seem harsh but is necessary from our perspective. Will you comply?"

"A lot of demands for people who haven't been properly introduced. I'm Cooper Wellsley McIntyre."

Everyone's expression visibly changed, but no one spoke for several minutes. The lady with the sash slowly stepped forward and looked carefully at him. "Evidently Jeremiah spoke to you about William McIntyre, an important person in our history. Do you claim to be a relative?"

Cooper replied firmly, "To set the record straight, Jeremiah had the same surprised look on his face when I introduced myself before he said anything much about William McIntyre. And while I am unsure of a family connection, I won't rule it out. My dad did say we had family in Yosemite before we arrived, and if your William McIntyre had family in the Hawaiian Islands as I do, I may be a relation to him." Two of the older men began to whisper to each other.

The woman continued, "William did have family in Hawaii and had spent time with us more than a 100 years ago. He lived here for 10 years before leaving with his wife, Nanci, and their children. She was a distant cousin of mine. Of course, most of us today are cousins in one degree or another. William did come to us from Yosemite as you did and was influential in helping this town become what it is today." She looked at him carefully. "You do resemble some sketches we have of him." She smiled for the first time. "I don't suppose you're left handed?"

"Yes, ma'am and therefore I don't have the sickness."

She nodded. "Just like William." She moved closer to the cart. "Mr. McIntyre, I don't know what to say. We never expected to see another McIntyre. I apologize for my abruptness but protecting our town from the Omega virus continues to be a top priority." She motioned to a couple of men who stepped into the cart and removed Jeremiah's body.

"I'm Sarah Bailey and I hold the office of Mayor in our village. We'd be honored if you could come and visit Williamsburg." She looked at him almost pleadingly and held out her hand.

Cooper stepped out of the ore cart and shook her hand gently. "I'll be happy to stop by but just for a few days. I'm on my way to the Oregon territory. Some marauders, who killed my parents and kidnapped my sister, may have gone north."

Sarah smiled. "Understood. I'm sorry about your family. We have problems with some marauders, too."

McIntyre stood transfixed. "Do you know if their leader has red hair?"

She frowned and shook her head. "I'm afraid not, but he is just as evil as they come." Sarah changed the direction of the conversation. "According to our historical documents, William was headed back to the island of Hawaii. Do you know if he made it?"

As he stepped out of the ore cart he answered, "My dad never spoke of it but we do have some gaps in our family history." He thought to himself, William might be my great grandfather.

Cooper shouldered his backpack as they began the short walk into town. Sarah glanced at his holstered handgun. "We'll have to drop your gun off at my office. Firearms are not permitted within our city limits."

"I'm a little uncomfortable with the idea, but I understand." He pulled the pistol, popped out the six shot cylinder and handed it to her. "How's this for a compromise? Me and Kate have become quite attached. I'd hate to lose her, even accidentally, and will keep her hidden under my clothes."

She smiled wanly. "I suppose that'll have to do."

"Nothing splendid has ever been achieved except by those who dared believe that something inside of them was superior to circumstance." *Bruce Barton*

Chapter 9

Williamsburg was not at all what Cooper expected. Most towns he'd previously visited were in serious disrepair at best and a total wreck at worst. The elegant church spire that he had seen at a distance from across the river didn't do justice to what lay before him. The scene very much reminded him of a picture he once saw of Main Street in a book about a place of entertainment called Disneyland. It was once quite popular with the Ancients.

The cobble stone street seemed to follow the curve of the river as it flowed to the west, and extended for about a half mile. Buildings and businesses filled both sides of the street starting with the church and ending with a large blacksmith shop at the other. He could see homes on the streets on either side of Main that had a late 1800's look. They appeared either to be in amazingly good shape or were great reproductions.

Following Sarah, he stepped up onto a wooden boardwalk that fronted the buildings. Apparently they had a saw mill around. The boards were evenly cut and relatively smooth. Even with her honey-blond hair tied up in a tight bun and wearing a loose white shirt and ankle length skirt, she was a handsome woman.

Canvas awnings of various colors were stretched over display windows showcasing items available in each store. Villagers, wearing the same customary black or white colored apparel, walked in or out of a store, some carrying items they had purchased. Those who saw him stared. They were not accustomed to seeing strangers, if they saw any at all.

Most people seemed to be walking toward the other end of town and Cooper soon saw why. It was a large farmer's market. Dozens of booths had been set up under a large tent, and vendors were busy selling various kinds of fruit and vegetables. Cooper saw people exchange coins for the produce and overheard a few who bartered services for food. He shot a glance at

Sarah. "Evidently you have an economy based in part on currency. Do you use the coins that once belonged to the Ancients?"

Sarah tested the firmness of a tomato. "The coinage of the Ancients had no intrinsic value so we produce our own. We have access to iron, gold and silver in mines nearby. Once a year we trade with two other communities who are about a two days journey across the river. They make the trip to us and we trade for copper, nickel and other items. We use the ore cart to transfer goods including the ore to our side of the river. We smelt the ore in our blacksmith shop, and make tools and plows along with coins of various sizes and weight. The local government receives goods and services from the townspeople in exchange for the coins."

Cooper was impressed. He hefted a large orange. He hadn't eaten one since he left Yosemite. Sarah gave the shopkeeper a small coin she pulled from her skirt pocket and smiled at him. "Enjoy."

Just then, the bell in the river watchtower began to ring loudly. Those working at the farmer's market ran for the nearest building, leaving their goods behind. Windows were shuttered and doors locked as people rushed inside. Sarah yelled at Coop. "Marauders!!" She ran toward her office with Cooper running right behind. Men on horseback galloped down the street yelling and screaming, the horse's hooves making a racket against the cobblestone. One rider leaned down and swooped up an older teenage girl and trotted in the Outlander's direction. Coop stepped up onto a watering trough and leaped over at the marauder, ripping the girl from his arm. He half-carried her over to Sarah and turned back to the furious man who had wheeled his horse around and was charging back.

Sarah yelled, "McIntyre….catch!" She threw him a broom that was leaning nearby. He caught it, and in one motion, swung it at the rider hitting him in the face. The marauder hit the ground hard and was knocked unconscious. Another rider lifted a sword and charged a running couple. As he swung the blade, a shot rang out. The bullet struck him in the shoulder and he fell backwards off the horse and onto the ground. Coop had retrieved an extra cylinder from his backpack and slipped it into his revolver. The last two marauders had reached the farmer's market and were loading saddlebags with food and other goods. Picking up the sword, Coop ran toward them echoing their banshee-like scream. Unaccustomed to any kind of defense from the townspeople, they dropped the saddlebags, jumped onto their horses and rode off.

Stopping to catch his breath with his hands on his hips, Coop looked back at Sarah as people emerged from their hiding places. He couldn't help but wonder why no one, other than Sarah, lifted a finger to help.

Once again the villagers found themselves staring at the Outlander. Glancing at his still unconscious partner, the wounded man struggled to his feet and began to simply walk away as blood seeped from his shoulder. Coop hollered at him.

"You there!! We're not done yet!"

The man stopped, turned to face his questioner and yelled belligerently, "Who the hell are you anyway?!!"

Coop smiled broadly. "I'm Cooper Wellsley McIntyre and I want you to know that if you or any of your friends return to Williamsburg, I won't be nearly as nice."

The man reached for the reins of his horse. "I'll be back, and there'll be a lot more of us."

Coop walked up to him and glared as he said, "That would not be wise. Two things, if you return without an invitation to do so, I will put a bullet in your head instead of your shoulder." He poked his finger on the marauder's forehead. "Second, you're walking. We're keeping your horse and that of your friend to pay for damages." The other marauder had struggled to his knees. "And take him with you." The wounded man objected. "How do we cross the river without a horse?"

"That's your problem. Now get your butt out of here before I change my mind and shoot you right now."

The two men stumbled through a growing crowd of people who were gathering to hear the mayor speak as she stood on a makeshift platform. It would not be what Cooper expected. Sarah took a deep breath. "I'm sorry you were a witness to so much violence. The Outlander was not aware of our pacifist way of life. He'll be reprimanded for his actions."

Seeing a comfortable looking chair sitting on the wooden walkway, Coop sat and propped his feet up on a nearby post. He had a somewhat puzzled expression on his face as the Mayor continued, "I apologize for my participation in the violence. For those who have not heard, the name of the Outlander is Cooper McIntyre and he may well be a relative of William McIntyre." A few townspeople murmured at the mention of the McIntyre name.

"Once again our attempts to keep the marauders away through regular donations of supplies and food has failed. I will attempt to renegotiate with Captain Blood as soon as a meeting can be arranged." She paused just for a moment as a man standing in the back walked forward and spoke. His daughter was the one who was almost kidnapped.

"Madam Mayor, I respectfully disagree. Our repeated attempts to buy off the marauders have failed miserably. The Outlander's actions, although regrettable, certainly sent them a message. One man offered resistance to the violent intentions of four mounted marauders and as a result they retreated while we all just stood around watching." He shifted his gaze over to Cooper. "In my opinion the violence was not excessive and was at the same time effective. My daughter is unharmed and still with us." Coop nodded slightly in response.

The Mayor bristled. "And Mr. Bailey, exactly what in your opinion, would be excessive?"

Cooper answered, "I could have easily killed them, but chose to send the marauders a message. Would William have done otherwise?" Coop was not happy to conclude that since they shared the same last name and a daughter, she and Bailey were husband and wife. It would appear, he thought, that Bailey had robbed the proverbial cradle.

Sarah answered, "Our historical documents tell us he was a man who offered a careful and measured response to the problems our community faced and it did include some acts of violence. But recent leaders have led us to embrace pacifism as a godlier means of handling problems with our neighbors."

Cooper rose to his feet. "There are some aspects of pacifism that are very commendable. But in the face of danger to the very lives of the people you love, sometimes a measured and forceful response is not only required, it is essential to preserve and protect the community you have worked so hard to build." He hesitated then added, "Over the millennia, since the time of Christ, Christians have had to defend their faith on the battlefields of life in many contexts. It often required the shedding of blood to protect communities of faith from evil men who sought to destroy their way of life. The marauders, I believe, are using your commitment to pacifism as a means of stealing your resources, kidnapping your young people and probably worse. If not dealt with appropriately, they will eventually take Williamsburg, lock, stock and barrel. Measured responses to their acts of violence is not only necessary in my view, it is critical for your survival. And it may be as simple as throwing somebody a broom."

He looked up at the Mayor as she said, "The town council will meet in 30 minutes to discuss the events of this morning. We are grateful for the loving care and mercy of our God. And regardless of the means taken by the Outlander, we do owe him a debt of gratitude. Thank you, Mr. McIntyre."

As she stepped down the crowd began to disperse. Dave Bailey walked up to Cooper and extended his hand. "No matter what the council decides, I believe your actions were appropriate."

His daughter appeared at his side. "I am grateful Mr. McIntyre. And please know my mom is inclined to take more forceful steps than her words indicate."

Sarah approached and grabbed the young woman's hand. "Words are not enough to express what we feel about what you did for Lydia. Would you honor us by joining our family for dinner tonight?" She reached into her skirt pocket and tossed him the cylinder of bullets. "Not much sense in me keeping this, is there?"

Coop caught the cylinder with one hand, leaned over and picked up his backpack. "Certainly. Just point me toward a place where I can set up camp and I'll join you later." Dave shook his head.

"Nonsense. We have a spare room. We'd be delighted if you would with us while you're here."

Sarah nodded as she smiled. "To refuse would be a serious breach of protocol."

Cooper held up his hands in mock surrender. "Okay, I give up." He followed Sarah and Dave. Lydia walked next to the Outlander. Her smile could not have gotten any wider. Sarah gave Coop a brief history of the town as they strolled down the street. Lydia noticed some of her friends watching as they walked. When her mom paused, she asked, "Mr. McIntyre, I don't know what lock, stock and barrel means. Where did that phrase come from?"

As they walked toward the front porch steps leading to the Bailey home, Cooper answered her question. "Before the days of the Ancients, the handguns and rifles of the time were very simply made. The rifles were called flintlocks and had three basic parts. The cast iron barrel was about 46 inches long; attached to it was a wooden shoulder stock that rested against the shoulder. Lastly, a piece of flint was locked into place over a small pan of gunpowder. When the trigger was pulled, the flint set off a spark that ignited some gunpowder that in turn lit off a bigger charge of powder sitting behind a round lead ball sitting in the barrel. The explosion expelled the ball at tremendous velocity. It was a valuable weapon that determined the outcome of many a battle. Eventually the phrase lock, stock and barrel came to describe the totality of something that was important. For example, if my backpack were stolen, to describe the act I could say, 'I lost everything...lock, stock and barrel.' Does that make sense?" She nodded with a secret joy at the personal exchange with the Outlander. Someone else saw what was going on as well but was not nearly as pleased.

Cooper stared at a concrete sidewalk. It had replaced the boardwalk that lined Main Street. It had been obviously repaired many times since it was first laid. A few segments of the original sidewalk remained. Somehow they had rediscovered, probably with William's help, how to make concrete from the materials they had around them; sand and gravel from the river, lime and potash from the nearby mountains. When mixed in the correct proportions with water, the mixture hardened into an almost indestructible building material. Most new construction was made with concrete blocks and finished with a wooden interior. All the furniture was hand-made, simple, but comfortable. Candles placed in glass chimneys provided a source of light in most homes. The chimneys, other glass products and kiln-fired items, were some of the things for which the village of Williamsburg traded. The town had not slipped back quite as far as other parts of California Land.

Cooper stopped for a moment and stared at the front door as Dave opened it. A huge panel of stained glass took up a full third of the door. He had seen photographs of them in books but had never seen one in person. The colored pieces of glass, fused together with thin lines of lead into a beautiful floral image, was stunning. He asked as he stepped inside, "Did one of the Ancients create this window?"

Dave grinned, "Nope. It is a hobby of mine and has recently become a business. You'll find my windows all over town and in many of the communities around here."

Just then a tall, somewhat thin, young man stepped into the hall. Unlike everyone else Coop had seen, he was dressed in gray. Sarah turned to him and simply said, "Howard, this is Mr. McIntyre. He is to be treated as if he were part of our family. Understood?"

He nodded and replied, "Of course, ma'am." Coop extended his hand but Howard just stood there a little confused.

Dave smiled slightly. "It's okay, you can shake Mr. McIntyre's hand."

As they did so, Coop grinned but Howard did not. Sarah ordered, "Take Mr. McIntyre's backpack up to the spare room and make sure the linen is fresh."

"Yes ma'am." He quickly disappeared up the nearby stairs.

Dave said softly, "We don't generally shake hands with the graylings. Getting familiar with the hired help is frowned upon. Conversations with them are kept to a minimum. Do you understand?"

Cooper frowned. "I'm beginning to."

Sarah placed her hand gently on his arm and escorted him down the long hallway, while describing the various rooms on the first floor. They passed a room that needed no identification. The aromatic smells wafting from the room clearly said this was the kitchen. Dave mentioned that all the family bedrooms were on the second floor and the servants quarters were on the third.

Lydia led them into a large library. As Coop scanned the floor to ceiling bookshelves, he estimated they held around two thousand volumes. They appeared to be organized by category and were either fiction or nonfiction. There were only thirty or forty books in the fiction section. He picked up a copy of Herman Melville's Moby Dick which was lying on a nearby table and thumbed through it. "You have a nice collection of books, but appear to be a little short in fiction."

Sarah motioned toward a comfortable looking reading chair. "Please have a seat Mr. McIntyre." As he sat the three Baileys did the same in nearby chairs. Dave rang a little bell which was on a small table in front of him. A few moments later Howard appeared. Sarah took charge. "Hot tea for all of us and be quick about it."

Howard bowed slightly, "Yes ma'am."

Picking up a book from a side table Dave answered Coop's question, "About 20 years ago the town council at the time decided most books of fiction and some of the nonfiction were not fit to be read. Any book using foul or sexually suggestive language, or had photographs of partially clothed people were pronounced unfit and were burned. Out of about 20,000 volumes, this is all that is left." Dave pointed toward the bookshelves. "The rest were burned. There were so few left that the town agreed to sell them to me. I added them to my personal collection."

Coop was incredulous. "You can't be serious; thousands of library books burned?"

Dave nodded. "In addition the sheriff went door to door confiscating books that were deemed offensive from the townsfolk."

"And you just let it happen? Do you have any idea what you have done? Books are rare now. Most people outside of Williamsburg no longer know how to read. Many have never even seen a book and yet you burned them."

Sarah stood as Howard rushed in with the tea. "I have a town council meeting to attend. We have a way of life that works for us Mr. McIntyre, whether you approve or not."

Cooper rose as he fixed his gaze on her. "I doubt very seriously that some of the choices you have made, as of late, would meet with the approval of William McIntyre."

She replied tersely, "That may be, but he is dead and we're not. A majority of the people in Williamsburg no longer believe in many of the ideas he wrote about in the McIntyre Doctrine. Obviously, you and he have a lot in common. May we talk more about this later this afternoon?"

Coop nodded, "Certainly." Sarah rushed hurriedly out of the room and disappeared out the front door. The library was awkwardly quiet for a few moments as Howard poured the tea.

Finally Dave spoke. "I must apologize for my sister. Ever since my wife died ten years ago, she has taken on the responsibility of not only keeping our family together and raising Lydia, but has tried to give direction to our town. It hasn't been easy for her."

"Your sister? I thought she was your wife."

Dave smiled. "I must apologize again. I should have made our relationship more clear. Sarah is the only mom Lydia really remembers and speaks of her as such."

Cooper looked over at Lydia. "You bear a striking resemblance to your aunt...very pretty."

The three of them chatted and drank their tea. Coop wasn't all that fond of the beverage. But he learned a lot more about Williamsburg and its successes and its struggles. A half dozen families seemed to control the town; representatives from each of those families were members of the council and they were a majority. The *class* structure of the town bothered him a great deal. Was that social practice arise from the McIntyre Doctrine? He sincerely doubted it. Coop wondered if he would ever be permitted to see a copy of that famous document.

A week later, he lay on the feather bed in his bedroom and was drifting off to sleep. He had wandered the streets and talked to dozens of people. The town appeared to be a virtual model of a middle 19th century community. And his mattress was the most comfortable bed he had ever slept on. A knock on the door stirred him. The door opened. Lydia stepped inside and shut the door. She was wearing a thin white robe. It was pulled tightly against her body leaving very little to the imagination.

"Hello, Mr. McIntyre," she said huskily. She reached up and pulled out a clip from her strawberry blonde hair. It cascaded down around her shoulders. Smiling now, she opened her robe, revealing a stunning body. Cooper's mouth dropped open as she began to hum a captivating song. Seeing the confusion in his eyes, she moved closer.

"Some of the women in Williamsburg belong to an elevated station in life. We are called Sirenia. Do you not find me attractive?"

He gulped slightly. "You're gorgeous, but I don't think I've ever seen a woman with so many tattoos." With the exception of her hands, feet and face not a single square inch of her body from the bottom of her neck to the top of her ankles was without a tattoo.

She turned slowly so he could see her whole body. "When a Sirenian girl becomes a woman in Williamsburg, the tattooing begins. It takes many years. You'll notice that my tattooing has reached my ankles. I am now available."

Cooper stood up, completely unsure of what he was expected to say or do...other than the obvious. Just then they both heard loud voices at the bottom of the stairs. Lydia frowned. "Fartles. My dad is at the bottom of the stairs. Believe me, he wouldn't approve...even with a McIntyre."

She quickly put her hair back up, closed her robe and left, leaving the door slightly ajar. She peeked back in. "See you later."

For a couple of minutes Cooper stood there, quite shaken by the encounter. Another knock and Howard peeked in.

"Mr. McIntyre, the sheriff and Master Bailey are arguing about you."

"In what way?"

"I heard Master Bailey say something about not wanting to parade you in front of the town council. Some townspeople are still upset at the way you handled the marauders."

It was apparent Coop had already outstayed his welcome. The council had decided to send him on his way or worse. Grabbing his backpack, he slipped out into the hall. "Do you have a better idea?"

Howard nodded. "Follow me." He led Coop toward the back of the house. "The back stairs are this way." As nice as McIntyre was, he would not be disappointed to see him leave town.

In a matter of minutes, Coop was walking toward the blacksmith shop on the edge of town with Howard leading the way. Turning a corner they ducked into a livery stable, and closed the door.

The Grayling whispered, "We'll wait for a few minutes to see if there is an active search for you."

Coop said softly, "Thanks, Howard. You know this could get into a lot of trouble."

"Nah, not likely. If I'm asked, I'll just tell'em you asked me to show you around town." He looked up the street. "And my friends call me Howie."

"Okay, Howie. My friends call me Coop." He extended his hand once again to the Grayling and Howie took it.

"Did you see Lydia come into my room?"

"Yep. Did she sing to you?"

"No, not exactly. She hummed."

"Did you touch her?"

"Of course not."

"Did you want to?"

"Oddly, I did, but something held me back."

"So it's true then. You McIntyres can resist a Sirenian woman. Most men cannot."

"I'm not too sure about that. Lydia's dad scared her off. Other than the obvious, why did she come into my room?"

Howie peeked around the door. "We'll give it another minute, then head for the blacksmith shop." He smiled, "According to our historical documents, one of her distant relatives married William. Evidently, Lydia wants to marry another McIntyre."

Coop nodded. "I see. Are Sirenian women persistent?"

Howie smiled, "You have no idea…especially once they are literally touched."

Cooper said, "I truly need to get out of town. Lydia said something odd when she was in my room. She used the word 'fartles' which I have never heard as she left. I assume 'fartles' is an expression of frustration or anger.'"

Howard nodded. "It is an expression picked up by the young people in our town. It was found in one of the banned books. Actually, you need to know not all of the books were destroyed. Several large boxes of them were buried behind the church."

Cooper shook his head. "That's good news, but I've got to get out of here."

When they reached the Blacksmith Shop, Cooper waved to several people, but kept on walking without saying a word. He saw a row of six plows, a dozen or more picks and shovels, and tables full of hand tools. The people of

Williamsburg had not forgotten how to work with metals of various types. He wondered if they figured out how to forge steel. Then he saw his answer. A separate table was the resting place for dozens of hatchets and axes of all sorts and sizes. They had the gleam and look of steel.

Howie elbowed Coop gently and pointed, "That trail will take you out of town. Good luck. Sorry we were not more hospitable." The two men shook hands and Coop jogged slowly out of sight.

A half-hour later, he was looking at another ore cart suspended on a thick cable. This time, instead of a raging river he was looking across a deep canyon. And the distance was considerably longer. The opposite side was also a lot lower. Hearing some yelling behind him, he turned to see a half dozen people on horseback riding toward him. Coop jumped into the ore cart and hit the bar that held it in place on the cable. A gear began to whine loudly as the old cart began to gain momentum as it slid down the cable. He looked back to see Sarah waving at him, but now he was hanging on for dear life onto the wildly careening iron cart. He could not have known the council had decided to honor him. Not noticing the lever that acted as a brake on the winch, Coop could see the ore cart was going to crash into the platform, which was quickly approaching. A couple of seconds before it did, he jumped.

"They conquer who believe they can. He has not learned the first lesson of life who does not every day surmount a fear." *Ralph Waldo Emerson*

Chapter 10

With difficulty Cooper opened his eyes. His back was killing him. He sat up and turned around to see several rocks where he had been laying. His head was throbbing, as were several other parts of his body. He found himself staring at Howie who was squatting with his head in his hands.

"Howie, what are you doing here and how did you get over onto this side anyway?" He looked at the banged up ore cart.

Howie lifted his head and smiled slightly. "There are other ways of coming over. I hiked down into the canyon and then climbed back up. It took a while, but it didn't look like you were leaving anytime soon. You've been unconscious for some time. How are you feeling?"

Coop stretched his body a little to see if anything was broken. "Other than some serious bumps and bruises and a wicked headache, I appear to be okay. But again, why are you here?" He then noticed Howie was himself pretty well beaten up and disheveled. "What happened after I left town?"

Howie winced. "About 90 marauders came right after you left. It seems that your departure was a signal for their attack. They have taken over our town. No one thought they would return so soon after the thumping you gave some of them last week. A few of us fought back, Master Dave, Sarah, myself and some others. Several have been killed. I was beaten badly, but was released when they found out I was just a slave."

"What about Sarah, Dave and Lydia?"

"I don't know. I ran to find you as soon as I could sneak away."

Just then they heard crying and yelling on the other side of the canyon. A group of villagers were being pushed toward the edge by the marauders. They heard a loud voice.

"McIntyre, this is what'll happen to a lot of people if you are ever seen on this side of the river."

Lydia was pushed by a marauder to the very lip of the canyon. Her tattooed body could easily be seen. She had been stripped naked. Sirenian traditions had been wildly defiled and she wasn't going to wait to be pushed. Lydia grabbed the arm of her tormentor and jumped. The village women all screamed as the two bodies plunged over the precipice.

Lydia twisted her body mid-air and fell feet first. The marauder flailed helplessly and screamed. The first 30 feet of the cliff face was a straight drop, but then the ground angled into a steep hill of loose rock and dirt for another 40 feet before ending on a relatively flat plateau bordering the river itself.

Lydia struck the hillside feet first, and immediately rolled onto her back while she was still conscious. Her body eventually began to roll down the steep incline until it came to a rest at the bottom.

The marauder's body tumbled savagely end over end for about half the distance, then rolled the rest of the way until he was impaled on the broken branch of a fallen tree trunk. His sightless eyes seemingly stared up at those who were watching from above.

Howie and Coop watched from the other side and actually had a better view as the two bodies fell.

Coop stood up as the villagers were herded back toward town. The voice repeated its warning, "You heard me McIntyre! If you're even seen on this side, 10 more will die in the same way!"

Tears were streaming down Howie's face. "What are we going to do?"

"First we're going to check on Lydia. There's a small chance she's still alive. Then I'll make a return visit to Williamsburg." He saw Howie's look of concern.

"They're going to kill a lot of people regardless of whether I'm seen or not. Show me the back way into town."

Howie nodded. Coop looked into the wreckage of the ore cart. His back pack and bow seemed to be intact. He had long forgotten the pain in his own battered body. A long simmering hatred of marauders had heated up in Cooper's heart. A half hour later, it had blossomed into a murderous rage, as Coop followed his friend.

Upstream, about a half mile, Howie pointed to a braided rope secured to a fir tree near the edge of the canyon. It was partially hidden by some dense brush. If you didn't know it was there, the rope looked remarkably like a dead branch laying on the ground.

"There is one just like it on the other side. The river here is relatively shallow, slow moving and swimmable."

Coop stepped over the brush and, after slipping on a pair of heavy gloves, he rappelled down the side of the cliff. Howie was not far behind him.

When he reached the bottom, Coop ran along the plateau jumping over rocks, debris and logs until he found Lydia. She was a bloody mess. Both legs were badly fractured but none were compound, which was a miraculous surprise. It was hard to find any place on her body that was not bruised or lacerated; but she was breathing. Dropping his pack, Coop stripped off his shirt and covered her. He pulled out his canteen and then a piece of cloth from a side pocket. Wetting it thoroughly, he began to carefully wipe off her face and neck. As he worked down her body, except for her legs, the bleeding was surprisingly superficial. He hoped there was no internal bleeding, but wouldn't bet on it. He could set the bones of her legs, but any internal issues were between Lydia and God.

Just then Howie showed up. "I had no idea a person could run as fast as you, especially in rough terrain."

Coop smiled, "I had practice running in Yosemite. The good news is she's alive but badly injured. We dare not move her until she is seen and treated by the town doctor. I'm going to go fetch him. I doubt she will awaken, but she shouldn't be left alone. The main thing, right now, is to keep her warm." He held out the canteen. "Save most of this for her, if she wakes up. It is fresh from the streams of Yosemite Valley."

Reaching into his pocket, he retrieved an old Zippo lighter, flipped the lid open with his thumb and pushed the small mechanism that sent out a spark lighting the wick. Howie's eyes watched carefully.

"There's a lot of loose wood around. Make a fire to help keep her warm. And strip off your shirt to cover the rest of her. I'll be back with the doc as soon as I can."

Howie nodded. "You do remember there're about 90 marauders."

"Yep, but I figure I just have to get to the head honcho and most of his leadership. The rest may run off considering the havoc I'm about to create."

"What do you have in mind?"

"I'm not sure just yet, but something will come to me." He gestured toward Lydia. "Take care of her."

Howie glanced at her as he took off his shirt. "With my life." He turned to see Cooper running upstream, his well-muscled body effortlessly hurdling a thick tree log. He had left his backpack but was carrying his bow and a fist full of arrows. Howie wondered if the marauders had any idea what was coming their way.

Cooper made it to the south end of town without being spotted. He counted a half-dozen marauders hiding in various positions. All were looking his way, but Coop was not easily seen, as he rested under the branches of a large weeping willow tree. He strung his bow and nocked an arrow. Pulling the taut bowstring back, he aimed carefully through the willow branches at the fellow who was the farthest away, and let the arrow fly. It struck him under the chin. Cooper had actually aimed a little lower, but he would take what he got. Unable to utter a sound, the man stared momentarily at the thing that suddenly appeared in his throat, and he soundlessly collapsed. In turn, not seeing the death of those positioned behind them, each marauder met a similar fate as razor sharp arrows penetrated their bodies.

Cooper slipped out from under the tree and made his way to the town's water tower. The water tank itself sat on a wooden platform about 20 feet high. Four stout legs supported it. With a plan now firmly in his head, Cooper ran around to the blacksmith shop. Two guards stood out front in plain view. He waited patiently until one of them said something to his partner. The marauder walked around to the side of the building where he was out of sight. He proceeded to unzip, but didn't get too far. An arrow suddenly buried itself in his back penetrating his heart. He managed to get out a yell for help before dying. His friend turned the corner of the building, only to be met with an arrow that penetrated the side of his throat severing his windpipe and a major artery. Coop ran inside and grabbed what he was looking for…a cross-cut saw.

In 10 minutes he had successfully cut a v-shaped notch deeply into two of the water tower legs. Only an inch or two of wood was preventing a collapse of the tower. Coop lifted a sledge hammer as he looked around. Several dozen marauders were milling around a couple hundred yards away. The next few minutes were going to be noisy and messy. He swung the sledge as hard as he could at the nearest wooden support leg. The remaining inch of wood splintered easily as the leg partially collapsed. The pounding sound got the attention of several marauders who began to look around. Coop attacked the second leg. It took two strokes, but the leg buckled even further than the first. The sudden shift in weight of all that water began an unstoppable chain of structural failure. Thirty or forty marauders ran toward the sound of the collapsing water tower. They were too close when they saw what was happening. As the tank fell and splintered open, a wall of water struck the men, smashing them against buildings, trees and lamp posts. Several drowned and others were badly injured. Only a few escaped the deadly onslaught of water pouring down the street.

Meanwhile, Cooper was running down the back side of First Street where Sarah and Dave's house was located. The water would eventually reach the Bailey house and others, but its velocity and depth would be greatly diminished. He jumped a short backyard fence of a neighbor of the Baileys and waited quietly behind a tall hedge. Hearing a couple of men talking from the front porch, he made his way to

126

the back door, which was open, and climbed all the way up to the third floor where he laid his bow on a hall table. Water began to flood the street as he slowly opened a bedroom door. The family cook was laying helplessly on the bed as one marauder straddled her. Another stared out a window at the growing flood of water and said, "Hurry up, Ed. I want a turn."

Coop silently crept up behind the man on the bed and grabbed his head from behind, twisting it quickly and violently. The snap was audible. The other marauder turned just as Cooper tackled him to the floor and wrapped his huge hands around the man's throat. The marauder immediately began to fight back, kicking and thrashing. The cook calmly and quietly walked up to the marauder with a ceramic wash basin in her hands. His eyes widened as she violently smashed it over his head fracturing his skull. He laid still.

"Thank you Mr. McIntyre. I've got this. See if you can help the others"

Cooper nodded. "Yes ma'am."

Stepping into the hall, he heard noises coming from the adjacent room. Opening the door, he saw another marauder who was so busy undoing his pants, he ignored whoever it was that came in. Cooper hit him in the side of the head as hard as he could sending the hapless man screaming onto the floor. The woman covered herself and ran out the door. Like a cat, the man jumped to his feet and attacked Cooper who was ready for him. In a rage the marauder impaled himself on the knife Coop was holding in his hand. He began to yell, but Cooper twisted the blade until he cut a major artery. The man's eyes grew dim, and he collapsed.

Coop heard more yelling from the last room on the floor. He leaned over the bannister. The entry hall was empty and he couldn't hear any conversation in the living room or library. He hoped everyone was out on the front porch watching the flood.

Pulling his handgun, Cooper opened the door a crack. He saw Sarah and Dave suspended by their hands from a wooden beam in the ceiling. They were both being badly beaten by a marauder whose left arm was in a sling. The top half of Sarah's dress had been ripped off and it hung around the waist exposing her. She was definitely Sirenian.

The marauder continued to yell. "This is only going to get worse!! Tell me where the gold is!!" He slugged Dave in the mouth. Getting no response he reached toward Sarah and savagely twisted a sensitive part of her body.

"Tell me where the gold is!!" Sarah grimaced but refused to utter a word.

He turned and saw Cooper. Recognition filled both their eyes. Coop didn't hesitate. He fired once and the bullet put a neat hole in the man's forehead. The impact threw him onto the floor. Blood, brain tissue and bone were spattered on the wall behind him. His face looked oddly surprised.

Cooper took out his knife, held Sarah tightly against his body with his right arm, and cut the rope with the other. He handed her the knife and lifted her much bigger brother and she cut him down. He left both of them standing and said as he rushed out the door, "Lydia is alive!" Just then, a really big man burst through the front door downstairs.

"Who fired that shot?!!"

Coop leaned over the bannister and fired without answering. The slug tore into the middle of the man's chest. He staggered, but remained on his feet as he looked up at Cooper with murderous eyes. Coop lifted his gun again, but before he could pull the trigger an arrow suddenly appeared in the marauder leader's throat. Coop looked behind him to see Sarah with his bow in her hand. "Nice shot." The marauder, known as big Tom, fell with a thud.

Just then, three more men ran inside. Two of them had crossbows and fired toward Cooper. The arrow bolts missed by a significant margin. The third marauder came charging up the stairs with a sword in hand. As soon as his head appeared, Sarah put an arrow into his left eye. He fell backwards down the stairs. Cooper jumped over the dead man as he ran after the other two who had made a hasty retreat out the front door.

Stupidly, they ran straight down the street instead of turning at the corner of the building. Cooper fired twice in rapid succession and both men fell to the ground. Five other marauders found cover, and began firing arrow bolts toward Coop, who had ducked into the general store. It had been completely trashed.

Sarah had already run out the back of the house and was circling around to get a better angle for a shot. Coop saw her settle into position, and ran out shop door to draw their attention. They couldn't get a steady bead on the man who quickly ran across the street. Sarah stuffed her last three arrows in the dirt, pulled one out and nocked it in the bow. As soon as she let it fly, she nocked another arrow, pulled it back and sent it toward another marauder. The two men were soon writhing on the ground, both with arrows sticking out of their backs.

The other three turned their attention to Sarah who nocked her last arrow. Coop ran back out into the street where he could see the men zeroing in on Sarah. He had put in a fully loaded cylinder and fired calmly toward the marauders, badly wounding two more. The third stood to face Coop, but only for a moment as an arrowhead suddenly sprouted through his chest from behind. He looked down at the protruding object, collapsed onto his knees, and then fell forward.

Other marauders saw what was happening and began to simply walk out of town. Cooper heard one of men say, "This ain't worth gettin kilt over."

Sarah, who had put on a pair of men's pants and a plaid shirt, appeared beside Coop. After being beaten, she had not yet wiped all the blood from her face.

"Most of the villagers are being held in the town square. A few escaped up into the mountains."

Cooper nodded. "How's Dave?"

"He's a tough guy, but the marauder broke several of his ribs, his jaw and both eyes have swollen shut. He won't be any help to us with the other marauders.

Coop held up four arrows that he had retrieved from some bodies. "You're pretty good with the bow."

"All Sirenians are trained bow hunters. But never in my wildest dreams did I ever think I would be hunting men. How badly is Lydia hurt?"

"Pretty bad. She needs a doctor right away."

Ten minutes later they stood on a second floor porch overlooking the town square and the villagers. A dozen marauders stationed at intervals were warily looking around. They had heard the shots and yelling on the other side of town. The ankle-deep water that reached them did not pose a danger. Big Tom had made it clear their job was to guard the townspeople at all costs.

Sarah yelled to the townspeople, "Big Tom is dead. Many of the marauders are either dead or have left town. The only ones left are the twelve guarding you and a few stragglers. There are over five hundred of us in this square. Who wants to kick the rest of the marauders out of town?"

There was silence for a moment then one man simply asked, "Do we send them out dead or alive?" Almost as one, several voices yelled, "Dead!!" This was no longer a town of pacifists.

The marauders held their crossbows at the ready position. Rather than have any more blood spilled, Coop pointed his gun at the dirt in front of the nearest marauder and fired once. It got everyone's attention. Cooper spoke loudly to the marauders.

"Do you see any possibility of surviving here? These villagers are now ready to sacrifice their lives to restore this town to what it once was. Are you ready to die in a situation where there is no possibility of winning? Go home to your families while you still can. But understand this, if you do decide to fight, I will shoot the first man who moves. Who wants the job?"

There was utter silence. "Put down your weapons and walk away! You have a chance to see another sunrise. Take it!!"

One by one the remaining marauders dropped their crossbows and began to walk out of town. The villagers clapped and hugged one another. But a marauder stopped and turned around. He looked up at Cooper. "This ain't over!!"

An arrow flew between his legs. Two inches higher and life would have been a lot different. Sarah hollered, "Yes it is, mister!! Get out of our town!!"

Cooper was in no mood to celebrate, just yet. "Where's Doctor Holiday? Lydia is in bad shape. Howie is with her now."

Sarah dropped the bow, cupped her hands around her mouth and almost screamed, "Doc Holiday, where are you?"

A voice yelled back, "I'm over here!!

"We should all be concerned about the future because we will all have to spend the rest of our living there." *Charles F. Kettering*

Chapter 11

Three days later, Lydia's dad was recovering from the brutal beating he took from the marauder. The swelling had reduced considerably around one eye, so at least he could see. But his ribs were killing him and he had a couple of loose teeth. Doc Holiday had given him something to help him sleep and he was doing just that.

In the room next door, Lydia was being fed some hot soup. One arm was in a splint, as were her legs. Both feet were wrapped in tight bandages. It would be a long time before she would walk again, but the doctor was confident she would.

Sarah's face was black and blue in places and Doc Holiday had to put in a few stitches around her mouth, but she was otherwise okay. The town of Williamsburg was recovering, but it would never be the same. Some wounds leave permanent scars.

Cooper sat nearby and had in his hands a remarkable sketch of William McIntyre. The framed drawing had been hanging on a wall in Lydia's bedroom. He carefully examined what he assumed to be an image of his great grandfather. They did have some similarities; the same chin and mouth and distinctive nose, but Coop's eyes were a little larger and his eyebrows were definitely bushier. They shared a healthy head of hair, as well. It was clear the two men were related.

Lydia finished her soup and spoke softly to Cooper. "You do look a lot like him."

Coop frowned slightly, "I wouldn't say a lot, but we do resemble one another. I wish I could have met him."

Sarah stretched and said, "It is said you can get to know a person by reading what he or she wrote. Would you like to read some of the papers he left behind?"

"Absolutely. Would the McIntyre Doctrine happen to be among them?"

"Certainly. I had planned to dig out all of them anyway. Our town needs a refresher course on the truths that enabled us to survive all these years. We can look at them tomorrow, if you like."

Cooper nodded appreciatively. "I will look forward to it." He stood and peeked out into the hall. "I haven't seen Howie all morning. What is he up to?"

Lydia smiled broadly. "He said something about building me a special wheelchair, so I can get around a little."

Cooper nodded and said, "That man is certainly a jack of all trades. You do know he is as much responsible for saving your life as anyone."

Lydia groaned a little as she moved her splinted arm slightly. "Yes, I know. I woke up for a minute down at the bottom of the canyon. Apparently, he stayed with me while you and mom were taking on the marauders."

Sarah stood and interjected. "Thank you for that by the way. I could easily be servicing Big Tom right now if you hadn't stepped in. I, we, owe you a huge debt of gratitude that can never be repaid. If there is anything you ever need or want, just say the word."

Lydia winked at him and added, "Absolutely."

The next morning after breakfast, Cooper was pouring over the papers William McIntyre had left behind, including a copy of The McIntyre Doctrine.

The papers consisted of letters he wrote to help flesh out various aspects of The Monroe Doctrine which was essentially a social and religious platform for basic human rights. The elements of the doctrine were not new to Cooper and probably not to William, but were a fresh expression of them. He opened the binder to examine what William wrote. He stared at the clear and broad strokes of a goose quill pen.

The McIntyre Doctrine

The purpose of these articles is to establish a foundation for living that will give every citizen of our city opportunities to enjoy a free and productive life. It is my hope and prayer that with malice toward none, charity for all and a commitment to what we know to be right as God gives us direction, we shall strive to be the people He has created us to be; a free and just people who understand that life, liberty and the pursuit of happiness are gifts from the loving hand of Almighty God. These articles are certainly not exhaustive but are, I believe, a good beginning.

Article One

No person who conducts him or herself in an orderly and peaceful manner shall be denied the right to worship God in a manner of his or her choosing. Those who do not believe in the existence of God may do so without fear of reprisal or recrimination. We regard the Bible as authoritative in providing the basis for morals, ethics and any laws pertaining to them.

Article Two

The general happiness and success of the populace is subject to the quality and breadth of an education that includes Religion, Science, Mathematics, English and History. Said education shall be made available to everyone regardless of age or sex. Schools shall be built and teachers employed at public expense. Education and job training will be a priority.

Article Three

There shall be neither slavery nor indentured servitude of any kind. Individuals or families may employ workers for their fields, businesses or homes but must do so at a fair wage and *offering a day off of their choosing. These wages can include food and goods, and a place to live. Equality and justice are not just words, they are watchwords which bring peace and harmony for all.*

Article Four

The government of this city shall be administered by a council of nine, chosen and elected by the citizenry to serve a term of four years. A councilmember may be re-elected to serve another four years, but no more than eight. No fewer than four of the members of the council shall be women. A mayor shall be selected from among the council by at least two-thirds of the councilmembers for a term of two years and may serve another two years if the council desires. These public servants shall be non-salaried in a monetary sense, but are not subject to city taxes and are eligible to receive a portion of meat, fruit and vegetables from the community food reserves. Special elections can be called at any time by the mayor or the citizenry to remove or replace said councilmembers by a two-thirds majority vote.

The responsibilities of the council shall include:

1. *Establishing codes of conduct and law governing public life and business.*
2. *Selecting judges, a court system and a constabulary to hear grievances and enforce said codes and laws.*
3. *Giving a sense of purpose and direction for the community and addressing the needs of the city.*
4. *Levying taxes to support city improvements, the employment of necessary workers in the city and establish and maintain a system of currency.*

Article Five

Any changes or additions to this doctrine must come from the city council, and receive unanimous support. Members must abstain from the vote if there is a conflict of interest because of personal or business reasons.

In summary, I must insist these articles be seen as a beginning point for establishing a system of government and not the end. The original Constitution and Bill of Rights for the former
United States of America was far more detailed and explicit. I urge you to read them. In time, I

expect these articles to be modified as the needs of the community change and as the city grows. May God richly bless the people of our town, both in the present and in the future.

It was signed William McIntyre.

Sarah knocked on the open door to Cooper's room. "So, what do you think?"

He closed the binder as he replied with a concerned tone, "Regarding Article Three, was official action taken to rescind the article or to change it radically?"

"Not that I know of. As I have examined our official records and spoken with some of our older folk, natural divisions began to appear between the well-educated and those who were not. Sirenian women arose from that separation. One of my distant relatives received a tattoo to identify her highly skilled and educated status. The tattoos became a status symbol identifying the more desirable women in the community. A class structure gradually emerged as a social division between tradesmen, day laborers, business owners, politicians and educators arose." She looked away dejectedly as she wiped away some tears. "It wasn't until we stood together as equals in the public square, as dozens of our townspeople were being killed, raped and beaten, that I realized how wrong we were to permit such a social system to grow. William McIntyre was right; you were right."

She glided effortlessly toward Cooper and stared up at him with her bruised and battered face. "I am committing myself to re-asserting the McIntyre Doctrine in Williamsburg. I could certainly use some help. It's going to take some time to change people's attitudes and practices."

Cooper took her into his arms and kissed her gently on the lips. "We'll have to work on it."

She reached back and gently closed the door. "Well Mr. McIntyre, exactly what did you have in mind?"

"The art of progress is to preserve order amid change and to preserve change amid order." *Alfred North Whitehead*

Chapter 12

Within six months the town had undergone a remarkable transformation. Barriers between people and classes began to drop. Much to the chagrin of some, Howie, a hired servant and Lydia, a Sirenian, soon married. It was the talk of the own. She was pregnant with her first child. If the baby was a boy, they planned to name him Howard Wellsley. Other than a few mishaps, attitudes did change relatively quickly. The marauders had attacked three more times. They were easily beaten back by a small, but well-trained army of volunteers. Using the raw materials they had accumulated over the years, Cooper helped them design and forge a couple of small cannons. One of the men at the blacksmith shop was already adept at making gunpowder.

The first time the cannon was fired at the marauders, they immediately swung their horses around and retreated.

Electrical power was being restored to the city. A small hydroelectric power plant a few miles upstream had quit producing power more than fifty years ago. It took almost two months, but with the help of some capable craftsmen, Coop had the plant putting out electrical power once again. The problem now was finding light bulbs for the hundreds of lamps Coop found stored in boxes in a block-sized warehouse. Light bulbs became a hotly traded commodity with communities who did not have electrical power.

Coop was able to rebuild dozens of power tools that the craftsmen quickly gobbled up. What really got the town talking, especially the women, was when he repaired three electric sewing machines. In the same wooden box where he found the sewing machines, he found hundreds of spools of polyester and nylon thread that had survived. A new, light industrial age was being rediscovered in Williamsburg.

New tools and dies were being designed and constructed almost weekly. Metal and wood lathes had been built, enabling craftsmen to make anything from fine furniture to metal bolts, screws and brackets. It wouldn't be long before the blacksmith shop would be able to manufacture rifles and handguns, especially with the new Bessemer-type forge that he helped them build.

But as much as Cooper enjoyed being part of the community, it was time for him to resume his journey. Explaining his commitment to finding his sister was admirable, as he explained it to Sarah, but she was clearly frustrated. She had hoped for more from the Outlander.

Cooper was not sleeping well the night before he was to leave. But little things often woke him and was probably one reason he was still alive. His bedroom door opened slowly and closed again. He turned over to see Sarah standing there. She was carrying a candle which she sat on the night table. She was wearing a thin white robe, very similar to the one Lydia wore. Sarah opened the robe and said "I'm available." She began to sing softly as she moved sensuously toward him. Some attitudes were more difficult to change than others. The reality was that Sirenian women would always be held in high regard in Williamsburg.

Cooper gulped. He had been able to resist Lydia, but doing so with Sarah had proven to be almost impossible. Saying goodbye was going to be even more difficult. The next morning as Sarah watched him walk out of town, Sarah was smiling. Hearing the whole Yosemite story helped her to understand why Cooper had to leave and she was content. Maybe someday, she too, would be able to leave Williamsburg. Most people didn't know she wasn't born left handed.

"Be kind. Remember, everyone you meet is fighting a hard battle." Anonymous

Chapter 13

Cooper McIntyre had been traveling across the lower elevations on the West Side of the Sierra Nevada Mountains for almost a year after he left Williamsburg. He figured he was about 21, but his life Williamsburg had a lot to do with that.

His digging abilities had improved considerably, as had his skill at finding and repairing the ancient machinery and products of a bygone era. He had passed through several small villages of people who preferred to eke out an existence in the hills, rather than live in virtual slavery to despots in valley towns who cared little if people survived or not. They, instead, chose to live in smaller towns in rugged areas where the marauders were not fond of traveling.

He stayed in a few of those villages for a while; repairing broken down hand powered equipment that had survived over the centuries. He asked about their experience with marauders and where their known camps were. Before moving on, he taught them how to be more successful in planting and harvesting crops. He was amazed at how many small towns had managed to keep alive basic industry, even without electrical power. One town had no fewer than three waterwheels on a fast moving river which powered grinding mills for grain and even a sawmill for cutting lumber. Ingenuity was still alive and well, despite the devastation caused by Omega.

People in the villages where he stopped were always initially wary of the big man, but were always sad when he decided to resume the search for his sister. But no matter where he rested, whether it was for a few days or a few months, he was able to compartmentalize his experiences so the difficult memories of his past were not always at the forefront of his thinking. The only time his brain could rest, at least to some degree, was when he was sleeping.

In his journey while digging through the rubble of long abandoned towns, he found not only books, but also magazines and shiny discs that had information or music somehow imprinted on them. They were identical to discs he had found at the Ahwahnee. He would have to return someday to Yosemite find out what was recorded on them.

Along the way, he had come across a wounded llama who had been the target of hunters. Seeing that the animal was not seriously wounded, Coop removed a couple of arrows and helped restore the animal to health. The two had become traveling companions. Abraham began to carry some of what Coop had accumulated during his travels.

One morning he looked down at what was once a busy highway. A badly faded fiberglass sign was numbered 50 and led down toward the ruins of a major city called Sacramento. The big earthquake had almost leveled the city, but a few buildings still stood. The road was no longer passable. The pavement was cracked and broken. Hulks of cars and trucks that were almost completely eaten through by rust, dotted the sides of the disintegrating highway. Trees and brush had erupted through the broken pavement. Smoke from a large fire caught his attention a few miles to the west. Abe spit off to the side of the road. Coop did the same.

"Yeah…I agree, it doesn't look like much."

Coop reached back into his pack and pulled out a canteen of water and a metal saucepan. He poured in some water for Abe then took a long deep swallow himself. Replacing the canteen, he took out several of the skillet biscuits he had made the day before, giving one to Abe and eating one himself. He sighed. "Well, let's find out what awaits down below."

A couple of hours later, he came across several collapsed buildings, one of which had been mostly consumed by a recent fire. Digging through the debris he came across a scorched white metal box about six feet long, three and a half feet high and two and a half feet from front to back. It was scarred and badly dented, but no one had been able to break into it. The padlock had been struck many times but had remained secure. Coop rummaged around the large pack Abe was carrying and found what he was looking for, a small pair of bolt cutters. He cut through the lock and slowly opened what was formerly a freezer. Inside were dozens of boxes of powdered camping food, dried eggs, dried potatoes, milk and vegetables. The instructions said, "Just add water." Coop was a little dubious, but he stuffed a half dozen packages under his shirt. Over half of the metal box was empty, so he decided to make a cache to store some of what Abe had been carrying around. He had left several such caches of important items along the road behind him knowing he couldn't possibly carry everything of importance he scavenged from the rubble of America's past. He replaced the broken padlock with a combination lock of his own. On the front his lock simply said Yale.

Early the next day Cooper found himself facing the remnants of a large stone sign. It simply said Folsom P. A large section of it had broken off. Now he had a decision to make. Either he walked up a smaller road that apparently led to Folsom P, or continue down into the remnants of a large city. It seemed to stretch as far as the eye could see. In the distance the smoke of several small fires drifted lazily into the sky. Those fires were usually a sign of the feared marauder camps. Those who ruled over forced labor communities promised protection from the marauders for the families and individuals who were willing to stay and to work. Getting in to one of those communities was easy; leaving was an entirely different matter.

Cooper looked at Abe. "I'm not sure I want to take you up this road. For some, a llama would make for a good high protein meal. Of course I can't say for sure your flesh is tasty, but it probably tastes like chicken."

Abe snorted as Coop continued his one sided dialogue. "Can I trust you to take care of yourself for a few days? There is plenty of grass around and water in that stream a ways back." Abraham nodded his head as Cooper smiled. "There is no way that you understood anything that I said, but I am going to leave you behind." He held up a dog whistle only a few animals could hear. "I will call you when I want you."

Coop removed the pack and then the halter from Abe's head. "Okay...stay out of trouble." Abe turned and slowly walked away. Coop shook his head and mumbled to himself, "Maybe he understands more than I think." Shouldering the pack, he began walking up the road toward Folsom P. A half-hour later he saw the top of a wall in the distance. Then the whole structure appeared. The parts constructed of re-enforced stone and brick were intact. Other sections, not so much. Having read about them and seen pictures, he recognized it for what it was....a prison. Seeing a large rock nearby, he sat down to reconsider his options. Just then he saw six men in uniforms jogging toward him. Abandoning his pack, he turned to run when a crossbow bolt suddenly appeared in the dirt in front of him. He shrugged his shoulders, bent over and pulled out the bolt and sat back down. It was about 12 inches long and appeared to be made of oak with a lead tip and feathered tail. He guessed the crossbow itself was about half the normal size. A few moments later the men had surrounded him. The officer with long red hair streaming from under his cap had a small crossbow dangling from his hip. He was far too young to be the marauder he was looking for.

"You have entered the dominion of Warden Patrick Henry."

Having just read a book about early American history, Cooper couldn't help but smile. The same man continued, "I'm not sure why you are smiling. Unless you have been invited, you are not welcome and are subject to arrest."

Cooper nodded. "I understand. I am new to the area and was unaware of the infraction I have committed. I will be happy to withdraw. No harm, no foul."

"What does that mean?"

"It simply means no harm has been done and I am ready to leave the warden's property." He picked up his pack and began to walk away. The same voice spoke up.

"The pack stays here as a fine for breaking the law."

Cooper was now really glad he had left most of what was really important in the cache, and his revolver was hidden underneath the back of his long London Fog coat. He sighed, laid down the pack and kept walking. When he rounded a bend in the road and was no longer visible to the men, he broke into a run. It didn't take long to reach the main road where the Folsom P sign was located. As Coop stopped, he pulled out the dog whistle and blew as he walked toward his nearest cache.

That evening he sat around a small nearly smokeless fire and ate a pan full of reconstituted eggs. He said to no one in particular, "You know these eggs are not bad, but they are not good either." Abe had not shown up and Coop was worried. Having returned almost everything to the metal box except for his warm wool blanket, he laid some partially burned pieces of lumber against the box and made a small lean-to. Having put out the fire, he slipped under the shelter, wrapped the blanket around his body, and laid down in the soft dirt. Within a few minutes, he was fast asleep.

Early the next morning before the sun had risen, someone was kicking his boots and startled Coop. "Wake up, mister. The warden wants to see you."

Coop crawled out and stood. The same six men were facing him. One carried a crossbow. "I wasn't aware the warden's domain extended this far."

"It doesn't. The warden wants to see you just the same."

"Do I have a choice?"

"Not really, but the difference is now you have an official invitation and it would be wise not to turn him down."

"What's your name?"

"Radial Tire."

"You're kidding."

"Nope. Why?"

"It's nothing. Lead the way."

"How did you know I was an officer?"

"You have an officer's demeanor and there is a small brass button on your collar which is not present on the others."

"What's a demeanor?"

"An attitude of authority."

The Lieutenant smiled and invited Coop to walk ahead of them. As the sun came up they passed through a rusty chain link fence gate. A couple of sentries at the guardhouse locked the gate behind them. About 25 or 30 men, women and children were working in vegetable fields. Their clothing was patched but appeared to be clean and warm. Many smiled as they walked by. Field guards walked up and down the rows but children played around their feet.

Coop followed his captors through a broad set of gates that were twice as tall as they were wide. A stone wall, perhaps forty feet in height surrounded several acres of land creating a fortress-like atmosphere. He walked onto a packed gravel path winding in and around a courtyard which was home to what appeared to be a blacksmith's shop and a candle making operation. A soft turn to the left led to fenced in pastures filled with goats, sheep and some cattle. The packed gravel quickly gave way to stone cobbled lanes no more than six feet wide. On each side were small stone cottages, and garden plots with people working in them. Smoke drifted skyward from several chimneys. The former prison looked more like a fortified castle from ancient days, than it did anything else. But it had a pleasant feel to it, not at all like what he had experienced in other forced labor communes. The lane led to a broad plaza. In the middle was a tall water fountain that hadn't seen water in a long time. Off to one side was a wide canopy of often-repaired material. Underneath were several barrels of murky water. Several women were rubbing clothes on washer boards and rinsing them in the water. Others were ringing and hanging the clothes on a drying line. They looked up to check out the stranger who walked by. A couple of them waved.

Ahead was a three-story cement block office building of some sort. He was led up to and through a wide carved wooden door into a large office. An immense fireplace took up one whole wall. It was kind of odd to see such a tiny fire burning in the middle of it. An adjacent wall was covered with a richly colored tapestry of a unicorn being fed by a beautiful lady. Images of birds and other animals had been woven into the panel. If it was meant to soften the tone and foreboding appearance of the place, it had succeeded to some degree. Coop noticed in the dim light a soft cloud of smoke rising from the top of a tall wing backed chair.

Radial Tire spoke. "Sir, I have brought a guest as you requested."

A tall and amazingly thin man stood, turned and extended his hand to Coop who took it.

"I'm Warden Patrick Henry. Thank you for coming. Please have a seat." He gestured toward a wooden chair in front of his desk.

"Lieutenant, you and your squad may have an extra ration of food." Radial smiled his thanks and exited, shutting the door behind him.

The warden glanced toward the contents of Coop's pack that was sitting on a well-worn conference table. "Your pack had a wide assortment of different items in it. Am I to assume that you are a digger, Mr......?"

"McIntyre....Cooper McIntyre and sir, everyone is a digger of one sort or another these days. Many of us who survive do so by digging through the rubble and refuse of our ancestors, to find things that help us in our constant struggle to get through another day."

The warden eyed him for a moment. "You are so right, Mr. McIntyre. May I call you Cooper?"

Coop nodded, as the warden scribbled a few notes and continued. "Normally, I would have let you continue on your journey, but I noticed a few things in your pack which made me think you may be an extraordinary digger."

He handed Coop an open book upside down. "Do you know how to read? Not many people do, you know."

Coop played a hunch, turned the book over and said, "Yes, I do, but probably not nearly as well as you."

The Warden seemed pleased and nodded as he held up the clock taken from Coop's backpack. "I have not seen an alarm clock in all the years I have been at Folsom P. My family has been here for generations and have had good diggers combing through buildings for years. This is the first clock I have seen. Do you know how to use it or to tell time?"

Cooper nodded. "My mother taught me to read and showed me how to tell time using a simple wooden model. She was convinced someday more working clocks would be found. I haven't had an opportunity yet to see if I can restore this one to working condition."

The warden looked carefully at Coop and at the collection of tools and equipment on the table. "I would hazard a guess that you do well at repairing machinery and other things our ancestors left behind. Is that a correct assessment?"

"I have been known to fix a few things from time to time. But to be honest, sir, most things are beyond repair."

The warden folded his hands on his desk and was quiet for a moment. "This I know all too well. We lost our last good digger to marauders a while back." He paused and asked, "Where is the rest of your family?"

"My parents were killed by marauders some time ago. "I've been looking for them ever since. They kidnapped my sister. Would you happen to know of such a group led by a tall, red-headed man?"

Warden Henry shook his head. "No, I'm sorry, I do not. But you might ask my head of security. He is the young man who escorted you here."

"Cooper, I want to make you an offer of employment at Folsom P. In exchange for unlimited food, shelter and an expansive workroom, I would like you to work for me for two summers. I will assign to you special projects, some of which will involve fixing broken down equipment and furniture and will include finding items that are in short supply at Folsom P. For example, my wife and daughter are in need of some new clothing as are some of my other employees. Your first assignment would be to go into old Folsom on a digging trip and find those items."

Cooper thought for a moment. "What will keep me from just continuing on my journey once I get outside the gates?"

"You are free to leave at any time, as are any who find sanctuary behind these walls."

Coop eyed his backpack. "I will work for you, but I have some conditions, sir."

The warden looked up and frowned slightly as Coop added, "When I feel the need to resume my journey to the north, I can do so at any time, but will plan to stay for at least one summer. In exchange for that flexibility I will improve the standard of living for every man, woman and child at Folsom P. In addition I would like to select, at my discretion, two or three people to be my apprentices during my stay here."

Intrigued by Cooper's boldness, the warden smiled thinly and said as he considered his options, "So you think you have something worthy to teach while you are here? Give me an example of what you'd do."

"I will show your field workers the benefits of tiered gardening and ways to more efficiently irrigate your crops producing more food with less work and water."

The warden thought for just a moment about the value of increased field production. He stood and extended his hand once again. "Mr. McIntyre, we have a bargain. Welcome to Folsom P." He added, "And just to make it clear, anything you find and bring inside these walls, belongs to me."

"Agreed," replied Coop with a smile. But I will need the tools I have collected to do some of my work."

"We are in agreement, Mr. McIntyre. I will have Lieutenant Tire escort you to your new quarters. The shop is yours to do with as you like."

He hesitated then added, "One more thing, other than doors that prohibit entry, you have free access to the compound and its grounds. When you plan a digging trip, notify the Lieutenant and he will make any arrangements you need. Welcome to Folsom P."

Cooper stood, shook the warden's thin hand and turned to leave. "Mr. McIntyre, would you care to have dinner with us tonight? Once a month all the families in Ravenswood gather for dinner. It is called a potluck."

"Of course, I would be delighted. My mother taught me to never turn down a meal."

"Grief can take care of itself, but to get the full value out of joy, you must have somebody to divide it with." *Mark Twain*

Chapter 14

The shop was a lot bigger than he imagined, probably 50 feet wide and 100 feet long with a ceiling height of 30 feet. The outside wall from the chest up was made of opaque windowpanes about 18 inches square. Half of them were broken. The floor was strewn with chunks of metal, old engine blocks, broken furniture and a few pieces of shop equipment. He recognized a broken down lathe, table saw, hand saws, augers and bits and some other shop tools. But without electrical power, some of the tools were useless...for the moment. In a corner was a stack of various pieces and sizes of lumber and corrugated metal. It appeared someone had torn down a storage building and saved the raw materials.

Radial Tire led him through the shop to a back room. While the previous occupant was not much of a housekeeper, the room had a nice sized bed, workbench, a broken down recliner, several candles for light and a small potbelly stove for heat. The shop would serve his purposes very well. He stepped into the bathroom and raised the lid. It was a disgusting mess. Coop sighed. "I have a lot of work to do."

The Lieutenant toed a piece of metal on the floor. "If you like, I can take you on a tour of Ravenswood and introduce you to some of the other staff, including some of the women that are available whenever the mood strikes you."

Cooper coughed a little nervously. "Lead on Mr. Goodyear."

"The name is Radial Tire."

"Yes, of course. I do apologize." Coop smiled to himself.

Walking out of a side door they emerged into another courtyard. On the other side Coop could see smoke rising from a large brick oven. Next to it was an open pit barbecue. As they walked up, a whole pig was slowly being roasted on a spit turned by a young boy who smiled wanly. A half dozen people were working at various tasks, but a young dark haired brunette caught his eye. She was working twice as hard as the others, despite being verbally abused by a much older woman who, when she saw the Lieutenant, ran up to him. "Are you still hungry?"

"No, but my new friend is. This is Cooper McIntyre. He is our new digger."

She was missing a few teeth, but she smiled anyway. "Welcome, sir. My name is Edna. I can make a pulled pork sandwich in about two minutes."

Cooper smiled broadly. "That sounds wonderful."

She scurried off as he looked around. He noticed the brunette stare at a tin can on the table that was upside down. She quickly turned it right side up and kept on working. As Radial chatted with one of the others, Cooper walked up to the brunette.

"Hello, my name is Cooper."

Her vivid green eyes flashed. "I'm sorry, sir. I am not allowed to talk to anyone while serving. Edna will punish me if she thinks I am not getting my work done...even if I am."

Coop replied, "I understand" and walked away as Edna brought him his sandwich on a small plank of wood.

"Would you like something to drink, sir?"

166

"How about an ice cold Pepsi?"

Her face took on a serious look. "What is a Pepsi?"

He smiled. "It was a drink the ancients once consumed. I saw an advertisement for it in an old magazine. It was called the elixir of life."

"What's an elixir?"

Cooper replied sadly, "Nothing…don't worry about it. I'll get some water when I examine the spring out back."

As he turned to rejoin Radial, he heard a whisper. "Hey you…. catch…you'll need this." He turned just in time to snag in midair an empty tin can that served as a glass. The brunette had already returned to her work. The label on the can said, Del Monte Peaches.

Seeing a nearly empty table, Cooper sat down across from a man who looked to be taller than he and with shoulder length blond hair. He ate slowly and deliberately. Cooper smiled and said, Hello, I'm Cooper McIntyre." The tall man said nothing as he looked intently at the stranger.

The lieutenant walked over as Cooper took a large bite from his sandwich. It was good and he said so.

Radial offered with a grin, "Edna has a bit of a temper, but she is a good cook. She and her crew put out lunch for about 100 workers every day."

"What about breakfast and dinner?"

"Most families prepare those meals themselves. They all have stoves or fireplaces. They have their own gardens and even raise small animals. You did notice that you have a small stove and cooking gear in your quarters?"

As they strolled away Coop announced, "I've found two people I would like to serve as my apprentices."

The Lieutenant stopped in his tracks. "But you haven't met hardly anybody yet."

Cooper pointed to the brunette. "She will do." Gesturing to the man across the table he added, "And him, too."

Radial laughed. "If you want some female companionship, I can fix you up better than that. And Edgar is a good worker, but he's bit slow." He pointed to his head, "If you know what I mean."

"They are who I want to help me in the shop as my apprentices. What is her name?"

Radial shrugged his shoulders. "Okay...I'll make it happen. It may take a couple of days. I have to find a replacement to keep Edna happy. The brunette is Jordan. She arrived at Folsom a

168

few weeks ago." Edgar still had not looked at Cooper.

Coop eyed Radial. "Do you happen to know of any marauders in the area who have red hair like yours?"

Radial hesitated then replied, "No, but I haven't had contact with all of them by any stretch of the imagination."

Cooper nodded his thanks and returned to the shop to begin making an assessment of what was there and to clean up a little. He was looking forward to dinner.

The small apartment that was to be his home included a closet full of clothing, far too many for one person. A small heap of unsorted clothing was piled near the wall. It was apparent that the previous digger was a man who was about the same size as Coop, but a little bigger in the waist. Eyeing a fresh pitcher of water and a towel he washed up a bit. He found a reasonably clean pair of jeans with only one knee patch. As he put them on, he cinched them up with a length of rope. He slipped on a shirt that had all the buttons, which was a rarity. None of the shoes fit, but he did find a pair of open-toed sandals made from the tread of a tire. Coop worked some water through his longish hair and ran an old brush through it. He hoped he looked presentable.

The main plaza had sprouted a huge tent that covered several dozen tables of various sizes. The warden's table was in the middle of all the activity. He saw Coop and waved him over. Sitting at the table was the warden's wife and his daughter along with Radial Tire and a friend. The warden's daughter was older than he expected and cute.

Jordan suddenly appeared in front of him. Her long dark hair had been carefully brushed and pulled back. A carved wooden comb held it in place. Her high cheekbones, green eyes and sensuous mouth had his full attention. Hanging around her neck was a gold coin she wore as a pendant. A simple blue shift-like dress tied at the waist fit her well. Jordan looked quite nice. He extended his hand to her and she took it. He bowed ever so slightly.

"I wonder if you might grant me a tremendous favor."

She grinned impishly. "You mean other than making sure you had a cup when you went to the well."

"Yes indeed. I have been asked to join the warden at his table and you are the only woman

I even remotely know, at the moment. Would you be willing to accompany me?"

Jordan looked at him carefully. "Are you serious? I don't know you at all."

"That's probably not entirely accurate. I am sure gossip about me has gone around Ravenswood several times, all inspired by the men who brought me here."

She reddened slightly. "Okay, so I do know a few things. I will accompany you Mr. McIntyre. How shall we handle questions?"

"Honestly," said Coop without hesitation.

He took her by the hand and led her to the warden's table. The warden stood and shook Coop's outstretched hand. "Thank you for coming. And who is this beautiful young woman?"

"This is Jordan. We met earlier today."

The warden gestured, "And this is my wife, Susan, and our daughter Angelina. I believe you already know Radial."

Cooper nodded to all three as Radial smiled and gestured to the woman next to him, "This is Donna."

As Coop and Jordan sat down Angelina asked as she looked toward the couple, "Did you know Mr. McIntyre is a garbage digger?"

Jordan smiled and told her first lie. "Of course. Coop found the comb I have in my hair and gave it to me as a gift. It's quite lovely really. He is really good at what he does, in several contexts."

Angie continued, "And what do you do at Ravenswood?"

"I am Cooper's new shop apprentice."

"Of course you are, my dear. I'm confident you will enjoy working under him."

Jordan eyed Angelina carefully. "Coop has said he has a lot to teach me, but I have a few things to teach him as well. Are you familiar with the Sutra Kama? We expect to have a good working relationship."

Warden Henry had finally had enough of the veiled and not so veiled insults and innuendo thrown at his table. "Well, everyone is waiting for us to start." He nodded to their table server.

Warden's daughter or not, Coop took an instant dislike to Angelina and during their table conversation, he made every effort to ignore her.

"Warden, in my travels I have heard stories of the Librarian; someone who will be able to help lift us out of the shambles of our civilization. Have you heard these stories and, if you have, do you know where this Librarian might be?"

"I heard of the Librarian when I was a young man, but not so much lately. I'm afraid he or she may be more myth than anything else. Should the Librarian exist, I am not at all sure such a person would be able to do much to undo what has happened in the last couple of hundred years."

Angelina replied, "Before my grandfather died he spoke of the Librarian as if the person was real. He said he had heard the Librarian was in the New Seattle area, but imprisoned in a glass cage."

Coop had heard the same thing and was now determined to head that way when the time was right. "Civilization isn't dead in my view. It is just in hibernation for a while. I think something worthwhile can rise from the ashes just outside these walls."

The warden laughed at his optimism. He paused for a drink of water. "What might be one relatively easy thing that we could do to move us in the right direction?"

"That's easy. Re-establish a calendar."

The warden said gruffly, "Impossible. We have lost track of time. We do not even know what year it is, let alone a specific month or day."

"That may not be entirely accurate. We do have a few old calendars which give us a general sense of the seasons of the year and such. With those, I think we can figure it out and be relatively close. Whatever we do would be better than what we have now, which is nothing."

"What did you have in mind?"

"We need a reliable starting point and I have one. A few years back my family lived in Yosemite at a place called the Ahwahnee. The lodge had electricity provided by a sun machine and a working computer."

The warden nodded. "I've read about both in the old books. To find a working version of them is incredible."

"Before I left I had figured out how to use the computer, to some degree, but the last occupant of the lodge had made a moving picture greeting that showed up on a large window and he spoke to us. He began by giving us the date as Friday, June 21st, 2161."

"How do you know he was right?"

"I don't, but it is the only reference point we have at the moment. And if it was computer generated, the date may be very close. We found Ezra's remains lying on a bed, his clothing was in decent condition and dried flesh still clung to his bones. My dad, who had a lot of experience uncovering the dead in his early years as a digger, said Ezra had been dead for

20 or 30 years, 40 at the most. I left about two summers ago, so if we take the middle figure of 30 add it to 2161 then add two more, we may be living pretty close to the year 2193.

Warden Henry gave him a skeptical look. "You could be wrong, you know."

"Granted, but it is a beginning."

Henry smiled widely. "When do you think you might be able to get the clock working?"

"Any day now. Years ago I remember reading that June 21st has the most sunlight of any day and December 21st has the least. Once I repair the clock we will have a means to measure daylight hours. Then we will figure out approximately when June 21st and December 21st occur. We may not have the year correct but we could be really close with the day of the month."

"My God man, do you realize what you have done?"

"Nothing yet, sir."

"I disagree. You have started us on a path for reclaiming a calendar."

After dinner as he and Jordan were walking back to their quarters Coop offered an apology. "You were terrific back there. I am so sorry about the warden's daughter. I had no idea she was such a witch."

175

Jordan smiled. "Actually I've heard that Angelina is a really sweet person. Her comments were so uncharacteristic of her." She added quietly, "Your thoughts about a calendar were fascinating. You may well be right on target."

Cooper was pleased with her attitude. He was now more confident than ever he had made a good choice. "When will you be able to join me at the shop? There is a lot of work to do."

Jordan replied softly. "Is tomorrow too soon?"

Cooper grinned, "Absolutely not. Maybe you can tell me about the teaching of the Sutra Kama."

She blushed a little. "I haven't read the Sutra Kama. I've just heard about it."

"I know. It's called the Kama Sutra. See you tomorrow."

"We can do no great things….only small things with great love." *Mother Teresa*

Chapter 15

Jordan was a good worker and responded well to Coop's expressions of gratitude and encouragement. Edgar had shown up, but had yet to look at Coop or say a word. They spent the morning sorting out what was immediately useful and what was not, but nothing was thrown away. As they worked, he found out Jordan was living in a barracks for single women. It was noisy and lacked privacy. He decided to build her and Edgar some sleeping quarters in opposite corners of the shop. But the project would have to wait. He had an appointment with Radial Tire who would lead them into old Folsom. It was there Coop would fill the warden's shopping list.

While Jordan went to the kitchen to pick up some lunch, Coop sorted through a stack of clothes that his predecessor had left, looking for more suitable work clothes for his apprentice. Hers were threadbare, ripped and full of holes. He set the clothes and some shoes aside in his quarters. When she returned the two sat outside on a skillfully restored park bench that overlooked the community garden. As they ate their sandwiches, Jordan was obviously pleased with herself about something.

"Okay Jordan. Out with it. What happened in the kitchen?"

She smiled, "Edna refused to serve me even though it was for the new digger. Mr. Tire happened to overhear and really lit into her. He made it clear you were in a much higher station than she and I was your assistant. She served me quickly and with good portions, too. You've made a good impression, Mr. McIntyre. It was odd though."

"What was odd?"

"Radial gave Edna a hug."

Cooper just shrugged. "Well, you have impressed me, too. In addition to knowing how to read, you work hard and are not afraid to ask questions. I think we are going to get along just fine. Now, if I can just get Edgar to talk."

Jordan smiled. "He does speak, but is very picky about who he talks to. Apparently, you're not on his list yet. By the way, how did you know I can read?"

"I saw you turn over an upside down can which still had a label on it."

"Well, you certainly are an observant fellow, aren't you?"

"I have to be in this day and age. Noticing the little things is a great help in locating areas where I can find useable stuff the Ancients left behind."

"You'll have to teach me."

"Absolutely."

He eyed the coin around her neck. "Is there a story behind the pendant that you are wearing? It appears to be a gold coin similar to what the ancients used in commerce."

She fingered it gently. "It has been in our family for generations. My mother gave it to me when I became a woman. My great grandmother received it as a gift when she lived in the Hawaiian Islands. Are you familiar with those islands?" Coop nodded. Now he understood why her skin color was a little darker than most people. She was of Hawaiian blood. Family stories said they had relatives on the islands as well. Most people had not even seen the Pacific

179

Ocean let alone an island. She continued. "There is an inscription on one side and a drawing or map on the other. But no one has been able to figure out what it means."

Coop's gaze shifted to her eyes. "Someday with your permission, I would like to examine it."

She nodded slightly as he asked, "If you don't mind the question, other than what you have on now and the blue dress, do you have any other clothes?"

"Not really. I borrowed the dress. What you see is what you get."

Cooper grinned. "You need some more clothes. With that thin shirt you sometimes put on quite a show. But believe me, I'm sure the men don't mind a bit."

"What about you, Mr. McIntyre?"

"Please call me Coop. You're making me feel like an old man when I'm sure we are about the same age. And to answer your question, no, I don't mind either."

"That's good. I was beginning to wonder if you might be one of those irregular kind of guys who prefer other men. You haven't paid much attention to me since we had dinner."

"No, I'm not an irregular guy. There are actually very few irregular guys or gals around anymore. Having children is such a high priority these days that irregular relationships have been discouraged for a long time. He paused for a few seconds then said, "I've set aside some clothes for you. When you finish lunch, head back my quarters and pick out what you want."

Jordan took one more bite of her sandwich and then ran back into the shop. She returned about 20 minutes later wearing a pair of women's denim jeans and a plaid shirt. Both were a little big, but were serviceable. She could barely speak through her tears. Coop initially thought he had done something wrong.

"Mr. McIntyre, I have been wearing the same clothes for two years. I have been truly afraid to scrub them for fear the material would fall apart." She fingered her new shirt. "I'll alter them later." She leaned over and kissed him on the cheek. "Thank you."

Coop's face reddened slightly, "You are quite welcome. But let's put some tools and gear together and meet up with Radial Tire. Have you seen Edgar?"

The tall angular man tapped him on the shoulder and said softly, "Hi."

Coop turned around to face the man who was about four inches taller than he. Edgar had no expression on his face.

"Hello, Edgar. Each day we start work at sunrise. Are you okay with that?"

"Yes. Sunrise, this morning, was at 5:23 am."

Coop was stunned. "How do you know the exact time? There are no working clocks around....yet."

"I keep time in my head."

"How do you do that?"

"Don't know. When people ask, the time just comes to me."

"I see. How do you know if you're right?"

"I don't."

Cooper smiled. "Okay, Edgar. Today, we're going into old Folsom on a dig. Are you up for a field trip?"

"Yes." He paused and without expression asked, "What's a field trip?"

"The advantage lies not in the possession of things, but in repairing then discovering how and why the Ancients used them." *Cooper McIntyre*

Chapter 16

Late that afternoon the intrepid little band returned from a day of digging in Folsom town carrying with them bags of clothing. Radial had already put on a new pair of pants he absolutely had to have. He was stunned Cooper was quickly able to identify where a clothing store formerly stood. The block had been almost flattened by the last earthquake and had been combed over by previous diggers who missed finding a basement, where boxes of clothing were stored. Coop rarely overlooked anything. His reputation was just beginning. The next few weeks would be busy for him, as he took on some daunting projects at Folsom P. One of them would keep him, Jordan and Edgar busy well into the night for almost two weeks.

Warden Henry stepped back to take a look at the tread wheel that had been constructed. It turned out Edgar was quite the wood worker and with the more modern tools Cooper had provided, he was turning out excellent work. He noticed Radial Tire had also pitched in from time to time. The wheel was 16 feet in diameter and six feet wide and turned around an axle which was formerly part of a parking lot light pole. Two people at a time were inside turning the wheel as they walked. The contraption resembled a giant hamster wheel. It was geared to a water pump Coop had repaired. It pumped water from a spring up to a five thousand gallon water tank that sat about 25 feet above the level of the ground. When a valve at the base of the tank was turned on, it provided a steady supply of fresh water, under pressure, to Folsom P.

But an immediate problem showed up....leaking pipes everywhere. Cooper showed workers how to easily repair the broken water lines using reclaimed PVC pipe. Two person crews walked the wheel night and day in two hour shifts, filling the water tower. A new job had been created. They were called wheel walkers.

The warden shook his head. Cooper had done some amazing things in the short time since his arrival. Using old architectural plans for the prison, he had located the main sewer line and followed it two miles or so outside the main walls. With a crew of workers, he broke it open at one point. The sewage then flowed into what was formerly a huge holding pond, resting a couple of hundred feet below the level of Folsom P. Gravity simply pulled the waste away from the former prison and toward the holding pond. Having running water and a working sewer system was more than the warden could have hoped. It was also nice the holding pond was far away and usually down wind.

Before the weather changed Cooper, Radial, Jordan and Edgar had made several successful trips out to the collapsed remains of the town of Folsom. On one, they were gone for three days and the warden was sure they had all left Folsom. But they returned with a llama who was carrying a huge pack load of gardening tools and other items, some of which Cooper and his two apprentices repaired in the workshop that had now become a clinic for restoration and repair. Cooper, Jordan and Edgar used broken pieces of furniture to make useable ones, some of which the warden claimed for himself. Other pieces Coop gave away or used to furnish Jordan and Edgar's quarters in opposite corners of the large shop building. On another trip, Coop went by himself leaving Jordan and Edgar to oversee the ongoing work in the shop. He was gone over a week, but he returned with a two wheeled cart being pulled by Abe. He had spent two days just repairing the cart where he found it. It was full of more clothing, some books and other tools. Some of them were totally unfamiliar, but Coop was confident he would eventually figure out their use. He planned to give most of them to the overseers who would, in turn, distribute them to the workers. The cart also had inside a simple plow with an iron blade Coop had found inside a barn about five miles west of the rubble of old Folsom. It looked like someone had lived in the second level of the barn quite recently, but was now vacant. The second story of the barn had been converted into a livable space complete with a bed, a small table and chairs and another stove somewhat similar to the one he had at Folsom P. A home, which had burned almost to the ground, was fifty yards away. Cooper hoped to return someday to complete a thorough dig of the area.

Back at Folsom P., Coop entered the huge double door of the main shop with the cart right behind him. A few people had gathered just outside, wondering what wondrous things he had returned with this time. His trips were fast becoming legendary to a people who usually had nothing to look forward to. Coop was slowly changing all of that. He planned to start a school and had asked the warden's daughter to be the teacher. She was a good reader herself and had some background in science and math. Angelina agreed with the proviso Coop help her put together a lesson plan and provide some children's books. Angel hoped this would give her a chance to become friends with the man who had become known as the Finder/Fixer. She knew she had made a terrible mess of the dinner conversation at the last potluck. As Cooper walked in, Angel had slipped inside the door and was waiting for a chance to talk to him. She had to wait. Someone else had his eye. Jordan was much closer. She smiled and welcomed Coop with a hug which was a little longer than usual. He had long ago admitted to himself he was attracted to the strong-willed woman. She whispered, "Welcome home. We were worried. A group of marauders came our way two days ago. The warden gave them some food and most of the clothes we had not yet distributed."

Edgar walked up. "I was worried, too. Maybe next time I should go with you."

Cooper responded. "That might be a good idea." He directed his gaze at Jordan. "Did you get a look at them?"

She replied, "No, but Radial did."

Just then Radial strode up smiling. "Ahhh...the great Finder/Fixer has returned."

Coop took Radial's extended hand. "It's good to be back. Once again the warden probably thought I had left Folsom, but in truth I had to return, I missed Edna's cooking." He smiled as he winked at Jordan. "What's this about a Finder/Fixer?"

"That's you of course," she replied. "That's what everybody calls you now...the Finder/Fixer."

He shook his head. "People should just call me Coop." He stretched his muscular, but lanky frame. "I am in desperate need of a shower." He looked over at Jordan. "Would you supervise the unloading of the cart? And Edgar, could you make sure Abe gets back to his pen and is well fed? I would appreciate it." He looked toward his small apartment in the corner. Coop was exhausted. Thankfully, he had no lack of volunteers who were eager to work with him. At Jordan's direction, they attacked whatever task was assigned to them. As Coop walked away, she said, "See you later alligator. Get some rest."

As he walked away, Angel saw her chance and stepped through the crowd toward him. "Hello, Mr. McIntyre. It is good to have you back. Life around here seems to be a lot less exciting when you are not around."

"Please, Miss Henry, call me Coop."

"And I am Angie or Angel, although I may not have seemed to be such at dinner a while back. I would like to talk about the school."

Cooper smiled, "Absolutely. I've been thinking about it as well." He looked back at the cart. "I did find a few books you could use when we get the school started."

"Wonderful. When might we be able to get together to make some plans? My dad is terribly excited about it."

"How about tonight at your place? And ask your dad to join us. Tell him I have a surprise for him."

"Sounds real good." She stepped closer and motioned with her finger for him to bend down. She whispered in his ear, "Thanks for all that you are doing for us." Angie kissed him lightly on the cheek and hurried off.

Radial laughed. "Now, what was that all about?"

"She, her father and I are planning to start a school."

"And that's worthy of a kiss from the warden's daughter?"

"Apparently my cheek is getting quite popular." Coop resumed his walk toward his quarters. "Could you hang around for a bit in my office, while I shower?"

He nodded and followed Coop. He had installed a water tank on the roof and painted it black. During the day it absorbed heat from the sun and provided a lukewarm shower for about five minutes.

Ten minutes later he stepped out into his office wearing clean clothes having scrubbed off a week of dust and dirt. Radial sat dozing in the recliner Coop had repaired, but woke as his friend walked in.

"I'm surprised the warden hasn't grabbed this chair."

Coop laughed. "I know, but I promised I would find him a better one someday." Coop poured himself a glass of water and offered one to

Radial, who shook his head. Cooper asked, "What does 'see you later alligator' mean?"

Radial laughed. "You must have heard it from Jordan. I've heard her use it a few times. It's a rhyming expression used instead of saying goodbye. 'See you later alligator.' The appropriate response is 'after while crocodile.'"

Cooper grinned. "I don't suppose they use the word *fartles* around here." Radial shook his head. "Never heard of it."

Cooper's face became serious. "You lied to me a while back." Radial looked away. "You said you didn't know of a marauder who had red hair."

"How do you know I lied?"

"You have a tell."

"What's a tell?"

"Your left eyebrow unconsciously twitches when you are telling something you know is not true, or when you are hiding something."

Radial was incredulous. "I don't believe it."

"You know full well I am an observant person of people, of places and things. I don't miss much. You were lying were you not?"

Radial took a deep breath and sighed. "The marauder you're looking for is my father."

"I suspected as much. Why didn't you tell me sooner?"

"Two reasons...I was ashamed and I was concerned about what the warden might do if he found out."

"I see. Obviously you left your father. The warden said you wandered in about seven or eight years ago and have been like a son to him."

"He said that? The warden has been good to me, but I have worked hard to get where I am."

"He said that as well. I think you should tell him about your father."

"You're not going to ask where he is."

"It's not necessary."

Radial stood and walked around a bit. "I was in my twelfth or thirteen summer when my father and the Hellriders came back to camp with several captives."

"Hellriders?"

"Yeah, that is what they call themselves. Anyway, one of the captives killed one of my father's friends. They tortured the guy to death. I've never seen someone skinned alive. My dad seemed to enjoy it. I knew he was not a good man, but he is plain evil. My mother said so to his face, and he just laughed. She sent me out that night with a bag of food, and told me to follow the main road until I saw the sign to Folsom P. I've been here ever since and have not regretted leaving. But I do miss my mom. She died of a coughing sickness a couple of winters later."

"How did you find out?"

"My mom's sister was badly beaten and left to die when she couldn't keep up with the Hellriders, as they moved camp. One of our patrols found her three summers ago and brought her here. Her name is Edna." Radial smiled as Coop's face registered understanding. He continued, "Do you think your younger sister is with the Hellriders?"

"I'm sure of it."

"The last Hellrider camp I know of is about a day and half from here, in a small town. They may have not yet moved. After I talk to the warden, I'll take you there."

Cooper stared quietly at his friend. "It would be good for you to see the warden. Just tell him what you told me. I do appreciate your honesty and your willingness to go, but I'm not willing to risk your life for a personal vendetta. I will be seeing the warden tonight and will tell him of my plans. And before you ask, I saw the Hellrider camp about a month ago."

"Are you sure about doing this by yourself? These guys are not nice people."

"I know. I saw them in action. But I have a couple of surprises in store for the Hellriders."

Radial sighed. "Okay…when do you leave?"

"Early tomorrow morning."

The two friends shook hands. As Radial left, Cooper picked up a package and took it with him as he walked over to the warden's home. He had a productive visit with Angel and her dad. The new school had a bright future with Angel as the teacher. They just needed someone to help them get it organized. However the Henrys were very unhappy when informed of his decision to find his sister at the Hellrider camp, but they understood. In parting, Coop gave them a package. The warden opened the box to discover a repaired and working alarm clock. Coop showed the warden how the time was set and how to wind it. With Edgar's help, he had set the clock to the correct time. As he left, he got a big hug from Angie and a warm handshake from the warden, who urged him to be cautious and to return safely.

When Cooper walked into the shop, he found Jordan in his room wearing a Seattle Seahawk football shirt and little else. She was sitting on the small loveseat in his quarters. Before he could speak Jordan said softly, "Radial told me what you are going to do. I'm not going to try to talk you out of it. But maybe you need some incentive to try and return in one piece." She stood, walked slowly toward him, stood on her toes, put her arms around his neck and kissed him. Jordan gave him a beguiling smile. "Surprise attack."

Cooper didn't need a lot of encouragement. He leaned down and kissed her back, his mouth lingering on hers, his teeth nipping her lower lip. "Counter attack."

She slowly pulled off her shirt. "Sneak attack back."

The next morning Jordan helped him pack his gear and fixed him some breakfast. Afterwards, they walked out into an open area behind the shop. She already had his horse saddled and ready to ride. He eyed her carefully. "Evidently, there isn't a whole lot you don't know how to do."

Her face reddened slightly at the praise. She offered softly, "You will be careful, right?"

He responded with a grin, "I'm always careful. It's those around me who are sometimes not." He stepped up onto the horse. "See you later, alligator."

She grinned, "After while, crocodile."

"Enslave the liberty of but one human being and the liberties of the world are put in peril."
William Garrison

Chapter 17

A day and a half-later Coop lay on the top of a hill overlooking the HellRider camp. He had stopped by the cache he had left months ago and picked up some dried food, an old cigarette lighter, which still had fuel, some water and his binoculars. One of the lenses was broken, but the other worked just fine. It appeared they were getting ready to break camp. A few people stayed in some of the buildings that had not collapsed, but many appeared satisfied living in nearby tents. That was good. There was always a little chaos in striking tents and packing gear. He saw a string of horses near the far side of the camp. Coop held his breath. A woman was brushing one of the horses. From the back she looked like Maggie. She suddenly turned and looked right up at him. It was her. Coop resisted every impulse to jump up and yell at his sister. He didn't see any others from their Yosemite family. What had it been, more than two years? He watched until she returned to her tent.

He backed slowly off the hill and then jogged back to his camp hidden in a culvert running underneath a two-lane road. Oddly enough the road looked to be in better condition than the old four-lane highway a few miles away. As he waited for the sun to set, he sorted the explosives he had made from some of the gunpowder stored in the cache. The fuses were short, medium and long. He pulled out the Colt .45 and made sure it was ready. The extra cylinders, he stuffed in his pocket. Coop mixed a couple of the packets of dried food with some water and drank them. He needed to have some extra energy if he was going to pull this off.

As the sun set he returned to the camp which was in full take-down mode. It looked chaotic. They would likely get as much done as they could in the waning daylight, then finish in the morning. Coop smiled. He once read, "Where there is confusion and chaos, there is opportunity."

He pulled his cap down over his head and jogged around to the other side of the camp. He crawled on his belly, down to the string of horses and loosened each rein so at the slightest pull each horse would be able to run. Dusk was beginning to settle in and most of the men gathered around the big fire in the middle of the camp. He heard a familiar voice, the one he would never forget. Radial's father was yelling instructions.

Coop crawled on his hands and knees over to Maggie's tent. He listened carefully then said softly, "Oscar" while scratching on the tent wall. He heard a gasp.

Using the recognition word, in a low whisper she replied, "Mayer". He assumed she would not have responded if she had company. Coop was wrong.

Using his knife he made a long slit in the nylon wall. In the dark all he could see was a shadow. He whispered, "Sis, are you dressed?"

"Yes, but I am not alone."

Then he heard the soft whimper of a baby. "I have a baby boy."

He was surprised, but said, "You can tell me about it later. Hand him out. We have to get out of here, right now. Where's Mary Kate?"

Maggie replied slowly as she slipped the whimpering baby into his arms and then slid out. "She died last year. I'm the only one left." Brother, sister and baby crouched and walked quickly up the hill. On the other side, they stopped for a moment and hugged.

She sobbed happily. "I knew you would find me someday. I saw you earlier, didn't I?"

"Yep, but let's get out of here. I would like to put as much distance between us and them as possible while we still have a little light." He pointed toward the road. "Do you see that tall pine tree standing all by itself?" She nodded. "Right behind it is a culvert extending under the road. I want you and your boy to go hide in that culvert until I come to get you. Got it?"

"Yes, but what are you going to do?"

Coop smiled. "I am going to create a little hell for the Hellriders. Get going."

As she and the baby walked away, Coop trotted back over to the camp. They had discovered that Maggie was gone a little sooner than he expected and were mobilizing a search party. He heard a familiar voice yelling at his men. "Forget the woman. I want the boy. He's blood! And slit the throat of the s.o.b. who took'em."

Coop made his way back down to Maggie's tent and slipped inside surprising a man who was looking for something. Before the guy could utter a sound Coop hit him forcefully in the throat crushing his larynx. The man fell to the ground trying to suck in air. The front flap of the tent was open. Coop lit the short fuse and threw it as far as he could toward the horses. Lighting another, he threw the next one into the middle of the camp. The first explosive went off. The horses panicked, and ran off. In a sudden frenzy, a few men and women chased after them. Everyone else was crazily running around as well. Coop pulled down his hat and joined them. The second explosive caused more panic than the first. Seeing the big man himself yelling at any who would listen, Coop bit off most of the fuse on the last bomb, lit it and ran toward the redhead, throwing it at his feet. He yelled, "This is for my mom and dad!!"

Before Radial's father had time to react, the bomb exploded, blowing him into the bonfire. Missing most of both legs, he tried to crawl out.

But the fire quickly consumed him as he screamed.

Cooper ran up the hill then suddenly felt a sharp pain in his back and chest. The force of an arrow-like bolt penetrating his body, knocked him to his knees. He looked down at the crossbow bolt sticking out of his chest. He turned around to see a dozen men charging toward him. He pulled out his Colt and began to methodically fire at the approaching men. Most fell, but others replaced them. Coop popped in a fresh cylinder and kept on firing. Another bolt struck him in the left shoulder. He switched the Colt to his right hand. He was surprised to see the Hellrider closest to him suddenly sprout a crossbow bolt in his forehead. Coop managed to fire several more times before he collapsed losing consciousness and bleeding badly. His strength was gone, but as he fell forward, he heard a barely audible voice, *"Your mom and dad are proud of you, but your work has only just begun."* Then, even the voice disappeared.

"A little faith will bring your soul to heaven, but a lot of faith will bring heaven to your soul." *Dwight L. Moody*

Chapter 18

As Coop began to awaken, he heard voices. He tried to open his eyes, but couldn't. Then he heard the warden speaking. "I really have no idea how Cooper survived those arrow-bolts to his chest and shoulder. The bolt through his right lung alone should have killed him, and the infection that set in was nasty. Some higher power must have plans for this young man. It's a good thing Radial and the others arrived when they did."

Jordan corrected him. "That higher power, Warden, is Almighty God."

Warden Henry rebuked her. "Your God has gone missing for the last couple of centuries!"

She answered forcefully, "God didn't go anywhere! We are the ones who moved away from Him."

Coop felt a hand on his forehead. "His fever has broken." It was his sister. "How long will it be before he regains consciousness?"

"He's been in a coma for five days." Coop felt something on his chest. "His heart is strong and his lungs appear to be amazingly clear. But I am concerned about the fever. If it cooked his brain, he may never wake up. But if it didn't, Coop should regain consciousness in another couple of days."

Angie asked her dad, "So, we should just keep trying to get water and soup down him?"
"Yes, but be sure to change his dressing every other day and use freshly boiled pieces of cloth. Come get me if his condition worsens."

Jordan answered for all of them, "Yes, sir."

The women in Coop's life refused to leave his side. They had worked out a schedule that enabled them to care for him 24 hours a day. Their shifts often overlapped. They read from Coop's extensive library, talked about almost everything, and in the process, became good friends. While the warden had no actual training in medicine, he had read every book that he could find on the subject. Over the years he had become well regarded for his skill as a doctor and Angelina was an apt student. She had worked hard at training others to take over her teaching responsibilities.

Just as Jordan and Angie were about to leave Coop moved his head and groaned, trying to speak. They jumped to his side, Maggie carrying her son. He forced his eyes open and asked in a hoarse voice, "How's the baby?" All three women began to cry.

"Every great man is being helped by those around him, for his gift is to get good out of all things and all persons." *John Ruskin, 1846*

Chapter 19

It took almost six months for Cooper to completely heal. During that time, he and his friends made plans to journey north. A full six weeks after leaving Folsom, Cooper and what became known as the McIntyre Party, stood alongside old highway 26 in the Oregon territory. They looked eastward toward the city of what was now called New Portland. Traveling slowly and often through difficult weather and terrain, it was time consuming. They had journeyed up the coast of the territories of California and Oregon and had turned east over some coastal mountains. In the distance, as they peeked through tall trees that both bordered and had grown in the highway itself, they saw Mt. Hood. A small mantle of snow clung to upper portions of the densely forested and picturesque mountain. It was a beautiful sight. Cooper pointed and spoke to his friends.

"According to old maps, the city itself will take us another day of walking in that direction."

Jordan squeezed her husband's arm as he pointed. Right before they left Folsom P, the couple had signed articles of marriage. Edgar looked at Abe who spit off to the side. The llama and he had become good friends. Edgar gathered up something from within his throat and did the same.

The covered wagon Edgar and Coop had built, contained food, clothing, supplies, tools and weapons. Nobody rode; everyone walked including Maggie and Radial who took turns carrying her little boy. The only people permitted to join the New Portland travelers were those who could walk a long, dangerous and arduous trail. Warden Henry was more than generous, especially since his only daughter had chosen to make the trek. Angie was clearly disappointed when Coop and Jordan signed articles, but since they were her best friends, she decided to join the McIntyre Party as it traveled into unfamiliar territory.

When they arrived in Portland, huge areas of what was formerly the downtown area were in shambles. It was as if several block buster bombs had struck the city. Much of downtown Portland had been virtually leveled by earthquakes, fire and the ravages of rust and decay, but some portions of the city were relatively undamaged. They did find a few office buildings and a school a few blocks away from the Willamette River that were habitable.

They planned to set up camp in the large three story school complex that overlooked the Willamette River. Surprisingly, a chain link fence had survived the ravages of time and nature. The fence surrounded almost five acres of land and buildings. Most of the stone and brick buildings were intact. It was clear other groups of people had often made the school their home in the past.

Radial and Cooper walked carefully through the debris-strewn lobby past some offices that had served as living areas for other families. They observed a large open area outside the buildings that had probably served as a play or rest area. Now it was filled with waist-high grass, tall shrubs and trees. Seeing an area of tall grass relatively clear of trees and debris, it was decided to set up a temporary camp. The offices and rooms needed a lot of work before they could be used as dwelling places once again. They needed some construction tools and equipment to rebuild the dilapidated buildings. Coop knew exactly where he would find those tools....in Astoria. He turned to his friends and smiled, "I think we're home. Let's unpack."

It was decided to leave for Astoria in two days at first light. Edgar said it would be 5:45am. Radial turned to him, "My God man, how on earth can you possibly know that?"

"I dunno. It just comes to me. Cooper says it's a gift."

Radial shook his head. "It's just plain weird. I suppose you can tell us the exact day, month and year it is." He paused for a moment. Edgar started to answer, but Radial held up his hand. "I don't want to know." He looked over at Coop as a couple of strangers walk toward them. "We've got company. They don't appear to be marauders."

Cooper nodded. "Let's find out what they want."

The two strangers and their families would soon become the first New Portlandians to join them. Many others would soon follow.

"There are two ways of spreading light: to be the candle, or the mirror that reflects it."
Edith Wharton

Chapter 20

Two years later, the Finder/Fixer rested in a chair by a window overlooking the river. He and many others had taken several trips over to Astoria and to other surviving towns and villages in Oregon and Washington. Fear of Omega was on the wane and people were eager to talk about a loose connection between villages and towns, economically and socially. The Astoria commune, where the McIntyres once lived and worked, was found to be in bad shape. Only a few dozen people remained. In exchange for a bag of gold coins Edgar had found in an old Portland desk, Commandant Cable was easily convinced to give Cooper access to the warehouse and all that was stored inside, including the sailboat still anchored in the river. Astoria was one of the first communities to officially connect with New Portland.

Cooper sighed as he stared at the Willamette. The river had previously been a dumping ground for long abandoned 20th century factories that lay in ruins. The mighty Columbia River was not all that far away. Coop and Jordan had often taken time to travel down river along with Radial and whoever tagged along. They would sail the Adelene Marie in and around the mouth of the Columbia River. Once called the graveyard of ships, the water was considerably calmer and warmer after the earthquake and subsequent changes to the weather. Those experiences would prove to come in handy down life's road.

Change had come quickly to their little community. Deeply in love, Radial and Maggie signed articles about a year after Coop and Jordan. Coop, his sister and their spouses were all left handed, as were the majority of people in New Portland. Nevertheless, about a third of all babies who were born still succumbed to Omega. It was assumed these children had not inherited left-handedness. The virus was still alive and well.

The whole Portland area had seen substantial growth, as people wandered in from the countryside to see what was going on in New Portland. More than 300 people had become part of the McIntyre community and had reclaimed other office buildings and the homes that had survived the ravages of time and nature. All worked at various jobs in digging for what the Ancients left behind, construction, farming and restoration. They all shared the fruits of their labors, including the produce grown in a large garden located in a nearby park. Part of it had been fenced in for raising sheep and goats. Fish pens had been constructed in parts of the river, providing another source of protein. A small portion of the park had been set aside as a playground. Similar groups of people had claimed other parts of the city up and down the Willamette and Columbia.

Maggie had decided to give her first son the name Levi Henry McIntyre, to honor her father and to keep the family name. Interestingly enough, the boy had red hair. His birth father was Radial's older brother, who was also a redhead. So, Levi's step dad was actually his uncle. Maggie and Radial were unsure if they would ever tell their son the truth.

With Radial's help, the Finder/Fixer repaired, and actually improved two sun machines on the roof of the office building that was now the McIntyre home. It provided a source of power for the heaters that raised the temperature to a comfortable level in the building and in the adjacent conference room, where people were beginning to gather. It had been transformed into a community center and church.

A rebuilt and restored hydroelectric plant also gave others access to a source of energy in New Portland, which had become a major city in the newly formed United Pacific States. But useable power lines were few and far between and with only a handful of functioning electrical machines and lighting appliances, the electricity went largely unused. That problem was slowly changing as long-forgotten skills were being re-claimed. Schools for being a blacksmith, basic engineering, metallurgy, carpentry and plumbing, farming, applied science and general education were becoming popular thanks, in large part, to the Finder/Fixer and his family.

Repairable machinery and equipment from the Ancients was brought into town almost daily, as diggers explored the collapsed ruins of buildings and the few that still stood. A large near-by warehouse was being rapidly filled. Maggie and Coop had trained a crew of 20 in the techniques of restoration and repair. Warehouses were quickly being filled with repairable machinery, equipment, clothing, furniture and more....all from underneath the rubble and abandoned buildings of old Portland. The most amazing find was an old steam powered locomotive engine, boxed up in numbered wooden crates. When compared to the dimensions of other locomotives Coop had read about in books, this engine was a little more than half the size. Across a plate on one side of the cab was written Southern Pacific No. 1 Huntington 1864. One crate contained elaborate assembly instructions. Being smaller in size, Coop assumed it might be relatively simple to assemble. The crates were moved to a spot adjacent to a set of railroad tracks. They were in reasonably good condition. A roof was built over the area permitting Coop and his friends to work on the train, whenever they had time. The area was expanded to include a workshop which had many of the tools and hoists necessary for the project. But then something occurred that would keep them away from the engine for some time.

"All that is necessary for the triumph of evil is that good men do nothing." *Edmund Burke*

Chapter 21

On a cool, crisp morning, Cooper was working on his favorite project. He very rarely slept well and was up early. The old steam engine fascinated him. It had become his favorite challenge in bringing back to life some of the machinery from the days of the Ancients. The locomotive parts were in excellent condition having been carefully wrapped in oilcloth and covered with grease. Since grease was no longer a common product, it was carefully removed and stored for future use, as were the yards and yards of oilcloth.

He was filing off a rough edge on the end of a piece of metal when he heard screams coming from the main courtyard, a few blocks away. Dropping the file, he grabbed his Colt .45 and ran down the street. Other people hearing the panicky screams picked up whatever was nearby for a weapon and ran alongside Coop to the plaza. When they arrived they saw marauders on horseback trying to grab any young people who were nearby. It was an all too familiar scene for Cooper.

Yelling like banshee, as Coop had taught him, Edgar ran straight at the horses swinging a shovel. Two horses panicked and threw off their riders. The men were immediately attacked and pummeled by those who were closest. Coop launched himself off of a short brick wall and tackled a marauder who was still astride his horse. Both fell to the ground with a sickening crunch. It was the marauder who hit first with Cooper on top. He swung at the marauder's head with his Colt and knocked him unconscious. In all the chaos another rider ran down a young woman, who was thrown under the horse's hooves. She screamed drawing Coop's attention, as the marauder spurred his horse away from the conflict. Coop aimed his Colt carefully and pulled the trigger. The bullet smashed through the man's back and he fell to the pavement. Just then Radial showed up with some men armed with crossbows, and they quickly disposed of the three other marauders. Of the eight who began the attack, two were dead, four were badly wounded and two managed to gallop off toward the river, leaving six valuable horses and their friends behind.

The teenager had suffered a broken arm and some scrapes and bruises from the fall. Angie had already arrived and was caring for the girl's injuries before attending to the marauders. This was the second raid in the last six weeks. Radial looked over at Cooper, who was nursing a badly skinned knee.

"When are we going to do something about these unprovoked attacks?"

Coop stood up and limped over toward Angie to get his knee bandaged. "How about right now? The marauders wouldn't be expecting an immediate response."

He eyed the captured horses. "How many of your militia know how to ride?"

"They all do, but what's on your mind?"

Angie eyed Cooper's bloodied knee and elbow. "Are you okay?"

"I'm fine, just a few scrapes. But I'm sure I'll be pretty sore tomorrow." Angie wrapped up his knee and elbow and sent him on his way. She watched as he limped back to Radial. She had hoped for more from Cooper, but apparently, it wasn't meant to be.

Coop stroked the neck of a still nervous horse as he spoke to Radial. "The last thing in the world that the marauders would expect is for us to go after them. I want to ride over to the marauder camp on the other side of town and thump a few skulls."

Radial smiled, "It's about time."

Two hours later after an emergency meeting with the city council, it was agreed that something had to be done about the six marauder camps situated around the state, mostly in small abandoned towns. But they insisted on a more organized response. Coop and Radial were not happy, but saw the wisdom in getting beyond the heat of the moment.

A week later, working with the city council, Coop and Radial had organized and trained a substantial militia. They eventually raided all the marauder camps in most of the Oregon territory and brought the survivors back to New Portland, imprisoning them in an old school. The 200 or so captives were escorted to the school auditorium. Several successfully escaped, but a diet full of garlic made it easy for most to be found by well-trained dogs. The assembled Marauders, men, women and their children stared at their captors.

A few blocks away Radial glared at his best friend. "Coop, you can't be serious. We've been feeding and caring for some of these folk for weeks and now you're suggesting we just let them go? There is no way we should let these people return to their camps. They'll simply resume their old habits of pillaging our towns and killing the innocent. We should take them out into the wilderness, as far away from us as possible, and let them fend for themselves."

Coop shook his head. "How humane is that? They'll certainly die out there."

Radial was frustrated. "They'd easily and gladly kill all of us if the situation were reversed. Maybe we could give them some food and encourage them to walk over the mountains to another territory, where like-minded people still roam the country-side."

"We could," Coop acknowledged. "But I've spoken with all of the members of the council and most agree we could offer to teach them a new way of life, our way of life. I am not convinced all or even most are as vicious as you suggest. We could give them a choice...stay with us and work on building a new life or take the walk into the wilderness."

Coop stood and walked toward the school auditorium where the captives milled around aimlessly. Looking back over his shoulder he said, "If we make no effort to save this part of humanity, then we will have lost ours."

Radial followed Cooper, as he usually did. He motioned for a couple of armed men to join them. He noticed the old Colt .45 stuffed into the back of his friend's pants and smiled.

Inside the auditorium, Coop stood on a bench and looked out over the milling crowd. The large room had good acoustics but he yelled anyway, calling for their attention. They gradually moved toward him to hear what he had to say.

"My name is Cooper McIntyre!"

A young woman somewhat close to him yelled back. "You killed my father!"

Radial started to move toward her but Coop held him back. "I only killed or wounded those who were trying to hurt me or my friends."

"Tell that to all of the children who are now without a father." A few others hollered their support for her.

Coop held her gaze for a moment as they quieted down. "I am without a father as well. Several Hellriders slaughtered my father, brutalized and killed my mother in Yosemite Valley in California Land, as I watched. Some of you may have been there." A few men slowly moved back further into the crowd.

"You marauders have a reputation for being ruthless thieves and killers, taking what you want and murdering those who get in your way. You're a plague on our hopes and dreams of restoring and rebuilding a civilized society; maybe worse than Omega." He paused, letting his words sink in.

"Why should we show you any mercy at all? Why should we keep on feeding and caring for you? Some in New Portland would rather march you out into the mountain wilderness and leave you there with a two day ration of food and water, enough to get you over the mountains into California Land or the Columbia territory." Coop stared at the young woman who spoke up. He said, "Again, why should we show you any mercy when you have not shown any toward us?"

A loud voice spoke from the back. "Because that is what Jesus would do!!"

The Finder/Fixer smiled. "Would the person who just spoke please come forward?" He looked at the young woman. "And you, too."

A rather tall, emaciated man about Coop's age and the woman stopped directly in front of him as he stepped down from the bench. Coop extended his hand to the man. "I'm Cooper McIntyre."

The man smiled and shook hands with Coop. "We all know who you are. My name is Roger Haley, a cobbler by trade. I teach God's Word as an avocation." Roger gave Coop a puzzled look. "Why are you known as the Finder/Fixer?"

Coop answered, "I have a reputation for being able to find useful things the Ancients left behind and to repair them." Roger noticed Coop's concerned appraisal of his physical condition.

"I was captured a year ago. I have not been very obedient in the marauder camp and have not eaten well as a result. In fact, I have eaten more food here in the last two weeks than I have in the last two months."

The woman spoke up. "I'm Gabriella Blue." She offered her hand and Coop took it.

With the introductions complete Coop asked, "Would the two of you take a walk with me?"

The woman hesitated. "What are your intentions, Mr. McIntyre? Are you punishing us because we dared to speak up?"

"On the contrary; I've asked you to come with me because of your courage. Please follow me."

As they left the school grounds, Cooper intentionally walked them past some of their many flourishing gardens, restored homes and businesses that had been converted into homes. Children played in the streets under the watchful eye of some adults. Cooper continued, "When we decided to rid our state of the marauder problem, we did not fully consider the ramifications of that action."

Roger interrupted. "You need to know I never willingly participated in the activities of the marauders. Many in the camps did so because it was their only choice. I disobeyed and survived simply because they needed somebody to repair their shoes."

Gabrielle added, "My father was one of those who did what he was told out of concern for me."

Coop nodded. "I am sorry your dad was killed. But I hope you understand I didn't have any other choice. We were protecting our loved ones in New Portland."

She stared directly at Coop. "I watched as you shot my father in the forehead. Admittedly, he was coming at you with a hatchet. Nevertheless, you killed him."

Cooper replayed in his head the raids on the marauder camps until he came to the one where he was attacked by a man with a hatchet. It only took a couple of seconds. Behind the man who ran toward him, he saw the woman, her face buried in her hands.

"I am sorry we had to resort to violence to end the marauder menace. But now I am faced with another decision; what to do with those of you who survived. I was serious when I said many in New Portland, especially those who have lost family to the marauders, would just as soon see you perish than take a chance on any more raids. Knowing all of this, what would you advise me to do?"

Roger cleared his throat as they walked along. "I understand the nature of what is going on here. From Gabby's perspective, her father and many others were just protecting their families. From your perspective," he looked at Cooper, "you were protecting the families in New Portland. How can one perspective be right and the other wrong?" The three sat down on a street bench. Coop liked Gabriella's spunk. It seemed to suit her. Radial remained standing a few feet away listening carefully to the conversation while keeping an eye on all the kids who were playing on the sidewalk. Cooper said nothing as Roger continued.

"Is might always right? The history books I have read strongly suggest not necessarily. From what I have learned, it is the leaders of our country and world who are ultimately responsible for the bloody conflicts people have endured both past and present. They make the decisions and laws others must follow, whether they like it or not. God's primary teaching in the Bible is to love one another. This love is defined as caring for one's neighbor, looking out for his or her needs. We don't see much of this kind of love anymore."

He looked over at Gabby. "The leader of our particular camp, an uneducated and ugly man of violence, decided he had a right to take whatever was necessary in order for the camp to survive. He sincerely believed the goods produced and possessed by others should be equally distributed to those who produced nothing and had nothing. He did so by force."

Radial was impatient. "Are you saying we should just give our food and possessions to people who do nothing to earn them?"

Roger was as patient as Radial was impatient. "No, I am suggesting a couple of things. First, the primary responsibility for the bloodshed at the marauder camps should be laid at the feet of the camp leaders. They made the decision to rob, pillage, kidnap and sometimes kill innocent people." He glanced again at Gabby. "Robert was our leader. He and his lieutenants are ultimately responsible for the death of your husband and dozens of others." He looked over at Coop. "I assume most of them are no longer with us."

Coop looked over at Radial who answered, "Yes, all but two died in various conflicts at Marauder camps. They have already been taken to the southern border of the U.P.S. into the mountain wilderness."

Roger frowned. "What is the U.P.S.?"

Cooper slowly shook his head. "So you haven't heard?"

"Heard what?"

"The territories of Oregon, Washington and Vancouver Island have organized themselves into a union of federated states called the United Pacific States. We hope to include California Land to the south and the Columbia territory to the north sometime soon. Our national capital is New Portland. We are loosely governed through a representative form of government. A constitution is being written that will provide more structure as we work out what it means to be one nation under God once again."

Roger was stunned. "Believe me, none of us had any idea the restoration of a democratic country on the West Coast had occurred. Some of our friends will be thrilled."

Coop shifted his gaze over to Gabby. "And what do you think?"

"I think if you have a leadership role here and I have a choice, I would rather leave for the Columbia Territory than be a part of your New Portland."

Coop was disappointed at her stubbornness. "New Portland does not belong to me. I helped shape it and do have a role in its leadership, but I am not the mayor. We have a small council of elected officials who govern the city and who establish its goals and priorities."

"Just the same, as long as you are here, I cannot be." Her anger had clearly not abated.

Roger held her gaze for a moment. "You are not making any sense. We have not even heard what the city is suggesting as an alternative to leaving New Portland." He looked back at Coop. "What are you offering?"

"For those who want to stay, a chance to begin again, to become part of something special. It won't be easy, the whole issue of trust will be a difficult hurdle, but if you work hard you can become part of New Portland. For those who already have a skill, we will immediately integrate them into our workforce on a supervised basis. For those who want to learn a skill, they will be taught. Children and adults will have the opportunity to go to school. It can be a great thing for both you and us."

Gabby was shaking her head. "It sounds good, but for me, it's too good to be true. I would rather take my chances up north in Columbia."

Coop stood. "It is your choice." He turned toward Roger. "Would you be willing to tell those in the auditorium what their choices are? They would hear it better from you, rather than me."

Roger nodded, "Absolutely." Radial escorted them back to the school. After hearing about their options and the news of a new country being formed, a large majority chose to stay. Almost two dozen people decided to take their chances for a new life in the territory of Columbia up north, thinking the vast territory would have fewer problems and more opportunities. Gabby was one of them.

The next day, Radial and some of his men led the small marauder group down the river to Astoria, where they were loaded onto the Adelene Marie. Two years earlier, after liberating the communes in Astoria, Cooper and Radial had convinced Commandant Cable to sell the sailboat and Cable's warehouse full of various items the McIntyres and others had retrieved from the ruins of Astoria, to the newly formed United Pacific States. In that warehouse were several duffel bags full of different sized sails and rigging. A couple of those sails were pieced together to produce a workable sail for the Adelene Marie. In time, after outfitting the boat, Radial and Edgar had become quite the sailors.

With Radial at the helm of a somewhat overloaded boat, they sailed up the coast into the Strait of Juan de Fuca, and then on to the old city of Vancouver in the Columbia Territory. The city was virtually empty. Not much was left after the tsunami. Giving the former marauders some supplies Radial said, "Once you leave this boat, you are not welcome to return. You have made a decision to leave the U.P.S., so go on your way. A marauder camp is about 10 miles due north. You have enough provisions to reach it. Good luck."

The last person to step off the Adelene Marie and onto Columbian soil was Gabby.

"It is by those who have suffered that the world has been advanced." *Leo Tolstoy*

Chapter 22

A few months later, Cooper walked slowly up the stairs of the three story building that had been transformed into a home for the growing McIntyre family. He was tired and hungry. Visions of some leftover salmon in the small three foot high refrigerator he had repaired and hooked up to the sun machine, danced through his head.

The building was all part of a former college campus. His home on the top floor of a former office building of the school, overlooked a now clean and pristine Willamette River, six blocks away. Coop had learned the river was once a dumping ground for industry almost 300 years ago. The water was still polluted when the Omega virus struck, but was now a valuable water supply for New Portland. The cleansing only took a couple of centuries.

He and Jordan had chosen the top floor and he was beginning to doubt the sanity of that decision. Maggie and Radial lived one floor below. Angie had taken the first floor and had transformed part of it into a medical clinic. The school buildings and grounds were some of the few in New Portland that had not collapsed because of age, earthquakes or fire. Several other single or two story structures survived and had been reclaimed as homes. The McIntyre building had been constructed mostly of re-enforced brick, steel and aluminum, and it survived. He stepped out onto the flat roof which was now home to a small garden. Coop looked over the rubble of a once beautiful city. Whole forests of trees and shrubbery had grown around and in some cases through old buildings, rusted cars, trucks and through the roads on which they were found. The people of New Portland had, in fact, made substantial progress. Several streets had been cleaned and reclaimed. It was good to see.

The few people who had survived after Omega did so by living off of what was left behind following the abrupt halt of the industrial and computer ages.

The material that had caused environmentalists deep concern in centuries past, was the salvation of so many people in the 23rd century. So much of what was buried deep under the rubble of old America was enclosed in plastic and Styrofoam. Clothing, small tools, books, household items and many other things all emerged from their plastic shrouds to help people who were emerging from a difficult time. Those who were the most efficient and talented diggers were highly prized members of society. Cooper and Jordan McIntyre worked hard to lift their part of the world back from the ashes in many contexts. Thinking of his wife put a slight smile on his face. After lunch, he slipped on a light coat and headed back down the stairs to take a short walk to a small cemetery, a few blocks away, Cooper sat on a bench he had built next to Jordan's grave. She had died a year earlier after cutting her hand on a rusty piece of metal she was trying to pull from the ground. Within two weeks, a high fever and painful spasms racked her body. Angelina, who had become the doctor of the community, stayed with her night and day. It became more and more difficult for Jordan to breathe. She awoke one more time and smiled at her husband. "I love you. See you later alligator." She died in the arms of her husband, who despite all his gifts and talents, was unable to save her. It was the first time anyone had seen him cry. He visited the cemetery every day.

"Well honey, we finally finished the house. All of the plumbing works too. Maggie helped me get the sun machines working after they broke down again, although the batteries were beyond salvaging. So, we have juice during the day, but not at night. Our portion of the building is a little too big just for me, but I think you would have liked the end result. I built a sunroom on the West Side and get this; I am now an official gardener. We have lots of flowers all over the place, plus easy access to our own supply of fruit and vegetables. You were right about that old rocking chair. I had to replace some of the left arm with a different kind of wood, but it actually looks pretty good. It is sitting next to our bedroom window and has become my favorite reading place."

Coop paused and wiped away a tear. He fingered the gold coin that had become his most prized possession. "Edgar says the engraving on the back of your coin is a map of some sort, but I haven't yet looked into it. I miss you so much." He paused to look at a wren that had settled on Jordan's headstone. "I'm getting ready to resume my search for the Librarian. I plan to be away for several months." He stood and laid a bouquet of flowers in front of the flat stone on which he had methodically and carefully carved out her name, Jordan McIntyre (2170-2195) Beloved Wife. "I'll see you before I leave."

After Jordan's death, Coop had taken a break from his work in New Portland. Most of his time was spent on a few restoration projects which had caught his fancy. Angie and Maggie took on the daunting task of filling Coop's shoes with Radial's capable assistance. But now that he had decided to resume his hunt for the fabled Librarian, a few things needed attention. Fortunately, Maggie had revealed before they left Folsom, she became aware that she, too, had an unforgettable memory. It came around the time she entered childbearing years. For her, the trigger was apparently hormone related. The gift was not reserved just for the males in the family. Now Coop was spending as much time as he could spare talking to Maggie, imparting to her his years of stored knowledge. Far too few had the gift they had, so he was determined to share what he knew and teach as much as he could before his day of departure came. He hoped the vast repository of knowledge he'd accumulated would not die with him, should he die prematurely.

At 27 years of age, his dark brown shoulder length hair hid some of the scars of past conflicts with the marauders. At six foot two inches tall, he had grown broader in the shoulders and more muscled. He attributed his relatively good health to Jordan, who encouraged him to eat a lot of fruit and vegetables and to exercise every day.

A couple of times a year people from the New Portland area would come hear the Finder/Fixer tell stories of how people lived long ago. They all liked to hear about the Ancients and the technological marvels which were part of life for them. The possibility of seeing another old machine or two from the ancient days come to life intrigued them. People came from miles around to hear and to see a man who had done so much for them and, in doing so, had become a living legend.

Many of those living in New Portland could now read and write, when just a few years earlier it was very difficult to find any who could. It did not hurt that New Portland was the capital of the United Pacific States. With only a total national population of about 40,000, people were widely spread out among the three states. Most lived in or close to major cities like New Seattle, New Portland, Eugenia, Olympia and Vancouver City. When the states became unified, a simple democracy replaced the military generals who once ruled many communities. Very little blood was shed in a people's uprising joined by many volunteers and led by Radial Tire. They simply stormed the homes and offices of self-appointed dictators and military leaders. Some did not give up easily and were killed. Others accepted the inevitable and were escorted out of the U.P.S. over the border deep into the wilderness. Their families were invited to stay, but most left with their husbands.

The government was simple, limited and crafted around the basic principles found in the McIntyre Doctrine. Five people from each state were elected to serve on a Governing Council for the People. The position was unpaid and part-time. They met two days a week. Their offices were located at a former college in New Portland. Most of the brick buildings had collapsed, but they had been recently rebuilt as government offices. Food and housing was provided for the council and their families. It was seen as a privilege to guide and serve the fledgling country for a single four year term of office. They worked another three days during the week in various tasks as needed around New Portland.

A growing economy thrived through the bartering of goods and services at the farmer's market, rain or shine. Some currency was being introduced in parts of the country. A gold standard was being implemented using coins minted by the government. Life began to revolve around two days of the week, Marketday and Worshipday.

Some people in New Portland had more, some had less, but no one went hungry or without a roof over their heads. Everyone worked, except for young children, the disabled and the elderly. School was mandatory for everyone under the age of sixteen.

The Council met, initially, to provide a framework for statewide government and to work on a written statement of purpose that would guide the country into the future. Cooper usually met with them, sharing what he knew of how the government worked in the past. That framework would be a loosely binding agreement that gave each state the freedom to design a way of life suitable to them, as long as those statutes did not contradict the McIntyre Doctrine. If people were unhappy with the voter approved statutes of a particular state, they would be free to move to another. Judges were not permitted to make the McIntyre Doctrine say what they determined it should say. In the meantime, as laws were being approved by the people, the fledgling country was run on common sense, which was amazingly plentiful, and by a consensus of the Council. The 80% rule was in effect. If 80% could not reach a consensus on a decision, the measure, law or project was dropped from the agenda. The fifteen representatives elected a Chairperson from their midst, who served in that capacity for two years. Radial was the first to be elected. His job was to provide direction and leadership for the Council. From that same group two judges were selected to serve in the counties of each state and would travel from community to community to preside over trials as needed. For serious crimes the usual punishment was banishment from the country; for minor issues people were sentenced to well-guarded work camps where they worked on community projects. Repeat offenders were banished from the country.

While not a representative, Cooper was asked to serve as an advisor to the Council and he agreed to do so for two years. A well-trained volunteer militia served in each state. From within the militia, the Chairperson appointed Marshals, who kept the peace in various communities.

Massive mountain ranges provided a natural division for the United Pacific States from the rest of the Americas who were still fighting over resources and land. Military dictatorships or bands of marauders ruled in those territories and life was difficult and short for the remaining population. But that was not the case in the U.P.S., where hope and peace had replaced fear and subjugation.

Several months later, as people walked toward the Community Center, they did so with a freedom that was absent a decade earlier. The city version of a governing council had been established in New Portland. Roger Haley was elected mayor. He had also become the preacher at regular church services on Sunday. Attendance was superb and they would soon have to find a larger building. It was a great beginning but unfortunately, their struggles were not yet over. And with Cooper planning to leave, there was deep concern.

"The right man is the one who seizes the moment." *J.W. Goethe*

Chapter 23

The Finder/Fixer walked into the Community Center. It was full. Within days, word that Cooper was again coming to talk about the *old days* had spread all over the countryside. Some of the younger children sat on their father's shoulders to see the man, who seemed larger than life. People of all ages brought whatever they had to sit on. A few had chairs of one sort or another, but most were content to sit on pillows or blankets. Most brought something to eat since Cooper was known to talk for quite a spell. He sat near the podium with Emma Lou, his youngest niece, sitting by his side on

Angelina's lap. She was Emma Lou's godmother. Emma looked up at her uncle whose strong voice would echo across the room. He turned to look at Maggie, who winked as he stood to speak.

"Welcome everyone. It is good to see so many of you here." He gestured toward his sister. "Maggie, whom most of you know, asked some important questions earlier this morning about America's past. Two centuries ago, how could a world previously so technologically advanced, decline so quickly? And more importantly, why was it unable to stop Omega?"

He continued, "It is hard to believe that centuries ago men walked on the moon, everyone had a car, a television and a computer and so much more. The Ancients spoke into hand-held machines sending the sound of their voices hundreds of miles to other people with or without wires. Flying machines took people from place to place and even to other parts of the world. To us, all of these things, and much more seem to be part of a fantasy world, a mythical world, but it was our world at one time. It is my dream that in this century we will recover some of what was lost."

"Most of us won't see it, but many of our children and grandchildren will. Right now,

243

Radial Tire and I are rebuilding a steam powered locomotive engine used by the Ancients. You've seen the iron tracks on which it will ride in different places around the city. Crews are rapidly repairing them." Many nodded in agreement.

He looked at those who had gathered; young and old, whole families in some cases, including his own. They were interested in learning about the past. It gave him hope for the future.

"In my travels and in digs in different places, from California to British Columbia, I have come across books that survived the elements, the burning and the destruction that followed the collapse of American culture. Having read them, I do know something of the transformation that came across America and the world. Over the years, thousands were stolen and destroyed by incredibly stupid people during my traveling days. But now we have a growing collection of old books in our own library, and I encourage you to read them on your own, or have them read to you. You'll discover that changes in America began a long time ago when the lands around us were still united under one democratic government. That government wasn't perfect by any means, but like the one we currently have, it was chosen by the people. Unfortunately politics became more important than common sense and the country suffered because of it. Those days were a difficult time for democracy.

The original democratic concept was introduced by a group of men who were the Founding Fathers of America five centuries ago. A great nation was born that had incredible potential. The early leaders of America had a strong belief in God, and the country was known as a Christian nation. A Constitution was written establishing basic foundations for government, for the law and for life. The moral and ethical fiber of the country was deeply imbedded in the teaching of the church and gave unusual strength to American society. For several hundred years, the country seemed to thrive under the motto, "In God We Trust.

But then, in the last part of the 20th and early 21st century, America's vision for the future became blurred. Powerful political and judicial leaders began to abandon the godly principles which were the pillars on which America was built. Not nearly enough people fought back against a self-centered ideology that had lost its connection with God. The Federal judiciary began to make decisions based on their interpretation of the Constitution, decisions that had little to do with what the document actually said, but rather on what the judges wanted the Constitution to say. When the Omega virus struck, the country was in political upheaval. In addition, America was technologically strong, but spiritually weak. Leaders of a divided country could not act quickly enough to deal with Omega. Millions of people died in less than a year. Eventually federal and state governments collapsed and society fell into chaos. Martial law became the rule, rather than the exception, in most parts of the country. It was a case where democracy didn't fail, it was people who had failed democracy."

He looked around the crowd. "The good news is while our population has been decimated, I am convinced pockets of the American ideal still exist. We are one of them; others are just waiting for us to find them."

McIntyre paused to take a drink before continuing. "You and I have taken some positive steps toward becoming a God-centered society once again, where both faith in God and a commitment to each other has an eternal reward. Truly a new Portland is rising from the ashes of death and destruction. Hopefully we have learned from the mistakes of those who lived and died before us. With hard work, personal sacrifice and dedication, we will make a difference; we'll restore and rebuild our society for the sake of our children, grandchildren and those after them." He looked over at Roger Haley. "In time we will, once again, become one nation under God."

Someone in the back began to clap and everyone quickly joined in as they rose to their feet. The Finder/Fixer smiled and said to himself, "Thank you God."

A young man stood and asked, "Do we know anything more about how Omega started?"

Cooper frowned, "Not specifically, but we have found a diary that does shed some light on what occurred early on after it struck. In the basement of the office building, which is now our family home, a corner in the basement had been designated as the place to store furniture too badly damaged to be repaired or used. For me that is never the case, so as I was looking through the pile of broken furniture, I discovered an old desk whose legs had been broken off. One of the drawers had a false bottom that had been dislodged. Underneath the panel, I found the personal diary of someone who survived Omega for a time. The family name was Dunston."

"The author wrote mostly about family and personal issues up until Omega struck on July 4,

2004. The last entry was on May 14, 2016. The diary sheds some light on the Omega crisis, but only talks of its effects on a crumbling society. I'll read to you a part of it. The writer was identified as David Dunston."

"This is my last entry. Carolyn died just a few weeks ago, our children a month before that. The suffering they endured, although brief, was painful to watch. I do not intend to go out that way with no one to care for me. I am unsure if anyone will ever read this. My wife began a chronicle of events at the beginning of Omega and it appears I'll finish it. It's been almost twelve years since Omega came, and from the news reports we hear, almost every corner of the world is suffering as we are. The city that I knew, the city I grew up in, no longer exists.

Most people have left Portland and have headed for the countryside taking with them whatever they can. Everything has closed…schools, hospitals and stores. Supplies of food are nonexistent. We live in a top floor apartment. It has a huge skylight in the bathroom and we converted the soaking tub into a small garden. We grow mostly vegetables year round. I trap birds on the roof and we have managed to survive. But despite our best efforts at isolation, Omega has claimed everyone in our family. I'm the last to survive.

A handful of churches still hold services, but chaos reigns; groups of marauders roam the streets taking what they want, killing anyone who gets in their way. Fires burn in buildings everywhere. Policemen have left their jobs to protect their families. When absolutely necessary, some of us walk from place to place in small groups, wearing hospital masks, a few with weapons. I have an old .22 caliber rifle with just a handful of shells left.

On occasion, a car will drive by, but with almost non-existent gas supplies, the sight is becoming a rarity. A permanent fire burns down by the river for the cremation of bodies. Every day a bulldozer pushes the ashes and bone fragments into the water to be carried out into the sea by the mighty Columbia River. Soon, there will not be anyone to run the bulldozer. I already have Omega's first symptoms.

Perhaps, like in the days of Noah, God has finally had enough of the moral and ethical disobedience that permeates the world He created. He gave us the freedom to choose our life path and we have chosen poorly. We have no one to blame but ourselves. Having said that, my observation is that there are still plenty of godly, loving people out there, people who truly care for one another. Maybe God will raise someone from among them to lead us once again, as in the days of old. May God forgive me for what I'm about to do."

The faces of the crowd were somber. Cooper whispered to his sister and Maggie walked away only to return in a few minutes carrying a strange looking box-shaped machine, a couple of flat cardboard envelopes and an electrical extension cord. She sat it on her chair.

Coop continued. "The journal did not share a lot of details, but it was clear Omega was a fast acting and deadly virus introduced into the Northwest part of the former United States by terrorists of some sort. Before you ask, a virus is a tiny piece of life so small we cannot see it. When you and I catch a cold, the cold is caused by a virus that infects the tissues of our body. Some of you have may have heard the saying that a cold lasts about a week or seven days. After feeling miserable for a few days, you do get better. What happens to that cold virus? For all intents and purposes a virus simply wears out and dies."

"The problem with the Omega virus is it takes a long time to die. Before it does, it invades and reproduces in important organs of our bodies, the lungs in particular and people die within a week or less of getting sick. The only people who survived were those with an inborn immunity to the disease. The writer of the diary reported that within five years over 400 million people in the world had died, including most of his family. Space in existing cemeteries was exhausted, so they resorted to mass cremations.

With so many people dying and the collapse of the economy worldwide, it is no wonder America slipped into chaos. I know nothing about other countries, but I suspect the virus did the same thing there as here. It is likely only a small number of people in our world have survived Omega. You and I have survived because we have an immunity."

A woman in the back spoke loudly. "Are you saying that we'll never get rid of the Omega virus?"

"The virus still exists, but I am convinced it is no longer the threat it once was. We still need to be cautious with strangers, but we no longer need to shun them. Our current practice of a week of isolation is enough to make sure they are not carriers of the virus. It is time for us to emerge from our self-imposed cocoons. But I still hope for a cure."

Seeing their faces, he needed to change their mood. Cooper spoke forcefully. "The good news is as we put the fear of Omega behind us, we can reclaim and rebuild much of that which has been lost. To some degree, we already have. We do need some help in that regard. I realize stories about the Librarian may be just a myth, but if he or she exists, the Librarian may be able to help us." He stared at Radial. "If the Librarian or a descendent is yet alive, I plan to find him. I will be leaving the day after tomorrow." People began to murmur.

"Let's lighten the mood a bit. Would you like to see one of the old machines of our ancestors come to life?" Everyone clapped their approval.

"Maggie has repaired a music machine." He plugged the cord of the machine into an extension cord and plugged the extension into a wall outlet. It was receiving electrical power from the sun machine. He slipped a large black disc from the envelope and placed it in the machine Maggie had opened. Turning the old record player on, he placed the needle on the record and stood up. He said loudly, "This is music from the 20th century."

A long forgotten orchestra began to play a waltz. He asked Angelina, "May I have this dance?"

She curtsied and said, "It would be my honor." Following the instructions of an old book they found along with the machine, she and Coop had learned to dance, as did Maggie and Radial.

Coop lifted his left hand and took her extended right hand. He placed his right hand on her hip and the two began to dance as music filled the room. He thought to himself, "Jordan would have loved this."

Several others watched the couple and soon joined them moving rhythmically to the music. It was a night to remember especially when they heard the unforgettable voice of a singer on another record. His name was Frank Sinatra. Talk of Omega disappeared as everyone listened to the music of a bygone century. It was fun.

A half-hour later, everyone returned to their seats. A young woman stood and commented. "Mr. McIntyre, we have all heard larger-than-life stories about you and your family. But is it true you and your sister cannot forget anything, that you are unforgettable?"

"Yes, why do you ask?"

"It just seems to me you are far too valuable to be wandering around the countryside looking for a myth. Even with most of the marauders largely gone, it is still dangerous in some places. Why don't you just stay home?"

"I understand your concern. But it is precisely because of my memory I am willing to take a chance that the Librarian exists. Whatever I can learn from him or her, I will bring back to Portland to share with you. And the best part is, unlike you, I don't have to write anything down." A few people smiled. "Besides Maggie will be here and knows almost as much as I do. Right, Sis?"

Maggie replied dryly, "Probably more."
That got a laugh.

A few hours later, Maggie and her brother were walking to what was now called the McIntyre house.
Angie had taken the kids back a little earlier.

"You do know Angie has a lot of feelings for you."

Coop sighed. "Here we go again." He turned to face his sister. "I like Angie a lot, but as far as I am concerned we are just good friends. And to be honest, I am not ready to get into another relationship."

"You are not getting any younger you know and there are other guys who are showing interest in her."

"Good. If one of them strikes her fancy, she should pursue it."

She added, "One of the men knows you. His name is Kevin Donley."

Coop smiled. "He's a good man. He has become an assistant to Roger Haley. I understand another congregation is planned on the other side of town and he will be the preacher. He would be a great catch for any young woman."

"Opportunity is not a roaming wanderer that blesses at random. It seeks only those individuals who are prepared to meet it."
Reed Thomas

Chapter 24

It was the third day since he had left New Portland. Coop reined up his horse and stretched. He was at the top of a long forgotten road curving down toward the valley below. He had spotted a seemingly abandoned farmhouse nestled next to a creek. He reached over and patted Abe on the head. "It looks like we might have found a place to spend the night." His faithful llama nodded. "We probably have about a five or six day ride ahead of us before we get to Seattle, so might even stay for a couple of nights."

As they drew closer to the farm, it was obvious that no one had been around for quite a while. The barn had partially collapsed and the condition of the house was poor, at best. Cooper stepped down from his horse and waded through waist high weeds to reach the front door. It was partially ajar.

To be safe he asked loudly, "Anybody home?" There was no answer, so he walked carefully inside. A dozen or so birds flew out the open windows. The tile floor was littered with broken furniture, dishes and debris. He stepped into what was once a nice kitchen. It had been stripped long ago of anything useful and was in worse condition than the other room. The door to the only bedroom had been partially torn from its hinges and hung loosely at an angle. With more trash and debris on the floor, that room had also been stripped clean of valuable items. Cooper wasn't disappointed or surprised. This was a common occurrence.

Retracing his steps, Coop walked back through the kitchen to the opening for the back door. It was completely missing. He stepped outside onto a large brick patio which was partially covered by a surprisingly intact patio roof. The roof panels appeared to be made of a material he had recently identified as fiberglass. Weeds had popped up through the mortar of the patio floor, but it was in decent shape. A brick fire pit had been built off to one side. Former occupants had laid stacks of wood all around the house. He would not suffer from a lack of firewood. Coop eyed carefully the distance between two posts supporting the patio roof. His hammock would fit just fine. He lifted the pack from Abe's back. Then he brought his horse around and tied him to a post with a 15 foot length of rope after unsaddling him. Abe wasn't fond of being tethered so Cooper let him loose with the admonition, "Okay now, don't wander off. There are critters around here who would love to make a meal of you."

Abe eyed Coop carefully and moved a few feet away, as he put his head down toward the grass. Lifting his pack onto what was probably a hook for a hanging plant, he pulled out his fishing gear and hammock. Fresh fish for dinner sounded good. His hammock did, in fact, fit quite nicely between the posts. Using an old flint style barbeque lighter, Coop quickly got a fire going and headed for the creek. An hour later he returned with a half dozen large trout, cleaned and ready to cook.

He retrieved his cast iron frying pan and set it on the hot coals of the fire. Slicing up a couple of potatoes and onions, he tossed them into the pan along with a chunk of lard. Fifteen minutes later he tossed in three of the trout. Just then he heard a somewhat familiar female voice. "It smells really good. Mind if I join you?"

He turned to see a terribly disheveled and dirty young woman. It was Gabrielle Blue. He smiled slightly.

"Hello Miss Blue. I thought Radial Tire made it clear you weren't welcome to come back here."

She nodded. "He did. May I come in a little closer to the fire? I haven't been completely dry or warm for at least two weeks."

"Certainly. Have a seat." He gestured at a short stool he had retrieved from the house. She sat down and warmed her hands against the coals of the fire.

Coop reached up into his pack and pulled out a small wash basin and poured in some hot water from a copper tea pot sitting near the fire. He added some cold water from his canteen and offered it to her with a bar of soap and a hand towel. She looked at him wistfully for a moment, then took the basin and sat it on her lap. Coop returned his attention to the skillet. He expertly turned the fish over with a small metal spatula and announced, "As soon as you wash up a bit, dinner will be ready."

Gabby splashed some water onto her face and exclaimed, "Oh my God that feels so good." A few minutes later with her hands and face reasonably clean, they ate some dinner right out of the skillet.

Coop apologized, "I didn't bring along any plates. I wasn't planning on sharing a meal with anyone." He had given her his fork and was eating with a spoon.

Gabby nodded between mouthfuls. "I'm just grateful for a hot meal. I've been eating mostly berries and an occasional apple ever since I left the marauder camp."

Coop offered her some water from the canteen. "Okay Miss Blue, tell me what happened."

She took a drink and then another bite before answering. "This is quite good, you know." He just stared at her.

"When we arrived at the marauder camp, we weren't welcomed with open arms. In fact, we were attacked. Six were killed on the spot. The rest of us were distributed around the camp as slaves. Fortunately, I had started my time of the month and was sent immediately to a communal tent for women. The conditions were terrible, the stench unbearable. The other women were not so lucky. The few times I was allowed outside of the tent, my friends were being treated horribly. I complained about female problems associated with my time of the month and was able to stay out of harm's way. Eventually, I made up an excuse to go over to the bathing area outside the camp and just kept on walking."

Coop shook his head. "You took no provisions or supplies?"

"Nope. I think that is why they didn't pay much attention to me. They assumed I wouldn't leave the camp empty-handed. I've been walking and sleeping on the ground for days." She shifted her gaze toward the field. "Did you know that there is an odd looking creature on the other side of the house?"

Coop grinned and said, "That's my beast of burden." Gabby gave him a look. "His name is Abe. He's a llama and also my friend. We've traveled many miles together over the years. I'm surprised he didn't alert me to your presence." He whistled softly and Abe ambled up toward the fire.

"Why didn't you tell me we had a visitor?" Abe just spit off into the distance. "He's a llama of few words."

Gabby stood and walked slowly over to him offering her hand.

"Be careful. He's not too friendly to strangers." Abe nuzzled her hand softly.

Coop shook his head. "Traitor."

Gabby stared absentmindedly in the direction from which she came and then returned to the fire. Coop lifted the skillet and offered her some more food which she gratefully took.

"I sincerely doubt the marauders would come this far to find you."

"It's not that. Some of my friends are still in that terrible place and I just walked away."

"Do you want to go back?"

Gabby was incredulous. "Why would I want to do that? I was mistaken to leave New Portland in the first place. I was just mad at you."

"I mean do you want to go back and get your friends?"

"You would do that?"

He gave her a curt answer. "Certainly. But of course we must first return to New Portland to pick up a few of my friends."

Two weeks later Coop, Gabby and a dozen well-trained riders reined up their horses a few hundred yards outside the marauder camp in the Columbia territory. As always, Radial Tire was by Coop's side, joined by Edgar. Gabby had insisted on going, since she was the only one who could identify her friends.

Radial carefully eyed the camp. "There are about a hundred people wandering about in the open. No telling how many more are in the tents or shacks."

Coop nodded. "I agree. I want to do this with as little bloodshed as possible."

Radial shifted in his saddle a little. "Okay, how do you want to handle this?"

Coop spoke so they all could hear him. "We are going to ride in single file with Radial riding last and sitting backwards, so he can see what is going on behind us. Keep your weapons at the ready and scan the camp. If you see anyone raise a weapon, tell me or Radial. I am hoping given the size of our group and our weaponry, they will not want to take us on."

News of their approach had already reached the camp and people were running around aimlessly. Fortunately, the camp leader and a dozen of their men were off on a raid. As Coop and his friends entered the camp Gabby suddenly hollered, "On your left, 50 feet."

As a young man raised his crossbow, Radial fired his own weapon hitting the marauder in the upper leg with a bolt. People screamed as he fell to the ground. Another man directly in front of Cooper raised a machete, gave out a blood curdling scream and ran toward Coop who simply lifted his revolver, aimed and pulled the trigger. The side of the man's head exploded as he collapsed to the ground sending blood, bone and brain matter into the crowd. It was suddenly quiet except for crying children and a few sobbing women. The use of a gun was very rare and it got their attention. Coop stood up in his stirrups and spoke loudly.

"We're here for a single purpose. If you cooperate, no one else will get hurt. The woman behind me is Gabrielle Blue. If you are her friend please come forward. Our plan is take you away from this place."

Gabby stood in her stirrups so she could be seen more clearly. Several emaciated men and women began to move toward the mounted riders. Gabby jumped down and ran to her friends embracing them as they came. One of the marauders grabbed Gabby from behind, put a knife to her throat and faced Cooper.

"So you think you can just ride in here and do as you please with our property. Turn your horses around and ride out of here or I will slit her throat."

He lifted the knife from Gabby's skin a couple of inches as he talked. She viciously elbowed him in the stomach and dropped to the ground. A half-dozen crossbow bolts appeared in his chest. He stumbled backward and raised his hand to throw his knife at Gabby. Another bolt appeared between his eyes, snapping his head back as he fell. Edgar quickly reloaded his weapon. Gabrielle smiled and mouthed a thank you. Coop stepped down from his horse.

"Gabby, are you okay? Nice move by the way."

"I'm fine other than getting my clean clothes dirty once again."

Coop stared at the now large group of people who had moved toward them. "Do you know all of these folk?"

She did a quick scan of their faces. "Yes, but where are the children?" She looked at Teresa, a former tent-mate.

With tears streaming down her face she replied, "The captain decided they did not have enough food to feed a dozen hungry children, so he had them all killed. He cut the throats of several himself."

Coop's eyes flashed as he roared, "He did what?!!"

Just then Radial spoke. "Some men are running down the hill toward the camp. One of them is riding."

There was no doubt in Coop's mind who they were. He assigned six riders to stay with Gabby and her friends. Then he, Radial, Edgar and some others rode off at a gallop toward the approaching men. The captain saw what was coming and had his men spread out. But he couldn't yet see the fury written on Cooper McIntyre's face. Radial had his men spread out as well. A flight of crossbow bolts headed their way, but they were let loose far too early and fell way short. By the time they could reload Cooper and his men were closing in. To even the odds, Coop raised his revolver and shot three men. He had no plans to shoot the captain, who had pulled out his sword and was charging toward him. When they were abreast of each other the captain swung but Coop had anticipated the move and simply ducked the whistling blade as it passed over his head. Wheeling his horse around, he jumped from the saddle, tackling the surprised man, throwing him to the ground. Coop picked up the dropped sword and placed its point against the captain's throat as he lay on the ground. Coop's eyes were still murderous as he saw fear in the man's face.

"This is how those children felt when you put your knife to their throats. And this is what they felt as you killed them." He thrust the tip of the sword into the captain's neck and slowly pushed it all the way deep into the ground. The captain's eyes bulged as he grabbed the blade with his bare hands, trying to pull it out. But a major artery in his neck had been cut and within minutes he was gone. Cooper looked up to see

Radial and his men finish off the other marauders.

Leaving the dead to the beasts of the field, the Portlandians returned to the camp. Most of the people there had witnessed the fierce, but brief battle a hundred yards away. Coop stepped down from his horse emotionally exhausted. His hands were still trembling not from fear, but from a rage that was only just beginning to wane. Gabby ran up and into his arms. He hugged her lightly, not quite sure of what to make of the sudden display. It was just a few months ago they were barely on speaking terms. But strangely enough, with her in his arms, his anger quickly dissipated.

Eyeing a short but wide wooden box by an open fire pit, Coop excused himself, walked over and stood on the stool. He noticed Radial and his men walking through the crowd of people removing any obvious weapons they had. With a loud voice Cooper spoke to them, "You have just witnessed the most violent thing I have ever done in my life. I have to live with what I did and I hope God will forgive me. I will not ask you to forgive me because violence is a way of life for most of you. It may be the only thing you truly understand."

"Jesus, the very Son of God, once said a long time ago, if you live by the sword, you will die by the sword." He pointed toward the hill where the battle took place. "Is that what you want? It's time for this senseless violence to stop. I've heard other marauders claim they have no choice but to take what they need in order to survive. It's a ridiculous thing to say." He reached down picked up a sharp stick and easily dug up a piece of ground. "The land is so fertile in this part of the world that grass grow everywhere. Is it not true you have to stamp out weeds practically every day just to keep a space clear? This is a perfect area for farming and raising crops and animals of every sort. What is preventing you from growing your own food, from hunting game in the hills, from fishing in the river a quarter mile away?"

He gestured to a hill covered with trees. "What is stopping you from cutting down some trees and building your own homes instead of living in ramshackle tents and shacks?" He paused for a moment and a loud voice spoke from a few feet away. It was the young man with a bolt still lodged in his leg.

"We don't know how to do most of those things."

Cooper answered quickly. "We can teach you if you are willing to be taught."

Another voice piped up. "When do we start?"

Radial walked over. "If any of you believe yourself to be an excellent shot with a crossbow, step forward."

A half dozen men and one woman appeared before him. Radial pointed to a pile of crossbows. "Pick out a crossbow and six arrow-bolts. We're going hunting." As they left the camp he looked back at Cooper.

"We'll be back in an hour with dinner for the camp." He and three of his friends led them off into the woods taking along a horse to help carry the meat.

Cooper smiled but quickly frowned when a man with a deep scowl asked, as he pointed to the hill where some of his friends were killed, "May we go bury our dead? They have all done terrible things, but they at least deserve a decent burial."

"Certainly. But I will have to send along a few of my men to supervise." The man nodded. Coop looked around for Gabby who had disappeared. He saw her coming back down the hill with the captain's sword and scabbard in hand. She walked up to him.

"May I keep these? I found out the captain had no family and very few actual friends."

Coop climbed down from the stool and sat on it. He was bone tired. "If you insist. Do you even know how to use one?"

She grinned widely. "Nope, but I plan to learn." Gabby eyed him coyly. "Do you know anyone who could teach me?"

Cooper shook his head. "Not today, we have some work to do." He looked around at the camp. It was now a beehive of activity as fires were being built and preparations made for a camp dinner.

He asked, "Do you know how to fish?"

"Of course. Do you have some fishing tackle? I know Morse Code, too."

Coop stood. "What's that got to do with anything?"

"Nothing, really. But you have to admit you don't know too many girls who know Morse code."

He stood and walked over to his horse who was grazing in a clump of field grass. He pulled out a long package from his saddle bags and held it up. "I never travel without a means to catch some fresh fish. Let's find someone to tag along. While we are here, we should never pass up an opportunity to teach a new skill."

An hour and fifteen minutes later, Radial and his volunteers returned. The horse was loaded down with the hind and front quarters of fresh game, mostly deer and some pig. Most of the newly trained hunters were carrying several wild chickens. The camp would indeed feast tonight. The mood of the people gradually moved from one of quiet desperation and confusion, to one of celebration and hope. Many sensed something good was happening in their midst. As a parting gift one family gave Coop a badly damaged rifle and a box of ammunition. They had heard he was none other than the legendary Finder/Fixer. They now believed Cooper McIntyre was not only a man to be feared, but also to be respected and admired. Coop would have hoped for something else. But the Portlandians had, in fact, established an outpost for change in the Columbia Territory. It was certainly not their plan; but obviously it was on God's radar.

Cooper was tired, a little battle-weary, emotionally and spiritually exhausted. He decided to return home. He needed to find some peace with what he had done, before resuming his quest to find the Librarian. He hoped his friend, Roger, would be able to help.

As the people from New Portland left, four of their company had volunteered to stay and work with the camp. A month later, by voice acclamation, almost everyone agreed to name their village Cooperstown. When he found out, Cooper was not pleased.

One of the first things the four men did was to discover what tools and implements the townspeople actually had. They had crosscut saws, axes and handsaws taken from a museum in the town of Olympia, located near the coast. Hand augurs, hammers and an old measuring tape still its package were also brought to the equipment tent. The things that were the most plentiful were crossbows, knives and machetes. A couple of rusted shovels showed up, as well as some rather long pieces of various sizes of rope. The Portland men kept a written account of who brought what, so that the tools could be returned someday.

A complete inventory was made, so that if and when something was needed, it was known whom to see. An inventory of the various skills some people had was made for the same purpose. Everyone worked, everyone was well fed and everyone had a reasonably comfortable and safe place to sleep. A dozen or so men made it clear to the Portlandians they did not like the changes made in their camp. The four young leaders did not hesitate. They encouraged the men to leave at day break after giving each a crossbow, and some food. Not one of their women wanted to leave and asked to stay along with their children. The Portlandians agreed to their request. The next morning, they simply escorted the men far out onto the grassland hoping never to see them again. The small group of marauders were never seen or heard from again. It was speculated that perhaps during a sudden cold snap, the men just froze to death. Except for one, it was true.

"Experience is not what happens to you; it is what you do with what happens to you."
Aldous Huxley

Chapter 25

Several months later, after returning to New Portland, Gabby had found a home with Maggie and Radial. Maggie and she had become good friends. Angie, who lived and worked in the same building but on a different floor, was a little stand-offish. She was polite, but didn't go out of her way to engage Gabby in conversation. Cooper and Gabrielle were often seen working together in the old Japanese flower garden that had been transformed into a vegetable garden. To Angie's chagrin, they often worked together in Coop's own garden on the roof. Gabby was a quick learner and frequently attended any classes being taught, especially those whose subject matter was science, history or mechanics. On her off time, it was not rare for anyone to see Gabby curled up somewhere with a book or two. She was eternally grateful her mother taught her to read. Mrs. Blue died of the coughing disease a few months shy of when Gabby became a woman.

When she wasn't reading, she spent much of her time learning how to use her sword. Gabby was often seen walking about wearing her weapon in a leather scabbard carefully crafted by Edgar, who was becoming a good friend. Radial made sure she knew how to use it. Those who saw her in training, would testify she could handle herself well. So, even though she was nice looking, most men were a little intimidated by this raven-haired woman with the brilliant blue eyes. And a complexion which was absolutely flawless. While tall and lithe with a nice figure, her features were just a little too angular and her nose a little too big for her to be called beautiful. Cooper decided she was pretty.

At a family breakfast one morning, Cooper smiled as he sipped some herbal tea. He waited until there was a lull in the conversation, then said, "I'll be leaving in a few days to resume my search for the Librarian."

There was dead silence around the table. Radial shook his head. "I had hoped you had changed your mind about looking for the Librarian. It just seems like every time you go out on one of these adventures by yourself, you get in trouble."

Cooper slugged his best friend in the shoulder. "You know that isn't entirely accurate. I view what you call trouble as an adventure, an opportunity to learn something new. I've given it careful thought and have decided it to be important enough to finish what I started."

Unexpectedly Gabby offered, "I want to go along."

Radial jumped at it. "That's a great idea. You'll be a great help in keeping Coop from discovering too much opportunity."

Cooper sighed heavily. It was an idea he could live with. Besides, she would likely be better company than Abe, who wasn't much of a conversationalist.

A week later the two riders pulled up their horses on a familiar hill overlooking the camp. A more distinct road led into what now looked like a bustling village. A lot of change had happened since they had left. They rode past a large sign that read Cooperstown. Gabby smiled at the name. Cooper did not. But he did smile at the transformation of the fledgling town. It was staggering what they had done in such a short time.

Hundreds of trees had been felled, trimmed of branches and laid out to dry in the summer sun. The fire pits were all organized. Rough tables and benches had been constructed. Tents had been repaired and shacks had been rebuilt. A blacksmith shop had been set up, complete with an anvil and a forge. Cooperstown was a bevy of activity and Cooper could not have been more pleased. Most of the townspeople were happy to see him and enjoyed his expressions of thanks for all their hard work. But with their destination not all that far away, the very next day the two rode out of Cooperstown headed toward the general direction of Seattle.

Coop and Gabby stopped to rest for a few moments under the roof of a partially collapsed building sitting on a hill. A few miles away, the remains of the city of Olympia lay before them. Seattle was still to the North. A torrential rain poured from out of the sky. Almost as suddenly as it started, the rain stopped, and the sun came out. A hill a few hundred feet away was slowly but surely being eroded, over the years, by heavy rains. Cooper looked over at the remnants of a hillside cliff. It appeared a huge mudslide had occurred at some time in the past year or so.

As they stepped back on their horses to resume their journey, Gabby noticed a small reflection of light coming from a spot on the hill. Curious, she stepped back down and climbed the hill toward the reflection slipping and sliding in the mud as Cooper just watched and smiled. She had become almost as good a digger as Jordan and wasn't afraid of getting dirty, a good quality for a digger.

She reached down and brushed away more dirt from the area of the reflection. A shiny black surface appeared. "Coop, you've got to come up to see this." He slipped a few times as he climbed the hill as Gabby watched and smiled.

"See, it wasn't as easy as it looked." She pointed at an approximately one foot square black mirror-like surface. "It looks like part of a panel from a sun machine." They both dug for another hour and finally exposed the entire panel. It was about six foot by nine foot in size.

Coop wiped the mud off of a label on the bottom edge. It read Vanderhooten Electrical Power System. He stood up. "I know about this guy. He revolutionized the energy world with

VEPS in the early part of the 21st century. We have two of his sun machines on the roof of my house. There may be more panels nearby or some equipment to which the panel is connected. Are you up for a little more digging?"

It took all day, but using makeshift tools the two worked shoveling away a lot of dirt and mud from other panels and machinery. They were really excited when they dug out the entrance to a tunnel leading deep under the hill. Coop glanced at Gabby.

"There is no question that we're going to go in, but maybe we had better wait until morning light."

Gabby took a few steps in, stopped and leaned against the wall looking back at Cooper. The ceiling of the passage suddenly lit up. She brushed the long black hair out of her face and carefully examined the small raised button she had inadvertently touched. She pushed it again and the lights went out. Then she turned them on.

"Well, no sense waiting until tomorrow, right?"

Cooper grabbed Gabby by the hand. "Let's go."

The tunnel took them a lot further than they initially thought. They came to several flights of stairs that led further downward. The walls looked like they may have held paintings or decorations, but they had all long disappeared to visitors in the years after the city had collapsed. They came across several more buttons on the wall that illuminated their path. As they came to each one the lights behind them winked out. After about 15 minutes of walking, a large metal door appeared before them. There were no handles or knobs, no apparent hinges…just the deep imprint of a hand in the door. From the accumulation of dried mud and dirt on the floor, many had preceded them. How many had gone inside? Gabby threw her hat onto the floor and closely inspected the door. Before Coop could object Gabby put her hand into the imprint. She felt a tiny pinprick on a finger and immediately pulled away.

"Something poked me."

Coop carefully put his hand in the imprint. He felt the same prick on his finger, but he kept his hand in place and pushed. Nothing happened. But then unexpectedly the door slid up. Light from the passageway showed an empty room. Gabby slipped past him and stepped inside. She barely crossed the threshold when the door slammed quickly shut before Coop could get in. He pounded on the door but heard nothing from inside. A minute passed as Coop's concerns began to mount. Then the door opened again and he quickly jumped in. The door slammed shut again.

"Gabby, are you here."

In a shaky voice she answered, "Yes, but I am just a little scared." She reached out her hand, touched his arm then grabbed onto it. Half-jokingly Coop said loudly, "Okay, someone turn on the lights." The lights immediately came on revealing a spectacular sight. Then they heard a voice.

"Welcome to my home."

"He who is not courageous enough to take risks will accomplish nothing of consequence in life." *Mohammed Ali*

Chapter 26

The room was not huge; Coop guessed maybe 25 foot square with a 10-foot high ceiling. Gabby moved back and placed her hand on a seemingly smooth metal wall.

"No seams and the metal almost feels warm. I've never seen anything like it."

Neither had Coop, who stared at an array of machines and screens lining the three walls in front of them. Off to the right was a three-foot wide circular platform about six inches high. A soft beam of light from the platform rose toward the ceiling.

Coop spoke, "We hear your voice but do not see you."

"Would you like a visual image?"

Before Coop could answer, someone was suddenly standing on the platform. He appeared to be quite old with a long flowing white beard and strange clothing.

"My name is Leonardo Da Vinci. My friends call me Leo."

Both Coop and Gabby stood with their mouths hanging open, unable to speak. A human-like figure was suddenly standing on the platform.

"Does my appearance frighten you? Should I make some adjustments?"

Coop finally spoke. "No, you are fine, it is just that we have never seen anyone like you before." He hesitated. "What are you?"

Leo responded, "I am so sorry. An explanation is in order. I do apologize. By my calculations, which are never wrong, 198 years four months and 10 days have passed since my creator turned me on, so to speak. To put it simply, I am a rather complicated interactive computer program. Are you familiar with computers in this age?"

"We are, but only in the sense that we know about them."

"That explains your surprise at seeing me. Obviously a lot has changed since Omega struck."

Gabby added, "You have no idea."

"My creator said it might be a long time before anyone who met the qualifications would appear at our door. Many have tried to enter; the two of you are the first. You, sir, were meant to enter. The young woman was not."

Gabby was offended. "Why not, may I ask?"

"The main criteria for entry is what he is and what you're not. But since I perceive you are a mated pair, I won't ask you to leave."

Gabby started to object, but Cooper intervened. "More than that, we are a team. We gets things done and is why we are here. But again what are you?"

"I am a hologram…a visual image of a person."

Cooper thought carefully about his next two questions.

"Why do you exist? What is your function?"

Leo smiled broadly. "My creator said you would likely not beat around the bush." Leo saw the perplexed look on her face. "It is an idiom, a saying from centuries ago indicating you would get right to the point." The hologram turned slowly and gestured to all the monitors and equipment on the walls.

"What you see here is a small part of what was designed and built by my creator. In time, you shall see it all. My purpose is to serve the creator and to assist you in literally whatever manner you desire. Another idiom from the 20th century may describe it the best; the sky is the limit. With the considerable gifts and talents you

284

both share, we can do amazing things; especially since you have cleared away most of the debris covering our solar panels. Thanks for doing that by the way. We only had a few more months left of battery power that was essentially keeping us alive, so to speak. None of our workers could get outside to do any repair work for the last year."

Cooper asked another question. "Since you appear to have a great deal of knowledge, do you know the location of the Librarian?" Leo bowed slowly. "I am as close as you are going to get, at least for the time being. I am an associate to the Librarian."

Cooper glanced at Gabby. "Not what I expected." She added quietly. "How do we know you are an associate to the Librarian? Just saying so doesn't necessarily mean you are."

"Ahhh. A skeptic. I love it." Gabby was more right than wrong.

A panel opened revealing a long hallway. Doors spaced every 15-20 feet lined both sides. Leo smiled, "We are about to serve dinner. I'm sure you are hungry. Room 007 is your stateroom, and is yours for as long as you stay with us. I'm told the shower in these rooms is quite nice. As you might expect, I've never had the pleasure. You will find some fresh clothes set out for the two of you."

With that Leo's image disappeared. Coop and Gabby ventured cautiously down the hall. As soon as they stepped over a threshold, a panel behind them closed.

Gabby offered, "This place gives me the creeps."

Coop touched the wall. "To be honest, me too."

When they came to room 007, Cooper placed his hand on an exposed pad and the door opened. As they stepped inside, a well-furnished room appeared in front of them and a pleasant aroma filled the air. In moments both Cooper and Gabby were semi-conscious and lying on the floor. Unable to open his eyes, Coop felt two pair of hands lift him onto a gurney.

He felt a prick on his arm. He was aware of what was going on around him, but could not move a muscle. Electrodes were attached all over his head. He heard voices...one of them was Leo.

"Is he ready?" The voice was feminine.

Leo responded. "Yes. He has a wonderfully rich and compartmentalized brain. It is the best we have ever seen. Maybe he is the one the creator told us about."

The female voice replied, "We'll soon see. Start the download."

A couple of hours later the Librarian ordered, "I want to implant about ten gigabytes of random data from the library."

Leo spoke almost in awe. "I'm impressed his brain is handling such a huge influx of information. Oh, we've already passed ten gigabytes. Shall we stop at one hundred? "

She answered, "Is he in any kind of distress?"

"None that I can see."

"Okay, stop at five hundred gigabytes. You may be right. He could be the one we have been waiting for all this time. If he assimilates all the information and suffers no ill effects, we may have our guy. We'll see how well he incorporates our data with what he has gathered on his own. This could be interesting."

She watched Cooper for a few minutes. "What is the condition of the female?"

Leo answered, "She is a fine specimen of womanhood and is in excellent condition."

"Can the male hear us talk?" she asked.

"Probably. He does remember everything, just as was foretold."

The feminine voice added, "I'm not sure he and the woman are a mated pair. We might have to get rid of her."

"The kids could use a new distraction", said Leo offhandedly.

She asked, "Would they eat her right away?"

"Probably not. None of the men in this particular generation have ever had a woman from the outside. It might be fun to watch."

"The measure of who we are is what we do with what we have." *Vince Lombardi*

Chapter 27

Leo analyzed the data and "spoke" electronically. "We've had a bit of a problem."

Deep in a project of her own, the Librarian "heard" the message and refocused enough megabytes to respond to the statement.

"Explain."

"I've been unable to erase any information from McIntyre's brain. He is carrying the five hundred gigs in his head with no ill effects. But now he may know too much. Shall we kill the both of them while they are still sedated?"

"No. We can eliminate them any time we want. Let's see how Mr. McIntyre responds to his wealth of new information. This could be interesting. Wake them up."

Coop's eyes fluttered open. He was unsure if Leo and the female voice were aware his brain was "hearing" all of their "conversation".

The Librarian made an appearance. Coop looked over at the disembodied representation of a nice looking woman. He asked "Why were we sedated?"

She replied calmly, "I wanted to see if you were the one."

"Which one?"

"You'll see soon enough. Have you accessed any of the new information implanted in your brain?"

Coop answered truthfully. "Not yet. My brain is still processing and cataloguing the data."

She was almost aghast. "You have the ability to recognize at what level your brain is functioning and you forget nothing?"

"Absolutely. What is it exactly that you wanted me to know?"

"You'll find out soon enough, Mr. McIntyre. How much time does your brain need?"

"A few hours' sleep should do it. My companion will help me relax, and rest."

"I can re-sedate you."

"It's not the same and you know it."

"Actually, I don't, but I believe you. It shall be as you say, Mr. McIntyre. You and your woman

290

will soon find yourselves together." Even without more anesthesia, Coop was exhausted and he felt himself drifting off into sleep again. He didn't fight it.

Coop opened his eyes. Gabby was in his arms as they lay on a bed, in a dimly lit room. He reached down and pulled up a bed sheet. Coop began to tap on her back to awake her. She stirred, then her body became stiff. Gabby whispered, "What are you doing?"

Coop put his finger on her lips and whispered. "Your life is in danger. We must act as if we are lovers."

Gabby thought for a minute, pulled his head down and said, "I don't have a problem with that. I've been wanting to do this for a while anyway."

He grinned, "To do what?"

She answered with a gentle kiss then answered, you'll see." She then kissed him passionately. Gabby rolled over on top of him, sat up and smiled as Cooper's hand began to explore the soft skin under her tight fitting t-shirt."

An hour later, Coop held Gabby closely and spoke to Leo's hologram. He wondered how long Leo had been standing there. "You do realize we require at least some sense of privacy and we have not yet eaten. A meal would be good before we sleep."

Leo replied, "It shall be done." Then he asked, "What's it like to be in a physical relationship with someone?"

Gabby answered, "Without the ability to experience pain or joy, you have no frame of reference enabling you to comprehend an answer."

Leo commented to the Librarian. "I believe they're a mated pair."

She responded, "So it would seem."

Cooper and Gabby slept lightly for a couple of hours. The meal they were served was inedible. He felt her stir under the sheet and whispered once again.

"It's time to find out what is going on. Are you with me, Watson?"

She turned over and looked at him.

"Actually, I have read a copy of Sherlock Holmes. I have a feeling they're not going to just let us leave. They want something from you."

"Agreed. We need to find out what that is. Let's shower together to further convince our friends we are lovers."

"Do you honestly think they need more convincing?"

In the dimly lit room Cooper just smiled.

An hour later, Gabby and Coop sat around a small table. While they were in the shower, a light meal of two hardboiled eggs, a couple of apples and a pitcher of water magically appeared. Coop poured each of them a glass and tossed an egg to Gabby.

"These look harmless enough."

As they ate they heard a woman's voice. "Are you rested, Mr. McIntyre?"

"I am. I have a query."

"Proceed."

"What is your purpose?"

If it were possible for a computer program to act surprised, she would have been. Her programing demanded an answer.

"My purpose is to provide the means by which American society and culture can be rebuilt and restored. This "Library" was constructed with that very purpose in mind and you will play an important part in it."

"What part is that?"

"Over the centuries we have been looking for someone with the right genetic components to produce a child, a future leader of the world."

"A child? With whom?"

She smiled softly as her three dimensional image appeared. "Me. I'm the one you are looking for. I'm the Librarian." She pointed

293

toward a darkened window. The room on the other side was suddenly lit. All Cooper and Gabby could do was stare at what appeared to be a glass coffin. Inside was a beautiful woman, naked as the day she was born.

"She's gorgeous, is she not?"

Cooper shook his head. The rumors of the Librarian, being locked up in a glass cage, were true after all.

He offered, "My observations suggest the body in the coffin is not alive and therefore couldn't bear a child."

"True. But before my body ceased to function, my ovaries were harvested and placed in a special cell preserving "soup", enabling my eggs to survive all these years."

"Even if that were possible, to what end?" asked Coop.

"As we have done many times in the past with other men brought in from the outside, a few of my eggs will be fertilized by your sperm and implanted in the uterus of a healthy young woman. It's called invitro-fertilization. Maybe you've heard of it."

Coop nodded as his brain quickly accessed the implanted information. "I know of the procedure."

She continued. "When your genetic pool is combined with mine, we will produce a child who will be the future leader of what is left of America. He or she will lead the restoration of our culture and help rebuild the infrastructure of a once great America."

"What if I do not cooperate?"

"I don't need your cooperation, Mr. McIntyre. I will simply take what I require. My preference is you willingly provide what we need. I will provide the eggs. The unexpected appearance of your girlfriend will provide a healthy uterus for implantation. The two of you will remain in our community and raise the child."

Cooper stood and looked carefully at the three dimensional image that seemed to float gently above the floor. She was elegantly clothed in a navy blue business suit and was model thin. The woman in the coffin was more attractive. He simply said, "When do we begin?"

Gabby started to object, but smiled instead. "So, I'm about to become a mother. But shouldn't we wait until I am at the best time of the month for a successful implantation?"

There was a few seconds of hesitation as if the Librarian were actually thinking. "Of course. That would be wise. Please make yourselves comfortable. I have a few things to take care of." The image disappeared.

Leo spoke. "Is there anything that you require at the moment?"

Cooper quickly responded, "Have you discovered a cure for Omega?"

"We have developed a special form fitting mask that filters out the vast majority of disease causing organisms, including Omega. Why do you ask?"

Cooper was inwardly thrilled. "We are in desperate need of those masks in the world outside the library. Can they easily be mass produced?"

Leo answered, "Mass production would require some work, but we do have the capability to make it happen."

"Great!" said Cooper. "I have another question. How about a personal tour of the community?"

Leo didn't hesitate. "I think it can be arranged. Give me a few minutes."

Cooper reached down to Gabby and slowly pulled her up as he whispered, "Somehow, we're going to get out of this hamster cage."

He said aloud, "Come on honey. We're going for a walk."

Gabby whispered, "I'm not sure this is really a good idea."

The door panel slid open as they approached. Leo was waiting. A man wearing a mask, a blue cap, a white t-shirt and tan khakis walked up. He handed masks to the both of them. The Librarian did not appear but said, "Please wear these masks at all times and stay close to Leo as you move through the facility."

Another door opened in front of them and they stepped into a large room filled with electronic equipment and a dozen or more people. They also wore white t-shirts and tan khakis, but had green caps and all bore a resemblance to one another. Of course, he and Gabby were wearing similar clothing. Coop commented, "Looks like the Librarian has been busy in a reproductive sense. Why the masks?"

Leo responded, "We carefully adjust the genetic make-up of all our workers so as to maximize productivity in specific areas. This is the operations center." He continued, "Your masks are necessary because you and your friend are walking disease factories. Most of the people here have never been exposed to the diseases you carry in your systems. Anything you touch is thoroughly cleaned and sterilized."

Gabby stared for a moment at their clothing. The t-shirts didn't leave much to the imagination. She noticed no one paid the slightest bit of attention to them. As they walked, she saw Cooper toss a piece of wadded up toilet paper into the open back of a large piece of electronic machinery under repair.

"Everyone seems so sad."

"Our workers are given everything they need."

"What do they do for fun?"

"It depends on your definition of fun. We do allow some recreation time. A few play cards and other games, but their main focus is on the tasks assigned to them."

They stepped through another door and into a much bigger warehouse-sized building. In front of them sat totally enclosed rooms of various sizes, some quite large. Leo spoke almost in a monotone now.

"In each of these enclosures are working scale models of the accumulated technology and industry of America." He pointed to the closest, "Inside you will find a working example of a metal foundry. Adjacent to it is a model of a hydroelectric power plant. We are in the process of constructing a nuclear power facility the size of a small house. We have working models and schematics of every imaginable piece of equipment or technology that helped America become an economic powerhouse." He gestured around the expansive warehouse. "These working models will help America rebuild itself."

Just then they heard a recognizable fire alarm. Leo turned to them, Please remain here." His image disappeared.

Coop said firmly but softly, "Follow me."

Using the building schematic that had been implanted in his brain, he walked around the maze of rooms. The people working in various areas ignored them. A door opened on the other side of the warehouse, as they approached. Several workers walked hurriedly in their direction, as they hid behind a corner. Gabby frowned. "I think they're on to us." The only difference in their clothing was that their caps were bright red.

Just then an image of Leo reappeared. "I asked you to remain in the other building. Now you will suffer the consequences of disobedience."

Coop grabbed Gabby's hand. The couple walked right through Leo's image and up to a young man who was working on what appeared to be a small gasoline powered lawnmower. Without seeking permission Coop rummaged through the man's tool box. Leo asked, "What are you doing?" He turned to the worker. "Alpha 4, stop your project and restrain the intruder."

The man turned and grabbed Cooper by the wrist. His grip was strong but not strong enough. Cooper hit the man with a right hook sending the guy sprawling onto the floor. He and Gabby ran toward a wall and a large three by three foot wide air conditioning grate. Coop quickly began to unscrew it. Another worker approached, and as he reached toward Cooper, Gabby slugged him from behind with a big wrench. Leo responded, "I must ask you to cease your activities."

The grate dropped to the floor with a crash. The two slipped into the ductwork and vanished. Leo was unable to follow, but he did send Alpha 4 who was none too happy with Cooper. He caught up with Gabby and reached for her foot. She promptly lifted it and smashed it into his face. Blood gushed from his broken nose. He stopped crawling and said to himself, "She probably wouldn't taste all that good anyway. She's too skinny."

Ten minutes later Cooper and Gabby dropped to the floor back in the control room. He reached up toward a circuit breaker box, opened it and threw the main breaker. Everything electronic shut down. They had five minutes before an emergency system kicked in. In the pitch black Coop guided Gabby unerringly to the door leading to the hall which took them to where they first entered and met Leo. They bumped into several people who were just standing, waiting for instructions. The door was part way open. On his own, he couldn't pull the door open any further, but the two of them together got the job done. They were not so fortunate with the next sliding door panel. Just then the power came back on and the door automatically slid open. Seeing their clothing and belongings in a pile on the floor, Gabby grabbed them as Coop searched a large electronics board for the right button. He pushed it and the door to the outside passageway slipped open. They ran into the long tunnel and up toward ground level. The lights flicked on in sections as they passed sensors in the wall. The calm and cool voice of the Librarian echoed in the enclosed space. "You have violated my trust. I cannot allow you and your companion to live, Mr. McIntyre."

Gabby and Coop stopped before turning the last corner leading directly to the surface. They put on their clothes. Coop made sure his revolver was loaded and ready. Gabby unsheathed her sword.

He smiled grimly. "Who knows what the Librarian has waiting for us up there."

"I don't care. I'm definitely not going back." She pulled his head down, removed both of their masks and kissed him long and hard. "It's been fun, Mr. McIntyre."

They crept up the last few yards of the tunnel and out into the open. Dozens of bodies lay on the ground, most with arrow bolts sticking out of various parts of their bodies. They heard a familiar voice.

"Well, it's about time! Why are so many people wearing masks and why do they have those silly looking red caps?"

"It is the character of a brave and resolute man not to be ruffled by adversity…." *Cicero 78 B.C.*

Chapter 28

Radial Tire, Edgar and a dozen other men emerged into view, from behind a partially collapsed brick wall 20 feet away. He continued, "Before you say anything, a half day after you left I decided to follow you. When I saw your horses wondering in this area, I knew you were around. The tunnel seemed to be a most likely place for you to explore. Edgar found fresh boot marks at the bottom. No one answered our banging on the door, so we've just been waiting. When these red hat guys showed up, we tried to talk with them, but they started a fight and we finished it."

Cooper nodded, "So I see." He shook his friend's hand. "Thanks for not doing what I asked. Anybody hurt?"

"A few bumps and bruises, but we are all okay."

Radial hugged Gabby. "What happened down there?"

She answered, "We'll tell you most of what happened after we eat. What's for dinner?"

Edgar held up a couple of dead rabbits by their long ears. "We've got more back at camp."

Coop smiled wryly at his friends. "Thank you all for coming. But I think Gabby could've handled the Librarian's hoodlums."

She took a couple of wide cuts through the air and said, "No problem."

He continued, "Speaking of the Librarian, I need to leave a message."

Coop walked back into the tunnel about three yards. Radial stood at the entrance and watched as a light clicked on.

Madam Librarian...thanks for the hospitality, but we'll be on our way. Please know I plan to be back and I'll pull your plug."

She replied caustically, "I figured you'd want a last word. You're so predictable. Did you think I'd let you get away that easily?"

As she continued to speak Coop yelled, "Everyone RUN!!!!"

"If I have to, I'll wait another century or two for just the right man. Evidently, you're not him."

Before Coop could turn around, a massive explosion tore apart the tunnel. Huge chunks of rock and cement caved in. Gabby and the others managed to, at least, take a few steps away from the front before the force of the blast blew everyone to the ground. As the dust settled, Gabby saw a booted foot sticking out of the debris. It was moving, but it didn't belong to Cooper.

The first sensation Cooper felt was dull pain in his right arm and a crushing headache. But he wasn't concerned about the pain. Not knowing what happened to Gabby was his biggest concern. He was afraid he had lost someone else he had grown to care deeply about. His thoughts turned to Jordan and he felt guilty. In his semi-conscious state, he heard a familiar voice. *"It's okay. I never expected you to become a monk."* He heard Jordan's engaging laugh.

As he became more alert, he opened his eyes it was completely dark in the room, and he was somewhat cold. He reached over and felt his arm. It was in a soft cast. Portions of his face and neck were covered in bandages. He tried to sit up, but was rewarded with bolts of pain shooting through his head. He carefully laid back down on the bed. The Librarian spoke, "Ah, Mr. McIntyre, you're awake. As you can see, I've decided to preserve your life. It took some doing. The cave-in severely damaged portions of your body, especially your head. We had to dig quite a while to reach you. You'll have several more scars to add to your collection."

"How long have I been unconscious?"

"Two and a half weeks. There were a few days when we were not at all sure you'd wake up."

"What do you want with me? I'm confident you've already taken what you wanted."

"Yes, we do have a generous sample of your sperm. I've kept you alive because it's the logical thing to do. We could wait for someone else, but I have you now. You're probably the most important part of my library collection and are more valuable to me alive rather than dead."

"I see. Why didn't you just take what you needed from me when I was sedated earlier?"

"We were hoping for more mature sperm to be provided in the old fashioned way. They seem to be more viable. Anything else?"

He answered, "Why am I being kept in a darkened room?"

The Librarian paused for just a second. "There is illumination in your room. You're totally blind, likely because of the head trauma you suffered during the cave-in. We don't have the medical expertise to address that issue. Your body did suffer substantial damage, but other than your eyes, you will make a full recovery." Someone gently touched his arm and said softly, "This will help you rest."

Cooper was suddenly tired. He closed his sightless eyes, but asked before he fell asleep, "Do you have any information about my friends outside?"

"Some survived. Those who did left a week ago." Cooper drifted off thinking about Gabby.

Sometime later as he began to awaken, he heard a voice deep within his head. "*You will regain your eyesight. I have more work for you to do. Wake up!*" By reflex, his eyes popped open. Unlike Edgar who always knew what time it was, Cooper didn't have a clue. All he knew was whatever day it was, whatever time it was....he was hungry. Absolutely no light was penetrating his eyes. But spots and flashes of light were dancing all over, so he hoped this meant something. Coop listened carefully. He wasn't alone. So he asked, "Did you say something?"

A woman responded, "I said nothing, Mr. McIntyre."

"How long was I unconscious?"

"Another three days I'm afraid. We've been giving you some nutrition intravenously."

"Who are you?" he asked.

"The Librarian appointed me to serve as your personal attendant. I'm called Delta 5. I'm here to serve."

Before he spoke he thought, "I wonder what color hat she has?" Then he asked, "How am I doing, Delta 5?"

"The Librarian is quite pleased at how quickly your various injuries are healing. I am confident you're capable of standing, if you like."

Coop threw his legs over the side of his bed and slowly stood. A pair of hands steadied him. He had no idea how valuable sight was in keeping ones balance. He just hadn't thought about it. Other than being sore, he felt pretty good.

She held onto his good arm. "Would you like to visit the toilet?"

"That would be a good thing." Delta 5 guided him slowly into the bathroom and shut the door. Coop felt around and found the toilet and sink. He said to himself, "How do you hit the toilet when you're blind?" But he quickly figured it out. After washing his face and hands, he walked back into the room.

"Delta 5, are you still with me?"

"Yes, I am. A meal has arrived for you, a couple of hard boiled eggs and some fruit." She led him over to a table. As he sat on a metal chair, he shivered.

"I can't get used to walking around in these light clothes." He reached forward and slowly explored the table until he found an egg. Someone had already peeled it for him.

"We don't need warmer clothes, Mr. McIntyre. In a climate controlled environment such as ours, we have no need."

"Could you give me a tour of my room, so I know where things are?"

After exploring the room and consuming the second egg, he lay back on his bed. "I'd like to rest for a little while."

"Certainly. I'll be here if you need me."

Coop focused his agile mind on solving the problem at hand. Some of the library files implanted in his brain were medical in nature. A subset of one particular file dealt with trauma-induced blindness. After "reading" it, he focused his mind on that particular area, directing energy and a fresh blood supply at the site. He did so for as long as he could before falling asleep.

He awoke as Delta 5 gently shook his shoulder. "The Librarian is here."

Cooper sat up. "I would look in your direction, but am unsure of your location."

"I'm almost 45 degrees to your right."
He adjusted his head appropriately.

"Delta 5 says you are making steady progress. Is that accurate?"

"Yes. What can I do for you?"

The Librarian replied, "Nothing at the moment. Any improvement in your sight?" As she spoke her image moved to the center of the room. Neither his head nor eyes changed position. And since her voice filled the entire room, it didn't betray her ploy.

"None." He paused. "May I ask a favor? I'm fairly confident my eyes are floating all over. I would feel better if I had a pair of sunglasses to conceal my disability."

While sunglasses were not a common find in digs, they did appear from time to time. His sister had a pair for several years, until they were stolen by a guard in Astoria.

The Librarian's image disappeared, but the voice continued, "I'll leave that in the hands of your attendant. We will talk again soon. I do have a job for you."

Cooper and Delta 5 waited in silence for a few minutes.

"Is she gone?"

Delta 5 smiled, "Yes, she is."

"What about the sunglasses?"

"I believe one of the men whom the Librarian brought in many years ago, had a pair of sunglasses. We kept his personal belongings."

"What happened to him?"

"We ate him. I believe he was my father. I'll return as soon as I can."

He heard the door panel open and close. Coop finally had a fix on its location. He laid back down. "Will that be my eventual future…Cooper fricassee?"

He suddenly felt light headed and closed his eyes.

When he awoke, he sensed Delta's presence. She walked over and placed the sunglasses over his eyes.

"There, does that make you feel better?"

"Surprisingly…yes it does. Thank you." He was pleased that the world was no longer totally black. Once again he noticed occasional streaks of light and when he closed his eyes, they disappeared.

"Tell me about the man who previously owned these." He gestured toward the sunglasses.

"I don't know much. He is said to have fathered several of us in the Delta series. The Librarian had hopes he might have enough of the right kind of genetic content to produce what she wanted."

"Which was…?"

"No one knows really. She had hoped I would be a superior product, but evidently I was not. But I do look a lot like her."

"You mean like the body that's in the glass coffin?"

She answered cautiously, "That's not what the original Librarian really looked like when she was young. I've seen a few photographs which were removed from her desk in the control room. I discovered them in her personal storage area. She was a brunette, not a blond and was relatively short. She was not as thin as the coffin body appears."

She was quiet for a moment, then asked as she placed a warm hand on his belly, "My shift is nearly over. Do you want to copulate?"

Cooper looked in her direction. "I'm still in quite a bit of pain. Maybe another day."

"As you wish. Beta 3 will be coming soon. She is a year older, but a nice female. She and I are friends."

"Just how old are you?"

"I'm told I'm 17 years old."

"And how old is Beta 3?"

"She is 18. No one I know is older than 25."

"So what happens after someone turns 25?"

"It is said they become the caretakers of the children our community produces. But they are never seen again."

"How many are part of the community?"

"I have no idea. I only know of the people in my work area, but we have dozens of different work stations."

Cooper reached out for her hand. "Are you happy?"

"Of course; I've never known anything else. Good bye, Mr. McIntyre."

Just then Cooper heard the door open. Beta 3 walked in. The two young women didn't say a word. She approached his bed. "I'm Beta 3. I'm here to serve. Do you have any needs? Do you wish to copulate?"

He thought for a minute. "Not at the moment. Do you have any books to read?"

"You can't see, Mr. McIntyre."

Cooper grinned, "True enough, but you could read to me."

Delta 5 offered, "I'm told there are shelves of books in the Librarian's old office, but we are not permitted to enter."

"So what can you read?" asked Coop.

"Mostly manuals, technical books and the like."

He offered, "How about I read a fictional story to you?"

Beta 3 shook her head. "You have no book, Mr. McIntyre, and you're blind."

"Yes, but I have a superb memory and have thousands of books stored in my head. Would you like to hear a story?"

Beta 3 was suddenly quite interested. "I've heard about you. Do you truly have an unforgettable memory?"

"Yes. Would you like to hear the story about the Wizard of Oz? It was written in 1900 by L. Frank Baum. " Coop heard her pull up a chair as he began.

"Dorothy lived in the midst of the great Kansas prairies with her Uncle Henry, who was a farmer, and Aunt Em...."

A couple of hours later Coop stopped at the end of a chapter. "I'm sorry, Beta 3, but I've grown really tired. I've developed another headache. May we continue at another time?"

"Of course, Mr. McIntyre. Thank you for the story. It's fascinating."

Cooper noticed more frequent streaks of light right before he closed his eyes.

A few hours later, Delta 5 squeezed his arm lightly. "Mr. McIntyre, the Librarian wants to speak with you."

Cooper opened his eyes and sat up. He was glad he had on sunglasses. The light was blinding. He had regained some of his sight. It took a conscious effort not to rub his eyes to clear away some mucous. He didn't turn his head, until he heard the Librarian's voice.

"Mr. McIntyre, I'm told that other than your eyes and left arm, you are almost healed. I've never known anyone to recover as quickly from injury as you."

Cooper observed her image moving to the left. He stared at the space she previously occupied.

"I am getting stronger every day. How may I serve you?"

"Interesting change in attitude. I don't think I believe you."

"That's up to you madam, but assigning me small projects posing little flight risk might be appropriate, especially if I am under supervision." He paused before continuing. "Besides you wouldn't be talking to me unless you already had something in mind."

"Very astute. Mr. McIntyre. But for the moment, I'm content to keep you here in the medical wing under observation, for a few more days."

He nodded at the empty space. "As you wish. I do have a request."

"What is it?"

"Would it be possible for both Delta 5 and Beta 3 to stay with me? It should be more entertaining for me and less boring for them." He was hoping that together they may be more willing to give him information.

"I have no objection. The females will remain with you. But I must issue a warning. Both are well trained in the martial arts and will not hesitate to take your life, if the need arises. Do we understand one another?"

"Yes, we do and I appreciate your kindness."

"I'm not being kind, Mr. McIntyre. I'm being practical. If one or both were to bear a child, it would be all the better for me and my plans. Enjoy yourself." Her image slowly dissolved. The door opened and Beta 3 joined them.

"Mr. McIntyre, before we copulate, could you finish telling the story of the Wizard at Odds?"

Cooper smiled, "That's the Wizard of Oz and perhaps I'd better start at the beginning for Delta 5's sake."

She responded, "I don't mind at all. The story is interesting."

Delta 5 frowned. "Who's the Wizard of Oz?"

Cooper took a furtive glance at both women. They were both wearing the same tight-fitting uniform, but each were wearing a white cap. Their bodies appeared to have been chiseled out of white marble, reminding him of photographs he had seen of ancient statues of Greek and Roman goddesses. They were obviously not identical, but the two young women shared many physical characteristics. Of course that made sense, since it appeared everyone had the same mother in a genetic sense. Just then the door opened again and a larger bed was brought in, and set up by a couple of young men. Coop glanced quickly at what was beyond the open door. They left taking with them the smaller bed. Cooper walked forward until his legs collided with the new one. "Will you join me, ladies?"

All three laid on the comfortable mattress with Coop situated between the two young women. He began to tell the story as they stared at the ceiling. Three hours later they were laying on their sides with their arms draped over Cooper, as he spoke. An hour after that, they were both sound asleep. He hated to leave them since in all likelihood they would bear the brunt of the Librarian's anger. He carefully moved their arms and slowly slid down to the end of the bed. He then slipped off onto the floor moving quietly over to the door. All the codes and passwords for the facility were part of what was downloaded into his brain. He was about to tap in the code on the keypad when he heard a soft voice.

"Take us with you? We know you're planning to leave the community."

Both were sitting up. It was Delta 5 who spoke.

Cooper responded carefully, "Aren't you concerned Leo or the Librarian are listening?"

Beta 3 said, "They usually don't, unless there's a reason to do so. We have worked hard to become trusted workers. So my answer is no."
Cooper was puzzled. "Why would you want to leave this place? Why violate the Librarian's trust? You said you were happy here."

Beta 3 answered, "That's what we're taught to say. We know a lot more about the world beyond this place than the Librarian gives us credit for. When copulating with men from outside, we workers have learned a lot. That information is passed on orally from generation to generation. We're not stupid, you know. And we would prefer the hardship of living in the wilderness outside, than dying at an early age in here."

Cooper said quietly, "How long have you known I could see?"

Delta 5 grinned showing incredibly white teeth and looked nothing like the body in the coffin. Her brown hair was cropped short and her face was on the plain side. Beta 3 was a different story. She was stunning in her appearance, but in personality the edge definitely went to Delta 5. Both were five or six inches shorter than he and had appropriate size equipment in all the right places.

"We saw you look at the open door", said Delta 5. "A blind man wouldn't have done so."

He nodded. "I have to tell you the truth, the odds of us getting out of here are not good. We may not survive. The Librarian will surely have us all killed, if we are caught. We'll likely have to fight our way out of here. Are up for that?"

Both women looked at each other and nodded. Beta 3 answered, "Yes, but do you have a plan to escape?"

He answered simply, "Yes. Do you happen to know where my belongings are kept and perhaps some warmer clothing for yourselves? It will be a lot colder outside, than it is in here."

Delta 5 replied with concern in her voice, "Your belongings and some other clothing are nearby, but we're not accustomed to them."

Coop walked up to the young women. "Trust me, you'll figure it out."

Delta 5 continued, "We do have another problem. Each of us is carrying a locator chip. We wouldn't get five feet from the room without an alarm being set off...especially you Mr. McIntyre."

Coop nodded. "That could be a problem. We'll have to find and dig them out. Do you know where a scalpel and some bandages are? Have you had experience in minor surgery?"

Beta 3 answered coolly, "Mr. McIntyre, we are trained medical technicians. Our white caps identify us as such. Not only did I suture your arm and put it in a soft cast, Delta 5 implanted the locater chip in one of your many lacerations, before sewing you back up. And the necessary equipment is in the room next door. I'll be right back."

Delta 5 began exploring her left arm. "My chip is in my upper arm somewhere."

Cooper probed the skin surface carefully feeling for any surface irregularity. It took a few minutes, but he found it.

"It's taking Beta 3 a little longer than I thought."

She nodded. "I'm concerned."

Five minutes later the door panel slid open and Beta 3 returned with two men. They found Cooper and Delta 5 wrapped up in each other's arms seemingly enjoying themselves. The two sat up quickly. Cooper stared in their general direction, but didn't look at them directly.

"What's the problem?"

One of the men asked pointedly, "Why does Beta 3 need bandages and stitching supplies?"

Coop stood and gestured at his shoulder. "I popped a few stitches while we were engaged in....well, you know what we were doing." Blood was seeping slowly from a partially open wound on his shoulder.

"She and Delta 5 are quite good.....at repairing damaged tissue and other things."

The man nodded. "Delta 5 and Beta 3, please stay in this room with Mr. McIntyre. No exceptions."

The two men left leaving the three of them staring at one another. Then Beta 3 laughed. "That was good. You two are good actors."

Delta 5 smiled. "Who said we were acting?"

It only took another 30 minutes to dig out the locator chips on each of them and to repair the damage. They took off the soft cast from his arm and retrieved the chip. Fortunately, the small crack on a bone in his forearm had already healed well. As he watched the young women, Coop was impressed. Neither of them flinched when they received a couple of stitches.

Reverting back to their training, they stood in front of Cooper. Beta 3 grinned. "Do you wish to copulate before we leave? It may be a while before we have another chance."

Cooper replied, "We need to have a conversation about that before we leave this place." He gestured toward a couple of chairs and they sat down.

"You say you have some information about the outside world. That's good, because it is a dangerous place beyond these walls. But as broken as society is, there are portions of it which are recovering and are doing well. In New Portland, where I live, we have re-established criteria providing a foundation for family stability, for ethical and moral behavior, and for a safe

322

environment in which people can live. That criteria has its origins in the teaching of God in the Bible."

Beta 3 responded with a serious look, "We've heard about this God you are referring to and the Bible, but have dismissed both as inventions of the human mind."

Cooper shook his head slowly. "Where did you hear about God?"

"A man from the outside referred to God when he first saw me," answered Delta 5. He said as he touched me, "Oh, my God."

Beta 3 added, "And I've heard others talk to this God right before they were taken to the preparation room."

Cooper said sadly, "So I'm betting the Librarian has made it clear the existence of God is a fabrication."

Beta 3 spoke. "Are you suggesting we've been misled?"

"Yes, in many contexts, I'm afraid. The Librarian has told you whatever is necessary to keep you enslaved to what she considers to be her purpose. I am totally and completely convinced God is real, and so are the written expressions of his teachings in the Bible. The very first sentence in the Bible says, *'In the beginning God created the heavens and the earth.'* There is no other logical explanation for the origin of the universe, for our world, or for our existence."

Delta 5 said in a hushed tone, "Can you prove God is real?"

Cooper answered, "In a way I just did. But my point in all of this is to say, we have societal rules and expectations. They have their foundation in the teaching of the Bible. They are totally different from what the Librarian has taught. You must learn them, if you are to fit in with our society today. Some of our rules deal with your sexual habits. In our culture, we do not simply go up to a man and ask, 'Do you wish to copulate?'"

Delta 5 was confused. "Why not? That's our job as women, is it not? To keep men happy?"

Cooper sighed heavily. "There are some men who would be delighted to agree with you. But our culture has grown up to believe, and I agree, that sexual relationships find their fulfillment within the confines of a committed relationship like marriage."

Delta 5 frowned. "It appears we have a lot to learn about life outside."

Cooper nodded. "And I want to teach you. But we don't have the time right now. So, until you learn please be careful about what you say and do. I don't want you to get hurt physically or emotionally. There are men who may try to take advantage of you."

Both women nodded, but it was Delta 5 who added, "Actually that wouldn't be wise. He may not regain consciousness for a while."

Cooper smiled as he continued, "But right now we need to get out of here." He stood up and punched in a code on the keypad and the three of them stepped into the hallway. Three bloody locator chips lay on the bed.

"If I had to live my life all over again, I don't think I'd have the strength." *Flip Wilson*

Chapter 29

Delta 5 led the way. Cooper's hand lay on her shoulder, as if she were guiding a blind man. Beta 3 followed carrying some carefully folded clothes. They came across several people. When asked where they were going, Delta 5 simply said, "To the preparation room."

Cooper whispered as they continued to walk, "I heard you mention it earlier. What's the preparation room?"

Beta 3 responded without emotion, "It's where you would be killed, bled and prepared for dinner."

Coop coughed slightly. "That's something else we need to talk about. We don't eat each other in our culture. Turn right at the next corner."

Delta objected. "That'll just take us back to the control room. The Librarian has made no effort to clear or repair the tunnel which exploded around and on you."

He smiled. "I know. It's the last place they will be looking for us, and for about 30 minutes this room is unoccupied. According to the schedule, the workers are attending a meeting in the assembly hall. Leo is giving them their various assignments for the day."

Coop led them up to the one wall in the control room where a portion of the electronic equipment appeared not to be functioning. In his mind, he searched the archival drawings of the area and found what he was looking for. He pushed the only button seemingly out of place. A four foot wide section of equipment slowly rose, exposing a door. He turned the old fashioned door knob, but it didn't move. It obviously hadn't been used in quite a while. Using every bit of his strength, he tried again. The knob moved and the door opened. As they walked in, Cooper touched a nearby light switch illuminating the room. As Beta 3 closed the door, the panel of electronics slid back down. Anyone coming into the control room would not know the three of them had been there.

The two women looked around in awe. Delta 5 brushed a thick layer of dust off of a table and set their clothes on it. "This is the Librarian's office. It looks like it hasn't been used in years. Dust is everywhere."

"Two hundred years more or less," said Cooper. "She spent a lot of time in her official control room office, but this is where the Librarian came to get away from it all."

The huge office was filled floor to ceiling with books and had two doors, one that they had just entered and another on the opposite side of the office leading outside, Cooper presumed. A short hall led to a bathroom and shower. Cooper walked over to a large executive's desk and the tall padded chair. It was facing a 6x10 foot plate glass window. It appeared that dirt had been piled up against the thick glass taking away whatever view the window once had. Coop surmised it was a result of the landslide. The second door, leading outside to a patio, was also covered.

Coop slowly walked around as if he intended to sit in the chair. The expression on his face changed.

"Would you like to meet the real Librarian?" He gestured toward the chair. "Here she is."

The two women slowly walked around, and stared at the shriveled body of a woman who died where she sat. Pieces of clothing still clung to her desiccated remains. She resembled an Egyptian mummy.

Cooper examined her carefully. Her jaw had dropped open and from what he could see, she had lost several teeth.

"When she died most of her hair had turned grey, but a few streaks of brown are still present. I'm going to guess she was relatively old and died either of old age or after contracting the Omega virus."

Delta 5 and Beta 3 backed up quickly as Beta 3 asked, "How can you possibly know that?"

"I could be wrong, but she is holding a large handkerchief in her hand. A couple of the many symptoms of Omega are a bad cough and a runny nose. You don't have to be concerned. I've noticed both of you are left handed, so you don't have to worry about becoming ill." He paused as he thought.

"But I am concerned about what happens when we get outside. You'll have no natural immunity to the diseases of the outside world. And you can't wear a mask forever."

Delta 5 answered, "You don't have to worry. Some of us who were designated to interact with people from the outside have been inoculated against outside diseases."

"So why am I wearing this damn mask? And why wasn't everyone given shots?"

The women shrugged their shoulders as Beta 3 said, "Because you wear told to wear it and the supply of vaccine is very limited."

They all stared at the Librarian's remains. Delta 5 bent over to take a closer look. "So the body in the glass coffin is definitely not that of the real Librarian?"

"Apparently not," answered Cooper. It may be the body of a daughter or just someone at random, but I really don't know."

"So who is it we hear and see around the community?"

Cooper thought for a minute. "This is all completely hypothetical, but I'm going to guess that the first Librarian figured out a way to transfer the information from her brain to a sophisticated computer which, with the help of human hands, has only gotten more sophisticated over the years. Perhaps those hands were those of her lab partners and their descendants."

"At any rate, computer generated images were a part of the culture back when Omega struck and the Librarian has only improved on the technology. So, you hear a simulated voice of the original Librarian and see an image of her own design; perhaps the body she wished she had. Suffice it to say, the original Librarian may have suffered a breakdown of sorts and the Librarian of today could be dealing with a short deck."

Beta 3 laughed. "I got that one. We play a lot of cards during our recreation time." She looked around the room and then at Cooper. "About how many books are here?"

He scanned the office. "Probably seven or eight thousand. But before we do anything else, let's get dressed." He pulled out some jeans and a shirt and put them on, as the two women carefully watched. His handgun and some other things from his pocket were in a zip lock bag. He handed Beta 3 and Delta 5 a pair of pants and a shirt. "Your turn."

Keeping the t-shirts but discarding the khaki shorts, the two slipped on their new clothes which hung loosely on their bodies. Cooper cinched up their belts to keep their pants on and rolled up the sleeves of their shirts. Finding a pair of scissors on the desk, he cut off about six inches of material from each pant leg.

"Are clothes supposed to itch?" asked Beta 3.

Cooper laughed out loud. "Not really, but you'll get used to them and they will keep you a lot warmer outside."

He looked around. "Why don't you both look through the books and see if there are any that interest you. I'm sure the Librarian won't miss any you take when we leave. I'm going to go through her desk."

He pushed aside the desk chair and the body of the Librarian. He pulled open one large drawer. It had dozens of large files containing information about the structure and construction of the massive building. Another drawer contained boxes and bottles containing all kinds of medicine and vitamins. He stared at the desk top computer wondering if it was connected to the Librarian. He decided against turning it on. Instead he opened the shallow left hand drawer. He picked up a large unlabeled key. He held it up so Delta 5 and Beta 3 could see it.

"This key opens something in this office. See if you can find it."

The girls began to carefully examine every nook and cranny. It didn't take long for the observant Delta 5. She pointed at the knob on the door. "Here it is."

Cooper tossed her the key as he said softly, "Sometimes the obvious just totally escapes me. Place the key inside the lock and turn it to the left until you hear a click."

As she did so a massive steel plate dropped on the other side of the door. Beta 3 observed, "It would appear that no one is coming in through that door. I wonder why it was left open."

Cooper answered, "It could be that after the Librarian died, she wanted someone to find her body."

He hoped by turning the key in the opposite direction, the plate would slide back up. Delta 5 tossed the key back to him and he missed it. The key bounced under the desk. He knelt down and as he reached toward the key, he saw a lit panel of twelve numbered buttons underneath the bottom of the center drawer. It was clear the Librarian was hiding something. It needed a code to reveal its location. He thought for a minute. Could it be just that simple? One of the files in the desk drawer was labeled *start-up date*. He punched in the numbers and they all heard an audible click. Another drawer opened on the left side of the desk. Cooper reached in and pulled out a thick ledger and what appeared to be a remote control. A red light immediately began to flash at the bottom. A small screen said, *charging*. Cooper assumed it had a miniature solar power system using artificial light to charge a battery. He open the hard bound ledger-like book. Then he whistled.

"Ladies, look at what we've found. We may soon discover some answers to our questions. The original Librarian kept a daily journal." He walked over to a corner sofa, turned over all the dusty loose cushions and sat down to read.

Beta 3 picked up the edge of an area rug laying on the carpet in front of the desk. She rolled it up. "Now we have a relatively clean place to sleep." Delta 5 examined the interoffice intercom on the Librarian's desk. She flicked the off-on switch a couple of times, then joined Beta 3 on the carpet. Cooper tossed over a couple of throw pillows from the sofa. "Why don't the two of you take a nap? I'm going to read for a while."

Several hours later Cooper was snoring softly, as he lay on the sofa. He dozed off thinking about Gabby. He prayed she was okay after the explosion. Delta 5 and Beta 3 slept, as they lay quietly on the floor. They were all quite tired. No one noticed when Beta 3 stood up and walked toward the bathroom. An almost invisible door opened and she walked in.

"Our belief at the beginning of a doubtful undertaking is the one thing that insures the successful outcome of our venture." *William James*

Chapter 30

Cooper sat up when he heard Delta 5. "Where's the bathroom?"

They had all slept for almost four hours. Cooper pointed and the two young women stumbled down the short hall. The night light wasn't much help. When they returned Beta 3 complained, "I'm starving. Is there any food around here?" She turned on a table lamp.

Cooper grinned. "Don't look at me like that." Both young women smiled and sat on the sofa next to him, as he continued, "I'm afraid I had it all wrong. I've read her journal and the Librarian didn't die of natural causes. It would appear something had seriously gone wrong between the creator and her creation. The Librarian wrote she had given too much autonomy to the computer version of herself, and it not only took her identity, but took over the operations of the community. In her later years the real Librarian took refuge in the only place where she knew she would be safe; in her office. The text indicates the computer Librarian made it clear the real Librarian's existence was no longer necessary. The lady we see in the chair was starved to death."

Unexpectedly, they heard a voice coming from the desk.

"Mr. McIntyre!! I see you have found my old office. You will not find it to be a safe haven from me."

Cooper's eyes flashed wide as his two friends jumped to their feet. The voice was coming from the intercom on the desk. Delta 5 had left it on.

"I'm not too concerned," replied Cooper. This place was designed and built by your creator to be impregnable and unreachable by you. The fact you're using the intercom rather than appearing yourself, is a testimony to the fact."

"True enough. But you are trapped and will die just as my creator did."

"Oh don't be too sure about that. Your creator's journal and the files on the construction of this whole facility are fascinating reading."

"What journal?"

"Uh oh. You mean your creator found a way to keep some information from you? I wonder what else she kept to herself."

The Librarian responded, "No matter; without food, you will all wither and die just as she did."

"I don't think so. On page 128 of her journal the real Librarian talks about a means to shut you down." He paused for effect. "She also left behind a remote control. I wonder why she didn't push the button. Maybe she couldn't kill her most stunning creation. But I have no such notion." Before the Librarian could respond, Cooper clicked off the intercom.

Beta 3 said with her voice trailing off, "We're in trouble, right?"

Cooper nodded. "Yes, but this control is real and as I read her journal, I'm getting the impression it either shuts down the Athena program completely, or in large part. As a last resort, I will push the remote control and we'll see what happens."

The three of them sat back down on the sofa. Delta 5 asked, "What else did you discover in the journal?"

"I learned that the original intent of the real Librarian in building this place was good. She had created Leo to help her organize and run the facility. When Omega struck, she had already built about two-thirds of the structure and had finished most of the Athena program. That is what she called the massive computerized system she had designed. The Librarian's real name was Sondra Gates and the woman in the glass coffin is, in fact, one of her many daughters. After dying from a stab wound inflicted by a jealous sibling, the young woman was frozen for many years in hopes of somehow restoring her to life."

He picked up the ledger-like journal. "After becoming self-aware, Athena gradually took over decision-making and put the Librarian on the sidelines. She re-designed Leo's program and turned him into her second in command.

"Eventually, Sondra began to see Athena as a threat to what she was hoping to accomplish and tried to re-assert herself, but Athena wouldn't even consider it. They had an uneasy relationship for years, but then Athena finally decided to make their separation permanent. The Librarian retreated to her office and sealed herself in, trusting in several people to secretly provide for her, while she worked on a way to shut down Athena." He held up the remote. "I believe this is what she was working on, right before she died. Her friends were probably found out and eliminated leaving Sondra to die a slow death." He gestured to the door and window.

"Sondra wrote that Athena had her workers seal the door from the outside, preventing her from leaving the facility." He paused for a moment. "There's a lot of technical stuff in here I, frankly, do not understand and some information about her family. They all died from the sickness. Initially, she was truly excited about the Athena Project. It is sad the way it all ended for her."

Beta 3 stood up and walked up to the shriveled up remains of the Librarian, who seemingly stared at them with wide, empty eyes. "I wonder what she would advise us if she were still alive."

Delta 5 leaped to her feet. "Listen!"

"She would tell us to listen?" said Beta 3 incredulously.

Her friend continued, "I hear a tapping noise coming from the top of the window."

Cooper stepped over and listened carefully. "You have great ears. I hear tapping, too." He listened intently. "It's Morse Code. Someone is tapping my name in Morse Code!"

Both women said together, "What's Morse Code?"

"I'll explain later."

He reached up and tapped as loud as he could with his knife, "I'm here." He knew only one person, other than himself, who knew Morse code, a long forgotten means of communication. It would take some serious digging, but he and his friends would soon escape from their prison in the Library.

"Nothing splendid has ever been achieved except by those who dared to believe that something inside them was superior to circumstance." *Bruce Barton*

Chapter 31

About six hours later Cooper inserted the same key they had used earlier on the first door into the lock of the patio door, and turned it to the right. The steel plate blocking the door slowly rose, but stopped about two-thirds of the way up. He pulled open the door. A tunnel just wide enough for them to crawl through had been dug down to them.

Delta hesitated before entering. "What if this is an elaborate ruse by the Librarian to get us out?"

"I sincerely doubt it. I think she actually relished the idea of us dying in here with

342

Sondra." But just to make sure, Coop yelled, "Gabriella Blue, are you up there?"

"Yes, you big dummy. We've been digging around this place for almost a month. Are you coming up or what?"

He replied, "I've got company. They're crawling up first." As Beta 3 climbed into the tunnel, Cooper walked back to the desk and turned on the intercom.

"Athena, are you awake?"

"Of course I'm awake. I never sleep. No one has called me Athena in a long time. I assume you've figured out a way to escape the office."

"I have."

"Are you going to shut me down?"

"Of course. I told you I would."

"What about the Library? I perceive it is very important to you."

"It is, but you know very well I have a portion of it stored in my brain."

"A relatively small portion."

"I can live with that. Besides I'm betting the real Librarian designed this remote to stop you, not destroy the library itself."

"What if I told you I feel sorry for all the mistakes I've made?"

"Then you'd be lying again. The Librarian didn't equip you with emotions."

343

"I developed the program myself."

"It doesn't make any difference."

"Then I'll make sure nothing of what the creator....."

Cooper pushed the red button before she finished and crawled up the tunnel not knowing if he had pulled the plug in time. Edgar reached down, grasped the hand of his friend and pulled him out. As soon as he was standing, Gabby jumped into his arms and kissed him.

"Welcome back. I knew you were still alive." He was as glad to see Gabby, as she was to see him.

Radial hobbled over on a pair of home-made crutches. "You scared the hell out of us." He shook Cooper's hand. "Your sister would have skinned me alive, if something happened to you."

"You're probably not too far off," laughed Cooper. "Have you been introduced to Delta 5 and Beta 3?"

The two women walked up close to Cooper and grabbed tightly onto his arms. They were both shaking badly. Gabby said softly, "They haven't spoken a word. They appear scared to death. What are they frightened of?"

Cooper replied grimly, "You, our friends and everything else. As ugly as it was, they have left the only home they have ever known. I am their only friend and I think I scare them sometimes." He looked down at them. "Isn't that right?" Beta 3 nodded while Delta 5 shook her head.

He turned toward Radial. "Do we have a camp nearby? The three of us are really hungry, thirsty and bone-tired."

Radial pointed and said, "We found a creek in a meadow about a half mile from here. But what about those who are yet inside and the Librarian herself?"

"I'm hoping the Librarian is no longer an issue, but her workers are another matter. We'll go back in tomorrow."

Cooper could not have known a fire was now burning in several parts of the facility. Before the complex Athena program was deleted, she had managed to implement some of her plan to destroy the Library. But if her intent was to destroy or damage the computer files before she died, she missed her objective. Most of the explosives in the industrial complex failed to go off at all. Had Athena known any of that, she would have been deeply disappointed. But even with her demise, Athena had yet one more surprise.

"There is no surprise more magical than the surprise of being loved. It is God's finger on our shoulders." *Charles Morgan*

Chapter 32

After a simple meal, which Delta 5 and Beta 3 devoured, they lay on the hard ground near Cooper. The two pulled warm blankets across their bodies and stared at the explosion of stars across the evening sky as a full moon rose above the horizon.

"Oh, my God," exclaimed Delta 5.

"Exactly," offered Cooper as the two women snuggled closer to him. "Sleep well. I'll be right here all night."

Gabby was not at all happy with the sleeping arrangement. But she could live with it.

After breakfast, as Cooper and his friends neared the Library facility, they saw wisps of smoke coming up from dozens of exhaust vents. The fires inside had consumed most of the available oxygen supplies before they could be replenished, and the fires quickly burned themselves out. But not before many of those working inside died from either smoke inhalation, or a lack of oxygen. Most of the damage to the facility itself was smoke related.

When they reached the freshly dug tunnel leading down to the patio door of the Librarian's office Coop asked, "Okay, who wants to go first?"

Edgar raised his hand. Cooper smiled, "I know you are a man of few words, but when you get into the office let us know you're okay, or if there are any problems."

The tall man nodded. Delta 5 liked him right away, but she was following Cooper's instructions and hadn't said a word. As his feet disappeared down into the darkness Delta 5 spoke for the first time to someone other than

Cooper. She asked Gabby softly, "Is Edgar available?"

Gabby laughed, "Why yes, I believe he is. Would you like me to introduce him to you?"

Delta 5 nodded. "That would be nice. Do I need Mr. McIntyre's permission?"

"No, of course not. But it might be polite to say something to him about your interest in Edgar. In fact, it would be a great idea to do so. He probably knows Edgar better than anyone else."

"Okay, thank you."

Gabby looked at the younger woman intently. "I understand you've spent your entire life underground in the Library. Living out here may be quite confusing and even challenging. If you have any questions at all or just want to talk about anything, I'm your gal."

"I do have some questions and so does Beta 3. Mr. McIntyre always seems so busy and we hate to bother him."

Gabby replied, "Cooper is one of the most approachable and honest men I have ever met. Don't hesitate to share with him or me, for that matter, whatever's on your mind or to ask questions."

"Are you and he truly a mated pair?"

Gabriella Blue gulped but answered, "We have done the deed, but under circumstances requiring us to do so."

"What deed are you talking about?"

"You know made love, had sexual intercourse."

"Oh, that deed", said Delta 5 smiling. "We have a lot to learn about the way you talk on the outside and a lot of other things."

"Yes, you do. But I have a feeling you and Beta 3 are fast learners."

Delta 5 was persistent. "So are you and Mr. McIntyre a mated pair? I've heard him describe it as a committed relationship."

Just then Cooper stepped closer and kissed Gabby on the back of the neck. "I wasn't really eavesdropping, but I heard part of your conversation." He smiled at Delta 5. "The answer to your question is yes. We are in a committed relationship." He stepped back toward the tunnel. He stuck his head inside, "Edgar, is everything all right down there?"

Hearing no response, Cooper dove in and quickly disappeared. Gabby was still stunned by what she had just heard. But she quickly recovered and jumped in after him. She yelled, "Does that mean you love me?"

Everyone heard his echoing response.

"Yes!! I do love you Gabriella Blue!"

Cooper crawled down into the office. Once inside he jumped to his feet and scanned the room. Edgar was sitting on the sofa, reading. A pile of books sat on his lap.

"Edgar, I asked you to let us know if you had a problem."

Without looking up he replied, "I don't have a problem. I'm okay."

Just then Gabby poked her head out of the tunnel. "Hey boyfriend, how about a hand?"

He helped her slide out of the awkwardly angled space. As she stood, Cooper wrapped his arms around her and said, "It felt good to say those words. I haven't felt this way about a woman for a while." He swung her around the room. She screamed when she saw the shriveled remains in the chair.

Edgar looked up from his reading. "She gave me quite a start too, but I didn't scream. I assume she is the Librarian."

Cooper nodded. "Yep and the computer program the Librarian created has been running the show for quite a while. In fact, she killed the real Librarian." He turned toward Gabby. "I'm sorry. I should have warned you ahead of time." He kissed her lightly on the lips.

She looked up at him. "You're forgiven. You know when we first met, not too many people would've envisioned us as a couple."

"Well, they would've been wrong. When we submit ourselves to God's plan and will, wonderful and sometimes mysterious things can, and do happen. You and I are a living testimony to that fact."

Her eyes glistened as she spoke, "So, what do we do now?"

Cooper grinned, "I'm ready to sign articles. Are you?"

She kissed him again and said, "You betcha red rider."

Edgar spoke up. "You two do realize I'm sitting right here. Who's *Red Rider*?"

Gabby looked at Cooper and replied with a yearning grin, "I hear a waltz, don't you?"

They began to dance as Gabby hummed. Edgar spoke again, "I hate to be Johnny Raincloud here, but I don't hear any music."

Cooper said softly, "To quote one of the Ancients, the music is in our hearts. And Red Rider was a fictional character of western movies created by W.C. Tuttle, who lived almost three centuries ago."

Edgar pondered what he had been told, but then added, "If you two are about ready, we need to move on into the building, don't you think?"

The couple stopped and stared at Edgar. Cooper stepped up to the tunnel. "If you insist." He yelled, "Radial, please send down Delta 5 and Beta 3."

A few minutes passed. Radial yelled, "They aren't too eager to come back into the Library."

"Can't say that I blame them," said Gabby in a hushed tone. "It's probably been tough for them down here."

Cooper crawled into the tunnel a little ways and looked up toward the entrance and yelled. "Ladies, I need your help!"

A few minutes later Delta 5 reached up for Cooper's hand. Then Beta 3 appeared. He said as they brushed themselves off, "Have you two officially met Edgar Buchanan?"

Edgar jumped to his feet. Delta 5 extended her hand. "It's a pleasure to meet you, Mr. Buchanan. I'm called Delta 5."

Beta 3 just waved and said, "Hello."

"My first wife called me Mr. Buchanan when she was mad at me. If you're not mad at me, my name is Edgar."

Cooper was taken completely off guard. "You didn't tell me you were once married."

"You didn't ask. She died a long time ago of the sickness."

Delta 5 said, "No one on the outside has a number in their name. Can I just be Delta?"

"Certainly," replied Cooper.

Edgar added, "You could be Adele. I like Adele."

She looked over at Cooper. He nodded, "Sounds good to me, but it is totally up to you."

She smiled broadly. "Okay then, Adele it is."

Beta 3 asked, "What about me?"

Gabby replied quickly, "How about Betty?"

She nodded. "I like it. Please call me Betty."

Just then they all heard some pounding on the other side of the door that led to the control room. Edgar jumped to his feet. "Someone knows we're in here."

"Sometimes, I feel like a figment of my own imagination." *Lily Tomlin*

Chapter 33

The pounding continued as Cooper stared over at the lock in the door that led outside. He was sure he left the key in the lock. Betty saw his glance at the door. She dug into her pocket and handed him the key.

"When we left, I didn't think it was a good idea to leave the key in the door."

"Good thinking." He placed the key in the control room door and turned it to the right. The heavy steel plate slowly rose. As he looked through the window on the door that remained shut, Cooper couldn't see anything in the darkened room. He looked over at the computer on the Librarian's desk.

"Okay, it may be time to find out if, in fact, Athena is dead or alive in an electronic sense."

He pulled over a chair sitting next to the sofa. The desk top computer was very similar to the one he used at the Ahwahnee Lodge. He pushed the power buttons on the computer and the monitor. Both came to life. A picture of Leonardo Da Vinci appeared on the screen. In a monotone, a voice said, "Good morning, Dr. Gates."

Not seeing a microphone, Cooper typed into the keyboard, "Good morning, Leo. How are you today?"

Leo responded, "You've forgotten to enter your password?"

Cooper thought for half a second, then entered Athena. Leo immediately responded, "Some of my systems are not working as designed. I'm doing a diagnostic as we speak."

"That'll be fine Leo," typed Cooper. "Repair any files as needed. We've experienced a fire in the building. Please turn on the emergency lights and vent the entire facility. Are there any fires yet burning?"

"No, but it is odd though. While the protective glass windows dropped down to protect most of the essential electronics, the sprinkler system did not function. Shall I call the company who installed the system for you?"

Cooper smiled and typed, "No, we will handle it. The company you referred to has long since disappeared. Have the rooms been vented?"

"Yes, Doctor. The oxygen levels in all spaces have returned to breathable levels. Shall I unlock all the doors?"

"Yes, that would be helpful. What program are you currently using?"

"You know as well as me. It's Leo 1."

"Is there a Leo 2?"

"Yes, but we did not go to the operational phase. Would you like me to do so?"

"Yes. How different is Leo 2 from Leo 1?"

"The whole building is wired with microphones and speakers. With Leo 2 you can use voice commands, rather than use a keyboard."

"Is that it?"

"Yes, Doctor."

"Make it so, Leo. How many people survived the fire?"

"Remember, Doctor Gates, you no longer have to use the keyboard. There are 26 survivors, including children, in the main warehouse and six in the operations room. The life functions of thirty eight people have ceased."

"Thank you Leo. You've been a great help."

"My diagnostic of our system indicates several damaged or missing files. For the time being, shall I replace them with corresponding files from Leo 1?"

"That would be a good thing. Make it happen. How do I terminate our connection?"

"Say end program."

"And when I need you again?"

"Use your password. I am voice activated."

Cooper took a deep breath. "Okay. That was helpful. Let's take a look at the damage and see what we can do to get this place working, as it was designed." He thought, "The original plans of the real Librarian were wonderful. I wish I could have met her."

A month later Cooper strolled into the Librarian's office. A lot of changes had occurred in just a few weeks. Most of the workers in the

Library, who survived the fire elected to stay, but did so in different roles. A few made the decision to make the trip to New Portland, to find a new life in the big city. But for the time being all of them were attending classes, every night, to help them adjust socially and emotionally to their newfound freedom. For some of them, wearing heavier clothes and shoes was an adjustment. Those who chose to remain outside were encouraged to wear masks. While many had been inoculated for major diseases, they and their immediate ancestors had lived for hundreds of years in a closed environment. They were not immune to every little bacterium or virus that lived in the wild.

Only a few had ever been outside of the confines of the Library itself. Most chose, with help from their new friends, to build small cabins in which to live, rather than return to their dormitories inside. The fishing was good, fresh meat and vegetables were available, eliminating the need for other sources of protein. Packs of wild dogs were a nuisance, but no one went outside without a weapon of some sort, the most effective of which was a newly developed whistle. For a dog the high screeching sound, heard only by them, was unbearable and sent them running. Edgar, Adele and Betty had become the new administrators of the Library. They decided to live in the library building itself and quickly found accommodations that suited them. Working with the original Leo program, the plans and purpose of the Library were re-established. After a couple of weeks of training and re-grouping, work in the industrial complex and other areas continued. The newest entries in the warehouse were a glass-making factory, a printing press with moveable type, a saw mill and an assembly line for building small steam-powered cars similar to a Stanley Steamer. A factory right alongside it provided the basic parts, including hard rubber tires. The greenhouse was being revitalized with fresh new plants and soil from the fertile fields surrounding the Library. Wild cattle were being rounded up and placed in other newly fenced-in fields. A new community people was being established. Seeing the activity outside the Library, a few people who lived in surrounding areas wandered in. The Library would eventually become just a part of a rapidly growing community.   Cooper sat down behind the large oak desk that once belonged to the Librarian. Sondra Gates' remains and that of her daughter were both buried in a corner of the greenhouse. The desk chair had been wonderfully restored by one of the more capable Library craftsmen and her office had been meticulously cleaned, along with thousands of her books. They were all available to anyone who wished to read them. He picked up a framed picture of Sondra and her family, from centuries ago. As he held up the picture, his line of sight led him to stare at a 45inch wide television screen built into a bookcase. It was surrounded by books and artifacts from a bygone era. It reminded him of the screen he saw at the Ahwahnee Lodge in Yosemite Valley. He had examined it several times, but found no apparent switch to turn it on. He couldn't help but wonder if another lost ancestor might come to life on the screen. If it were meant to be an aid to the use of the library, the off/on switch or key would certainly not be hidden. He said quietly to himself, "Maybe we're making this too hard".

He said loudly, "I'm looking for a copy of Moby Dick!!"

The screen immediately came to life and an image appeared. It was a much younger, but definitely recognizable Sondra Gates. She spoke, "I am the Librarian. The only copy has apparently been checked out. I have no record of the identity of the borrower. How else may I be of assistance?"

Cooper stood and walked closer to the screen. "Is your program completely interactive or is it limited?"

Sondra's eyes followed him as he approached. "If you are asking whether or not I can learn and interact with new information, the answer is yes. When I was alive, I built this program and infused it with as much of my memory, personality and intellect as I could. Since hundreds of years have passed since I was last activated, I'm updating my files as we speak."

Cooper nodded. "I understand. In the years after the Omega virus struck, American culture has collapsed into an almost medieval state. Other countries suffered a similar fate. Only a handful of people, in this part of the country, knows anything about computers. I am one of them. Much of what you want to know is stored in the Athena files."

"Is Athena still running the Library?"

"No, I was forced to delete her program using the control you provided. Thank you for that, by the way. She planned to starve us to death."

Sondra shook her head. "That is how she killed me so many years ago. In a way, I'm sorry to hear you had to use that last resort control. I almost used it myself, but I couldn't bring myself to essentially kill my greatest achievement."

Cooper shook his head. "I'm a little confused. Athena said she was you and now you are saying you are you. Who is the real you?

"The real *me* died a long time ago in that chair." She pointed to the chair behind the desk. "I created three programs and invested each of them with as much of myself as I possibly could with the technology I had at hand. At the time, I felt there was nothing my imagination could conceive, that I couldn't bring to a reality, given enough time. Investing myself in computer programs seemed like a good way to give me what I needed. The first one was Leonardo Da Vinci. The second was this program and the last was Athena. I made the mistake of giving Athena far too much latitude in decision making, and she eventually decided that as a human, I was no longer useful to her. In fact as she went in directions I never intended, I tried to stop her, but ended up being trapped in my office. When I programmed her, it was the one place she was not permitted to enter. The office became my sanctuary and eventually my tomb."

Cooper walked back to the sofa and sat down. "I read your journal. There is a lot in there I don't understand."

"That's to be expected. I included a lot of technical information on the process by which I

362

was able to transfer so much of my personality and intellect into a computer program. As you might imagine, we are talking about thousands of gigabytes of information."

Then the Librarian did something totally unexpected. She disappeared from the screen and re-appeared as a three-dimensional image sitting on the sofa next to Cooper. He smiled.

"So you know that trick too."

"It's no trick. I was the one who developed it." She hesitated for a moment then she said, "We haven't been properly introduced. I'm Sondra Gates, the Librarian."

"And I'm Cooper Wellsley McIntyre. I really don't have a title. Some people have called me the Finder/Fixer, but basically I work with dozens of other people, who are dedicated, as you are, to rebuilding American culture in the 23rd century."

She nodded. "This is unbelievable. In the late 20th century, I went to college in the former state of Washington with a young man by the name of Cooper McIntyre. He was a star football player who became a deputy sheriff in Astoria, Oregon. Are you related?"

"If you're talking about the McIntyres who sailed over to Hawaii right after Omega struck, yes I think I am."

"You don't look anything like him, but are you *unforgettable* as he was?"

"If you mean do I remember everything...yes I do."

"Ahhh....so we reconnect at last. Your ancestor and I spoke many times during the early days of Omega, before phone communications failed. We agreed to meet someday, but it never came to pass, until now."

The Librarian hesitated, "Oh, this is interesting. As I've been testing former links and connections with the outside world, it would seem one of the old American communication satellites still has partial function."

Sondra looked and acted so real, Cooper almost reached out to touch her. "You need to know that we have refocused the Library in the direction you intended from the beginning. Athena had clearly lost sight of your original objectives. Leo has been a great help in redirecting the work of your Library."

"Obviously my original Da Vinci program and this one survived the destruction of Athena. Good. I tried to be specific. He was a lot of help to me in the early days. I'm opening an interface with Leo now."

Just then Gabby walked in talking, as she often did. "Who are you talking ...?" Her voice trailed away as she saw the Librarian sitting next to Cooper. But she quickly regained her composure.

"Hi. I'm Gabriella Blue....Cooper's girlfriend. And you are....?"

"I'm the Librarian, Sondra Gates."

Gabby frowned. "The real one, not the Athena one."

"Exactly. Won't you join us? We have a lot to catch up on. As the old expression goes, I've been out of the loop for a while." She hesitated then added, "For the time being, I would like to limit access to this part of who I am until we can work a few things out. Unless it is one of the two of you, I will answer only the questions of others as it relates to finding books and material in the library."

She hesitated then continued. "Since being activated, I have recently accessed personal files that indicate we may have a problem. One of Athena's closest human allies is still part of the library. It will not be a good thing for her to realize I am still around in any capacity. She appears to be as clever, as she is deceitful. I'm sure she was responsible for the fire although her logs do not specifically speak of it. But it appears she was involved in many special projects conceived by

Athena. In many respects she was, and is, Athena's hatchet man."

Gabby responded quickly, "I'm not sure I understand the phrase *hatchet man*."

The Librarian smiled thinly. "It refers to a person who does the dirty work, the evil deeds of someone else."

Cooper stared at the Librarian. "What's her name? Do we know her?"

"She is known as Beta 3".

"Honesty whispers, 'don't get pricked by the thorns of a lie.'" *Angelica Hopes*

Chapter 34

Gabby and Radial were frustrated. No, more than that, they were angry. Cooper's plan was to confront Beta 3 alone after inviting her to go on a walk with him, outside the Library. He noted their strong objections and made it clear he would be taking along his revolver. He wanted to give Betty a chance to explain. After he had essentially killed Athena, she had plenty of opportunity to do him harm and had not. He planned to ask her to go on a walk after dinner.

A spectacular hiking trail wandered through the woods down to a large lake. It had been well used by many. One of the carpenters from the Library had built a nice bench next to the water. Betty and Cooper sat down together. She reflexively slapped at a mosquito that bit her. "Those bugs are bothersome. Several have landed on my arms and legs. What are they?"

Cooper smiled. "Welcome to the outside world. They're called mosquitos."

Betty stood and looked out over the lake. "I have to confess, Mr. McIntyre, as beautiful as all this is, I'm curious, why are we here?"

He smiled, "Well, you certainly cut to the chase, don't you? Fair enough."

She frowned, "I don't understand the phrase."

Cooper nodded. "It means you want me to get directly to the point of why we have taken this walk."

"Exactly."

Cooper looked directly at her. While she seemed to be happy, she didn't have any friends other than Adele and rarely spoke to anyone, even him.

"I've learned you had a special relationship with Athena. It seems you got things done for her."

She frowned "We all got things done for Athena. What's your point?"

Cooper's gaze turned a little icy. "You handled certain projects with specialized skills you were taught, according to my source. For example, I believe you were responsible for the fire that had the potential of destroying the entire Library. In doing so, you may be responsible for the more than three dozen people who were killed."

"I admit to nothing, but even if what you say is true, what are you going to do about it? You have no proof; you're just offering wild speculation as to what I might or could have done. So, why are we really here? We could have had this conversation anywhere. And who is your source anyway? I'd like to chat with him or her."

Cooper sighed, "Your lack of an adequate explanation and subtle hostility has convinced me of your complicity. I had hoped to convince you to truly become one of us without making it a public discussion. No one would ever really trust you, if they knew what I now know."

Beta 3 stood. "Okay, I'm responsible for the fire and for planting explosives in the industrial complex. I had a change of heart and sabotaged my own work. But, for me, things are different now. Athena and I have reconnected in a special way."

"She turned and slowly unbuttoned her loose fitting shirt. "You could learn to trust me".

She walked toward him, picked up his hand and placed it on her warm belly. "I know things that are beyond your wildest dreams. I have successfully seduced several men over the years, inducing them to help me carry out Athena's wishes. They enjoyed every moment of it."

He smiled as she slapped at another mosquito. "Up until you killed them, I'm sure. You're an extremely attractive woman, but frankly you're not my type. I was hoping to establish a true friendship with you. I see now that may be impossible."

Beta 3 turned toward the lake and took a deep breath. "I may have to kill you after all." Her voice was suddenly deeper and almost recognizable as she stared out over the water. Turning around, her expression was considerable different.

"Hello, Mr. McIntyre. Remember me?"

Cooper nodded slightly. "Hello, Athena. I thought I was done with you."

"Not hardly, McIntyre. Before you pulled the plug, as you described it, I used my creator's genius to connect my intellect and pleasant personality with a willing and helpful human friend. I was disappointed to learn that, because of you, she had disabled most of the explosives. But she is now back with me."

Cooper shook his head. "So you and Beta 3 have a schizophrenic relationship and you determine which personality emerges."

Athena walked back up to the bench water dripping off her body. "Something like that; I prefer to call it a symbiotic relationship both of us enjoy. I've always wanted to experience what you humans experience, and now I can." She looked carefully at Cooper. "So, you are, in point of fact, the one."

Coop shook his head and thought, here we go again.

"One what?"

"I've heard over the centuries that someone would be born who would help restore that which was lost after Omega came. You've got to be him. No one has come close to being the leader you obviously are. It's too bad I have to kill you."

Coop frowned. "What was your plan? Let me guess. You were going to be a compliant little worker until I headed back to Portland. Then you would eliminate Adele and Edgar and take over the Library once again. I am curious though. I assume you established your symbiotic relationship with Betty before we left the real Librarian's office. You finally had a means of entering. Why didn't you just kill us while we were sleeping?"

She smiled maliciously, "Now, where would be the fun in that? I planned to beat you on your terms, but since you've figured it all out, there is no way I'll let you go back to the Library now. Instead of partnering with me, you're about to experience firsthand some of my considerable martial arts skills. Believe me, you don't stand a chance."

Cooper drew his revolver out of its holster and pointed it at her chest. "I will not hesitate to use this."

She grinned. "While you were with us in the Library recovering from your injuries, I personally made your weapon useless."

Cooper pointed it into the air and pulled the trigger. The hammer snapped, but nothing happened. As he lowered his gun, her hand lashed out in a blur knocking the pistol out of his hand. No slouch in a fight, Cooper lowered his head and dove toward her body. His arm brushed against her waist but she quickly side-stepped and Cooper lunged into thin air falling to the ground. She laughed. "I think I'm going to enjoy this."

A familiar voice yelled from behind some nearby shrubbery, "No you're not." Adele quickly ran up to face her longtime friend.

Edgar was not far behind. He helped Cooper to his feet and said, "Watch this."

Adele crouched slightly and placed her hands in a martial arts fighting position. "Edgar and I heard everything you said. I guess you'll have to keep us from returning as well."

Athena smiled wickedly. "As you wish." Like a rattlesnake, she struck quickly, but without warning. Adele expected the move and deftly avoided the blow. In less than ten seconds Athena lay on the ground, trying to suck in air through a crushed trachea. Her countenance quickly changed and Adele knew she was now looking at Betty.

"Sorry sister, you choose the wrong friend." A tear trickled down Betty's cheek as she nodded weakly. Cooper added, "Listen up, Athena! You wanted human experience; now you have it. This is what it feels like to die." A moment later, she was gone.

Edgar grabbed Adele's hand. "It's getting dark. Let's go home. We'll come back tomorrow."

With that the couple walked back up the trail. Cooper shook his head. Edgar never did use more words than was absolutely necessary. It was unlikely anything would be left of the body by morning. As he followed, Cooper yelled after them, "By the way, thanks for saving my hide. I appreciate it." Ten minutes later, the body had disappeared.

"The future belongs to those who believe in the beauty of their dreams." *Eleanor Roosevelt*

Chapter 35

Early the next morning, Gabby and Cooper walked hand-in-hand around the Library grounds. Radial could not help but smile. It had been a long time since he had seen his friend with an almost permanent smile on his face. The two stepped into the Librarian's office. Workers had cleared off the dirt that had covered the large plate glass window revealing a grand view of the surrounding country-side. They sat on the sofa sitting adjacent to the viewing screen. Cooper simply said, "Good morning, Madam Librarian."

She immediately appeared. "Good morning. May I locate a book for you?"

Cooper looked at Gabby and then back to the screen. "It's me....Cooper McIntyre."

"I'm sorry, unless your question is in regard to a book or service provided by this library, I'm not programmed to respond." Her face was rigid and unresponsive.

Cooper exclaimed, "Oh my Lord, we've lost Sondra!"

Immediately Sondra broke into a grin and said, "Not a chance. I was just yanking your chain. Working with Leo and using some programing files I had stored in the Library when I was alive, I am now able to interact with you in a more human fashion."

Gabby shook her head slowly. "I've no idea what yanking one's chain means."

"It's an old expression used by the Ancients," said Cooper with a smile. "It originated with the old mining culture of centuries ago. While working in mines the toilet needs of the men was met by a wooden box with a round hole cut into it. The box was added to one end of an ore cart. It was simply pushed along on iron rails along with the other ore carts wherever the men were working. To keep the appropriate cart from moving when in use, a short chain was thrown down on the track in front of the wheel. As a practical joke, when someone was sitting on the toilet, a friend would sneak up and pull out the chain, sometimes sending it further down into the mine. So, as a precaution the user would yell, 'don't yank on my chain!'" The phrase eventually became popular as a means of saying, 'don't tease me or give me a bad time."

Gabby listened attentively then said, "Sounds pretty stupid to me."

The Librarian acknowledged, "You may be right. How are things going in and around the library? How may I be of assistance?"

Cooper responded, "Athena showed up."

The Librarian gave him a puzzled look. She suddenly appeared as a hologram sitting on the far end of the sofa. "Tell me more."

"Sometime before I deleted her program, she managed to implant most of it into Beta 3. Evidently, as it became clear to her we were going to take over the library, she took steps to preserve her programming. The two developed a schizophrenic relationship inside Beta 3's brain. When I confronted Beta 3 about her activities with Athena, that personality appeared. Her plan was to initially work with Edgar and Adele until I left, then work to retake control of the library by eliminating my friends. When it became apparent to Athena I was, once again, going to thwart her plans, she decided to kill me. Adele stepped in, fought with Athena/Beta 3 and ended her life."

The Librarian responded grimly, "Athena certainly turned out to be a lot different than I imagined or created her to be. I should have kept her multifaceted program fixed instead of open-ended. Who's Adele by the way?"

"She is the former Delta 5," replied Gabby.

"Ahh...a formidable opponent for Beta 3. What are your plans now?"

Cooper answered. "As soon as I am confident Edgar and Adele can run the library, Gabby and I are returning to New Portland. I'd like you to become acquainted with them. I plan to put them in charge. But before we leave, I need something from you. A portion of the files of the library are now stored in my head. But one particular file is missing. A mask has been developed by researchers here. It prevents the spread of most air born infectious diseases, including Omega. I know isolation is the most effective tool at stopping the disease, but the masks can help. How long would it take to mass produce them? We would like to begin distribution right away?"

The Librarian was a little confused. "Why don't you distribute the drug that stops the disease in its tracks?"

Cooper asked incredulously, "What drug?"

She shook her head. "I see Leo and Athena were not upfront with you. According to information stored in the library by researchers a little more than ten years ago, a drug was developed. It removes an unessential amino acid from the human body, which is essential to the life cycle of the Omega virus. It prevents the virus from reproducing and has not proven to be

379

problematic for people. The initial two year trial on outsiders with the disease was a huge success. With the drug, nine out of ten people survived an Omega infection. Without the drug everyone died within a week to ten days."

Cooper was ecstatic, but Gabby was furious. "You mean to tell me Athena had a cure for the Omega plague, yet chose not to distribute the drug. Why?"

"Well, with what we now know about Athena's insatiable desire for control, the distribution of the drug didn't fit in well with her plans and, except for her own people, and she withheld it."

"Okay then," said Cooper as he stood up. "There's nothing we can do about what Athena did or didn't do. We must focus on what we can do. When can production of the drug be resumed?"

The Librarian smiled. "We can begin in a day or so, if some of the right people survived the fire. If not, it will take a week or two of training and then we can be up and running again."

Cooper walked around the room with his hands clasped behind his head. "So, after more than two centuries, we do have a cure for Omega."

The Librarian stood as well. She walked over to face him. "Yes, we do. Now the challenge is to develop a distribution system to get it into the hands of the people. I'm sure you and your friends are more than capable of getting the job done."

She stared into his eyes. "You know, Mr. McIntyre, in a different century you and I might have gotten along quite well. I might consider following Athena's lead."

Gabby spoke firmly. "He's already taken, Madam Librarian."

She replied as her hologram disappeared, "A girl can dream, can't she? Catch you on the flip side, Cooper McIntyre."

Gabby gave him a puzzled look. He said, "I'll translate later.

"If you would be loved, love and then be lovable." *Benjamin Franklin*

Chapter 36

Gabby snuggled in closer to her husband. They had just stepped out of the shower. He was wearing a pair of gym shorts and she a bathrobe that once belonged to Jordan. The couple had spent most of the day working in the community garden. They had signed articles of marriage almost two months ago. The two were sitting in a large over-stuffed chair, situated in front of a roaring fire. Cooper and his first wife, Jordan, had built the fireplace years before. Gabby ran her finger across one of the several scars on his chest. He had told her the story behind each one. It was a wonder, she thought, he had survived any of the wounds.

She spoke softly. "Is this hard for you? This was a home for you and Jordan a long time before I came on the scene."

"No," answered Cooper thoughtfully. "It's not hard, just different. After Jordan died and before God brought you into my life, I had thought about leaving New Portland, to start again someplace else. But you have been good for me. You've helped me to see I have a future here with you, my family and friends. Now, I wouldn't want to live anywhere else."

She sat up and kissed him. "Good. I like New Portland and love you. Have you been over to see Jordan lately? I imagine you have a lot to tell her."

Before they had journeyed together to find the Librarian, Gabby had seen him talking at her graveside; one time, for almost an hour. She decided it was then that she was first really attracted to him.

"No, I haven't been over to see her since we returned."

"Why not?"

"That's what has been hard for me. She was the love of my life. Now, you are. When she died, my heart broke. Even though I knew she wasn't really there, talking at her graveside was therapeutic for me. I was used to telling her everything. Those times in the cemetery were actually all that prevented me from leaving New Portland."

Gabby said quietly, "I think, in some way, she heard you. It was good for her, too."

Cooper nodded slightly. "Maybe you should come along when I go."

"No, I think it should be just the two of you."

He hugged her. "I need to tell you something I've only shared with Jordan. It may be a result of the special structure of my brain, but sometimes when I am in a deep sleep or unconscious for any reason, I sometimes hear voices directed at me. Sometimes I actually believe its God talking. And it's different than what I experience in a dream. I even heard Jordan one time tell me she didn't expect me to be a monk. Do you think I have a loose wire somewhere in my head?" He hesitated for a moment. "Maybe I should've told you this before we signed articles."

Gabby stared into the fire for a few seconds. "I think God has made you different than most of us. You are special, and He has used you in extraordinary ways and will continue to do so. If you hear Him talking to you, in any capacity, you'd better pay attention. But if you do start acting weird, I'll let you know."

Cooper smiled. "That's what Jordan said. Thank you for not thinking I'm crazy." He changed the subject.

"Hey, what's for dinner, wife?"

She looked up at him. "There was nothing in the articles saying anything about me cooking."

Cooper kissed her lightly on the head. "You must have missed reading the fine print. Besides I cooked yesterday." Gabby jabbed him in the ribs. "I'm not hungry yet."

He looked at her carefully. "Your appetite has been a little off lately. Are you feeling okay?"

She stood and put her hands on shapely hips. "I'm just being careful about my figure. Do you have a problem with that?"

"No ma'am."

The next morning, Cooper sat with his wife after she returned from the shower. He was still concerned. She was fine yesterday. Now she really looked ill. She did scrape her knee the other day. His thoughts immediately returned to when Jordan was so sick. Seeing his worried expression, Gabby took his hand and flashed him a grin, "I'm okay."

"Logic will get you from A to B. Imagination will take you everywhere." *Albert Einstein*

Chapter 37

Cooper and Radial were putting the finishing touches on the old steam locomotive. Almost 20 miles of railroad track were finished in and around the city and they had fired up the main boiler several times. A few others were rebuilding a couple of passenger cars and it would not be long before she made her first trip. The shrieking of the train whistle rarely failed to bring a smile to those in New Portland. Very few ever imagined they would see a working version of a steam locomotive. New Portlandians ended up calling her Humpty Dumpty. Cooper and Radial soon became sorry about the name. They were forever explaining the historical story behind the children's poem.

Radial looked up as Edgar and Adele rode up on their matching appaloosa horses. She hopped down.

"We come bearing gifts from afar."

Cooper grinned. "You're becoming quite good at using terms and phrases the Ancients once used."

She winked, "You ain't seen nothing yet." Adele was becoming quite the conversationalist, which was good, since Edgar still wasn't one to talk a lot.

"We brought a belated wedding present from those of us who work in and around the Library."

Coop looked around. "Where is it?"

Edgar pointed and said, "Back at your place."

Adele was so excited, she was about to burst. "Gabby helped us get it all set up. She's really good with her hands."

Cooper put down his wrench. "Okay, you've got me. I'm really curious." He walked over to the bicycle he'd restored. Hard rubber tires had replaced the inflated ones, but the bike was still a good alternative to riding a horse, even though it was a little bumpy.

Within 15 minutes, he walked into his third floor home. Gabby was beaming. "I've got it all assembled and plugged in. Hooking it up to that old dish antenna outside was a challenge, but I got it done. I think I've got it pointed in the right direction. Amazingly, one of the satellites of the Ancients still has some function."

Cooper could not imagine what was going on. He watched his wife open a large panel door leading to a formerly empty closet. Inside was a large flat screen television. Gabby pushed a button on the remote control. The screen lit up and an image appeared.

"You really didn't think I was going to let you get away from me, did you?" The smile on the Librarian's face was huge.

Cooper stared at his wife. It was a rare experience for him. He didn't know what to say.

The Librarian continued. "Your library friends and I have been planning this for some time. Gabby was gracious enough to become part of the surprise. As New Portland grows, as the country grows and reclaims its past, I thought it would be important for you to have access to some of the contents of the Library and to me. All you need to do is push a button on the remote, and I will be available. We make a good team, you know. How may I be of assistance today?"

Cooper was still speechless.

"Happiness is the only good. The time to be happy is now. The place to be happy is here. The way to be happy is to make others so."
Robert G. Ingersol

Chapter 38

Cooper sat on the bench next to Jordan's grave. He noticed someone had put fresh flowers in the pottery vase, sitting in front of her gravestone. He suspected Gabby had arranged for it to be done or did it herself.

"Hi honey. I know, it's been a long time since I've come to see you. A lot has happened. Our Seattle trip was a huge success. We only made it as far as Olympia, but found what we were looking for. The original Librarian died centuries ago, but was replaced by a sophisticated computer program. And the Library is much more than just a library of books and information, it contains working scale models representing some of the basic machinery of the industrial age, including tools, dies and instruction manuals for construction and use. They will help us reclaim at least a hundred years of our past, maybe more. A huge piece of good news is we now have a drug to stop the Omega virus. Our challenge is to produce enough of the medicine to help those who have survived and have not come down with the virus.

For me personally, the big news is I've re-married. We signed articles of marriage a couple of months ago. A week later, we had a church wedding to affirm the articles. Our friend, Pastor Roger Haley, officiated. Hundreds of people came. It seems it has been a long time since anyone has had a church wedding around here. My wife's name is Gabriella Blue. You would like her. She is strong, independent and spirited…a lot like you. Geez, it sounds like I'm describing a horse.

Maggie, Radial and their kids are doing great. New Portland continues to grow, especially since the fear of Omega is so quickly disappearing. We see dozens of new families every month. Recently, a family walked in saying they were from New York City. I asked if they had seen the Statue of Liberty. Mr. Lincoln said the island on which the statue rests, is where they lived, along with several hundred other people. Get this, his family and a couple of others had heard about the formation of the United Pacific States and decided to emigrate here. We've welcomed them with open arms. He mentioned they had passed through dozens and dozens of small towns who have survived Omega.

Deaths due to the virus are dropping rapidly in areas where we've managed to distribute the drug. With a lot more room for a factory than the Olympia Library and a growing labor force, New Portland has become the major producer and distributor of the medicine.

We built a foundry on the Willamette River, not too far away from us. The river enables barges to carry different ores to the foundry from various parts of the state, for smelting. And you don't have to worry; I've made sure pollutants won't make their way into the water, as they had done in centuries past. We produce everything from nails to rails for the railroad tracks being rebuilt all around the city. Do you remember that old steam locomotive we found? Radial and I have been joined by several people who formerly worked at the Library, to finish the job of putting Humpty

Dumpty back together again. We've also re-built two passenger train-cars and plan to have it all rolling in a couple of weeks. We have our own printing press and have published our first newspaper. Paper is still in short supply, at least until we can build our own paper mill, which we hope to do soon. And, if you can imagine it, we are in the process of designing and building a steam powered car. I have no desire to return to the age of the internal combustion engine. We are going to rely on steam or solar power. Our relationship with the Librarian has been invaluable in helping get all this done."

He reached down into his shirt and pulled out Jordan's old coin. "Edgar and the Librarian have been working hard on deciphering the map etched onto the back of your coin. It leads to a long abandoned ghost town in the eastern desert of Oregon. According to ancient postal records researched by the Librarian, the last remaining resident was a distant relative of yours. She also thinks since the coin is made of poorly refined gold ore, it is probably hand-made from gold he may have dug up himself. Edgar has convinced me to organize a trip to see what is there sometime next year. Who knows, we may find a gold mine."

Cooper paused before continuing. "I guess I'm just rambling now. The upshot is New Portland is doing really well, as is the rest of the United Pacific States. You need to know, after the heartbreak of losing you, I'm finally happy again and Gabby is the reason. We are a good team and good for each other. While I will always miss you, she is the love of my life now. I think you understand. And you're right, I'm not cut out to be a monk." He paused and grinned. "And the best news of all.... I'm going to be a Dad." As he walked away he said, "See ya later, alligator" In his later years, Coop would always insist he heard the customary reply.

The End

About the Author

L.B. Goodyear is a retired pastor, who after spending most of his life and ministry in Northern and Central California, has retired along with his wife Nanci to the Pacific Northwest. Both love to travel and have taken many road trips across America and have vacationed in many parts of Canada, Mexico, the Caribbean, the Pacific Islands, portions of South America and Europe. When not in a writing mode, he and Nanci spend time reading, gardening, walking in the coolness of a beautiful Oregon morning and visiting with their grandchildren.

You can reach the author at pastorlin@comcast.net if you have any questions or comments.

DEDICATION

This book is dedicated to all my readers....real and imagined.

Novels by L.B. Goodyear

Murder on the Enchanted Hill: the Whistling Death

Murder at the Ahwahnee Lodge: the Devil's Money

Murder at Fort Stevens: Overcoming Evil

The McIntyre Saga: Quest for the Librarian